Fiona Harrison has been a freelance journalist, writing for a wealth of publications including the *Sunday Mirror*, *Daily Express*, *Prima*, *Woman* and *Grazia* for several years. Originally from Cornwall by way of Bath, this is her second novel, following on from *A Pug Like Percy*. She lives in Berkshire with her husband and when she is not writing can usually be found devouring other people's novels.

Also by Fiona Harrison:

A Pug Like Percy

A Puppy Called HUGO

FIONA HARRISON

ONE PLACE. MANY STORIES

HQ
An imprint of HarperCollins*Publishers* Ltd
1 London Bridge Street
London SE1 9GF

This edition 2017

1
First published in Great Britain by
HQ, an imprint of HarperCollinsPublishers Ltd 2017

Copyright © Fiona Harrison 2017

Fiona Harrison asserts the moral right to be
identified as the author of this work.
A catalogue record for this book is
available from the British Library.

ISBN: 9780008256791

MIX
Paper from
responsible sources
FSC™ C007454

This book is produced from independently certified FSC paper
to ensure responsible forest management.

For more information visit: www.harpercollins.co.uk/green

Printed and bound in Great Britain by
CPI Group (UK) Ltd, Croydon, CR0 4YY

For pug lovers
everywhere

Chapter One

There is nothing I enjoy more than catching the odd forty winks during the daytime. I am more than happy to curl up in most places, but my favourite has to be the large sunny kitchen at the home in Perivale I share with my gorgeous owner, Gail. It's there I have a lovely basket placed between the oven and the door so I'm never too hot or cold. And it's there I can always enjoy an undisturbed nap safely out of anybody's way, complete with the blanket Gail lovingly knitted for me when she first adopted me.

Now, I was in my very favourite spot enjoying a cosy few minutes of sleep when an ear-piercing crash, bang and wallop had me jumping out of my skin. Getting uneasily to my paws, I looked up at Gail's twinkling blue eyes, heart pounding.

'Was that what I think it was?' I barked, trembling.

Gail shrugged, her long, straight chestnut hair skimming her shoulders as she did so. 'Only one way to find out.'

Together we trooped out of the sunshine-filled kitchen and into the hallway where the slightly sickly sweet fragrance of dried flowers assaulted my senses. It didn't take long to discover the cause of all the trouble. There, by the front door, was my beautiful but mischievous four-month-old son, Hugo, surrounded by what could only be described as chaos.

My owner let out a gasp of horror as we both took in the mess that stood before us. It was like nothing I had ever seen before. Scatter cushions had been ripped to shreds, the stuffing from their innards covering the hessian carpet that lined the hallway. Elsewhere the vanilla and lime potpourri had been thrown across the doorway like confetti at a wedding, while large cream pillar candles had been chewed to nothing, wax deposited all over the wooden banisters and carpet. Quickly, footsteps raced towards us as Gail's husband Simon, clutching their baby son Ben, and their teenage daughter Jenny appeared.

'Is it Hugo again, Mum?' Jenny piped up.

'What's he done this time?' Simon sighed, his chocolaty eyes full of concern as he peered over Gail's shoulder.

Gail turned to each of them, despair written across her face. 'The house-warming presents, he's destroyed Mum and Dad's house-warming presents, they're ruined.'

As Gail stood rooted to the floor in shock, Jenny rushed towards the box and frantically rifled through in a bid to salvage something.

'You're wasting your time, love,' Simon called tightly. 'Hugo's done what he does best, ruined everything in sight.'

2

'Don't say that, Dad,' Jenny replied, ever the optimist. 'There has to be something here we can fix at least.'

But I knew Jenny's efforts were pointless. Shaking my head, I walked gently towards my son who was now standing next to the box and looking proudly at his destruction. With his blond fur, black markings and dark eyes he was without doubt a real cutie, but every day he was always getting into trouble, and today, on this super special day that was important to the whole family, Hugo had managed to ruin it with his tiny paws all over again. 'Look what I did, Dad,' he yapped excitedly. 'I never knew Gail had bought me so many toys.'

Fury rose, and I did my best to choke it down. 'Those are not toys. They are gifts for Gail's mum and dad. You were told that last night.'

'Was I?' Hugo asked, his brown eyes filled with innocence.

'You know you were,' I barked angrily. 'I explained that today was a big day because Doreen and Eric were moving into their new house around the corner and that all of these things in the box were presents, ready to welcome them into their new home.'

'But I thought you said they were toys for me,' Hugo protested.

I opened my mouth ready to bark, when there was a knock at the door.

'Oh Christ!' Simon groaned, passing the baby to Gail so he could open the door. 'That's all we need.'

'Simon,' Gail hissed, as she cuddled the nine-month-old

and kissed the fine blond hair that was springing up all over his head. 'They'll hear you.'

'Don't worry,' called Jenny, who from her position next to the front door was peering through the little spyhole. 'It's only Sal and Peg.'

'Well, don't just stare at them,' Gail said. 'One of you let them in.'

Immediately, Jenny pulled the door open and smiled warmly at a small blonde woman with kindly blue eyes and a beautiful blonde pug standing on the doorstep.

'Come in, guys!' She beamed. 'Welcome to chaos.'

As Sal stepped into the hallway she let out a low whistle as she took in the scene. As for me, I bounded over to my love, all thoughts of Hugo and his crimes temporarily forgotten.

'I didn't know you were coming over,' I barked gently.

'I suggested to Sal we lend Gail a paw,' Peg yapped, greeting me with a lick to my ear. 'Big day today, her mum and dad moving from Devon to London to help with the family.'

'Since baby Ben and of course our Hugo arrived Gail's been frazzled,' I admitted. 'I think she'll be grateful for all the support her mum and dad can give now they'll be closer.'

'How things have changed since Gail adopted you from the tails of the forgotten all that time ago,' Peg woofed with affection.

I realised that as always she was right, things had changed in the family, but it was all for the best. When Gail adopted me and brought me to the lovely semi-detached home she shared with Simon, little did I realise that their marriage was in jeopardy because they were both so worried about their daughter Jenny. The little girl was suffering from a life-threatening heart condition and needed regular hospital care but she pulled through, and now, Jenny is a very normal teenager with a perfect working heart.

'I thought you might like a hand today, but I think you need a full-on clean-up operation instead,' Sal exclaimed, interrupting my thoughts. 'What on earth's happened here?'

'Good question, Sal,' Peg barked, looking sharply at me and Hugo. 'What has happened here?'

Gail sighed, as she pulled Sal into the kitchen. 'Let me tell you while I make a coffee, I can't even think about what that puppy's been up to now. Honestly, Sal, it's something new every day with Hugo, I never realised having a puppy would be such hard work.'

With that, the two women trooped into the kitchen, followed by Jenny and Simon leaving me and Peg with a very jolly-looking Hugo.

'Mummy! Mummy! Look at all these toys Dad got me,' he barked excitedly.

Peg eyed him beadily. 'Don't try that with me. I was here last night, remember, when your dad very clearly told you these things were gifts for Doreen and Eric.'

Hugo at least had the decency to look contrite as he gazed forlornly at the floor. 'Sorry.'

But it wasn't enough for Peg who deftly grabbed him by the scruff of the neck. 'Are you sorry? Or are you just sorry we're cross. I don't know how many times your dad and I have to tell you, Hugo, you must do as you're told.'

'I didn't mean to cause so much damage,' he barked quietly as Peg released him from her grip. 'I just saw all the things and wanted to play with them.'

'But those things didn't belong to you, Hugo,' I yapped, the thread of annoyance still burning bright. 'Last week we had to have this bark when you ran off with Ben's toys. They're human toys not your toys and Ben was very upset when you snapped his rattle in half.'

I cast my mind back to the memory of the resounding snap when Hugo broke Ben's clown rattle into tiny pieces. The look on the infant's face had mirrored Gail's one of shock just moments earlier and then the tears had streamed down his little face. My heart had gone out to him, particularly as my son looked delighted with himself when both Gail and Simon told him off.

Peg and I had barked our frustrations out at Hugo last week and he had assured us there would be no more mischief, but he had managed to behave for less than a week. Something told me he enjoyed the attention he received from getting into trouble but I knew this wasn't the way to get through life, something I had tried to teach Hugo. For the minute, I felt defeated and I slumped to my paws, needing a minute to gather my thoughts.

Hugo was my son and I adored him but there were times he seriously tested not only my patience but the patience of my family. When Peg and I learnt she was expecting pups last year we were over the moon. We both felt it was the perfect way to seal our love, and discovering we were able to find our litter good homes nearby, we were delighted as it meant we got to see them all almost every day at the park. Our daughter Lily went to Sal's next-door neighbour, while our two other sons Roscoe and Ralph were taken in by a couple around the corner, who worshipped them as we hoped they would. As for Hugo, well, he was the tiniest little pup in the entire world but as the runt of the litter both Peg and I knew he would have difficulty finding a good home.

Gail wasn't deterred, however, and she placed an ad across all the local social media sites pleading for someone to offer him a good home. Consequently, we were inundated with people wanting to take a look at Hugo. Every time the familiar chime of the doorbell sounded, I, Hugo, Peg, Gail, Simon, Jenny and even baby Ben, held our breath as we each hoped this would be the moment Hugo would find his forever home. Yet as people shuffled into the living room and took one look at my precious boy lying in his sheepskin-filled basket they reluctantly shook their heads. They all wanted a cute little pug to trot around after them. What they didn't want was a dog who was all paws and squished face as he grew into his body.

I tried not to take it personally, but as a father I felt so cross on Hugo's behalf. To me, he was a beautiful bundle of joy and I knew that when he was older he would be just as perfect as his brothers and sisters.

Sadly, nobody seemed to share my view and I lost count of all the people who uttered polite thanks, but no thanks as Gail showed them the door. I couldn't help worrying over the boy's future. As dogs it was our purpose to serve our owners and shower them with love when we found our forever home, proving the bond between human and dog was the strongest one on earth. Thankfully, Gail had finally stepped in at the eleventh hour and said we could keep Hugo until he was bigger, and look for a home for him then.

She had done this for me even though space was tight with a new baby in the house, which had meant Simon had been forced to give up the spare room, otherwise known as his man cave that he had once treasured. I had been beyond grateful to Gail and had assured her repeatedly with plenty of loving barks that Hugo wouldn't be a burden. However, during the four months he had been with us, much as I hated to admit it, burden was the one thing he had become. He got into trouble every single day and no matter how many times I begged him to behave, my barks fell on deaf ears.

Looking at him now, still glancing at the mess he had made with a look of sheer pride across his face it was hard not to feel a sense of failure. I had taken it upon myself to show him the ropes, teaching him how to behave in a domestic environment. After all, nobody would want Hugo if he didn't mind his manners, something he didn't seem to understand. I myself knew more than anyone what it was like to be abandoned, and spending day after day hoping to find your forever home. My previous owner, Javier, had left me in the local shelter or the tails of the forgotten as it's better known amongst the dog community. Although I had been well cared for, it was by no means a substitute for a loving family and I didn't want Hugo to suffer the same fate. I had spent days performing tricks for would-be adopters and putting a brave face on my little snout as families adopted all my friends but left me behind. I had been broken hearted, until I met Gail, which was why I had made it my new purpose in life to get Hugo to grow up so he would find his own happy-ever-after.

I felt at the end of my lead with him. I glanced at Peg hoping she would have some answers, but she looked as worn out as me with it all.

'Come on,' she barked eventually. 'The least we can do for Gail is to clear this lot up. And, Hugo, you're helping.'

'OK, Mummy,' he said, bounding into action.

Together we worked, quickly pushing the potpourri into a big pile in the corner, and picking up the larger portions of the cushions into the box.

Suddenly, Hugo stood stock-still in front of me fixing me with a wide-eyed gaze.

'What is it?' I barked in frustration.

'I don't feel well, Daddy,' Hugo grumbled.

I exchanged knowing looks with Peg. Was this yet another drama created by my son to get out of cleaning up after himself.

Peg dropped the bit of cushion she was holding and glared at Hugo. 'How do you feel?'

'Very, very, very sick,' Hugo replied, his little voice lacking the vim and vigour of earlier.

I looked at Hugo again. I had to admit my boy looked green and, judging by all the candle wax and potpourri he had devoured, it was hardly surprising. I shook my head, waves of despair crashing over me as I realised that not only had my son cost my owner some gorgeous house-warming gifts but she would also need to pay for a weekend visit to the vet.

Chapter Two

It was several hours later by the time we finished at the vet's and arrived at Doreen and Eric's new home. To Gail's credit she took the entire incident much better than I expected. Instead of having a breakdown when she realised Hugo needed an emergency visit to the practice, she burst out laughing, her eyes crinkling with mirth and wouldn't stop no matter how much I barked.

At the vet's, Gail, Simon and Jenny all had great fun explaining what had happened to Hugo. As Gemma, our vet, had a good look down my boy's throat, I shuffled anxiously from paw to paw waiting for the diagnosis, the clinical smell of bleach making me feel even more agitated.

'Is it serious?' Gail asked anxiously, biting her nails as she waited for the verdict.

The vet said nothing for a moment as she tried to hold the wriggling pup still while taking his temperature.

'Yes, does he need medication? Or even surgery?' I barked desperately.

Gemma grinned at me as she removed the thermom-eter and patted Hugo gently on the head. As she turned to tap something on her computer keyboard, I pushed my anger to one side as I offered him a sympathetic howl. Even though it was clearly Hugo's fault, he now looked so poorly lying there on the long black consulting table that my heart went out to him. Usually Hugo made a monkey of everyone when we brought him in for a check-up. He would jump in the sink, run across the computer, climb the furniture, and once he even got his head stuck in the window. But today it was as though as he was a different dog, he was so quiet and sad.

'Well?' I barked in frustration.

Gemma turned around and smiled reassuringly at us all. 'The good news is, it's not serious, Hugo doesn't need any medication or surgery and this will all pass naturally.'

I let out a bark of relief. 'Did you hear that, you're going to be fine.'

Hugo cast me a baleful look. 'I don't feel fine, Daddy.'

Simon sighed as he looked from me to Hugo and then back to Gemma. 'When you say pass naturally, you mean Hugo is going to be going to the toilet a lot is that right?'

'Not necessarily a lot, but perhaps a bit more than usual,' Gemma explained. 'It's nothing to worry about, although Hugo might be a bit uncomfortable. All he'll probably feel like doing is sleeping.'

Jenny pushed her brown hair behind her ears and smiled. 'He does that a lot anyway,'

'Like father like son.' Gail chuckled, ruffling my ears affectionately. 'Do we need to do anything else?'

'No, just keep an eye on him.' Gemma grinned, writing something on her pad. 'Bring Hugo back in a couple of days for me to check he's on the mend. He shouldn't take a turn for the worse but if he does we'll have a poke about.'

'I don't want to be poked about, Daddy,' Hugo woofed with worry, as Simon scooped him up from the table and thanked Gemma for her time.

'Well, let this be a lesson to you,' I barked. 'Now, one of us will have to look after you instead of helping Doreen and Eric. Honestly, Hugo, it's vital we dogs put humans first rather than ourselves.'

'Sorry, Dad,' he yapped as we walked outside into the sunshine. 'It won't happen again.'

I barked nothing as I breathed in great lungfuls of fresh air, enjoying the scent of something other than bleach. Whatever Hugo yapped in his defence, I had a feeling that this, or something very like it, would happen again.

*

An hour later, all of us, together with a sleepy-looking Hugo, were inside Doreen and Eric's lovely new bungalow. Instead of the candles, cushions and potpourri Gail had planned to give her parents, she had resorted to a huge bouquet of gerberas and chrysanthemums from the flower shop on the High Street. After presenting them to her mum, Doreen professed to adore them and immediately put them in pride of place in the front windowsill.

Doreen and Eric's new house was only a ten minute

walk from Gail and Simon's and was what I heard lots of people describe as a new-build. I had never been inside a bungalow before and wasn't sure what it was. Yet my quick scamper around with Doreen as she gave us all a guided tour told me that the only difference between a house and a bungalow was that there were no stairs. It was, it appeared to me, like Sal and Peg's flat, just a bit bigger and with a huge garden they didn't have to share with other people.

Watching my owner's lovely mum and dad proudly take us from sunny room to sunny room, I glanced at each of them, noticing the happiness they basked in. Doreen was petite with hair in a neat bob and a warm, open face. As for Eric, well he was the double of Gail, with his chestnut hair that was now almost grey all over, and friendly, welcoming face that always made me feel at home.

As well as the huge garden there were three bedrooms, a bathroom, glass like in a greenhouse that Doreen reliably informed us was a conservatory, whatever that was, along with a huge kitchen and a funny-looking worktop that stood in the centre of the room.

'That's my island,' Doreen told us proudly, as she brought the tour to a close.

'It's beautiful, Mum.' Gail smiled.

'So pretty,' breathed Jenny.

'Very nice,' put in Sal, her blue eyes filled with admiration as she stroked the dark surface. 'It's lovely how it matches the slate tiles.'

'Well, you wouldn't have it any other way, would

you?' chirruped Doreen, her silver hair gleaming in the sunshine-filled room.

'You wouldn't, dear,' Eric grumbled good-naturedly at his wife. 'Shall I make tea?'

Doreen nodded her assent. 'Good idea. Let's all go through to the living room before we get stuck into some unpacking.'

As we turned to follow Doreen out of the room, I couldn't help wonder if I was missing something. I turned to Peg who was standing in the doorway with Hugo beside her.

'I thought islands were things surrounded by water,' I yapped in curiosity.

Peg nodded sagely, her blonde fur jiggling almost as much as her lovely jowls. 'They are. That's why you never want to get stuck on one. Unless it's England of course, that's quite big.'

I turned back to the island and looked at the floor and tiles suspiciously.

'I've got it!' I barked in excitement. 'Doreen's going to put the water around the island separately.'

'That's why it's important the tiles match,' Peg put in wisely. 'It all makes sense now.'

'Does that mean we'll go on boat trips then, Daddy?' Hugo asked, his pace matching mine as we joined the others in the lounge. 'Will I need to learn to swim?'

I nodded. 'I think there's every chance you'll need to do that, Hugo. But don't worry, us pugs are natural swimmers, you'll be doggy-paddling around Doreen's island like there's no tomorrow.'

Pleased to have solved that little problem, I looked around. There was no denying it, the place looked as chaotic as Gail and Simon's when we left it.

There were boxes everywhere, all piled on top of one another in various states of disarray. Some were half open, some had contents like duvets, pillowcases, lampshades and even cutlery spilling out and some had been emptied, flung to a corner of the room, to be dealt with some other time.

I looked across at Peg and saw her glance at the upended cardboard. She was rather partial to curling up in a box for a nap, just like me. For a moment I imagined the two of us snoozing the afternoon away nestled in the warmth of each other. But no, there was work to do. Shaking my head to free myself from such thoughts, I glanced up at Gail, who rewarded me with a beaming smile, just as Doreen came through from the kitchen. She was clutching a tray piled high with tea and cakes and I saw with delight Eric appear just behind her, carrying goodies for all us pugs.

'Water and a bone for you all,' he said, setting the treats on the floor.

'Thanks, Eric,' I woofed along with Peg.

We turned to Hugo to remind him of his manners. Only to find he had started on the chewy treats already.

I opened my mouth, about to tell him off, when Peg beat me to it.

'Hugo, that's enough,' she yapped. 'Do not show me and your father up in public. You know you don't eat a treat without saying thank you.'

16

At the sound of the sternness in his mother's bark, Hugo dropped his bone to the floor in horror. I could see the fear radiating from his eyes.

'Oh, Peg, don't be too harsh on him,' I whined, my heart full of concern for my poor boy. 'He's poorly, he's not himself.'

Hugo rewarded me with a gentle rub on my snout as he looked apologetically at his mother who was settled by the fireplace.

Peg gave me a lick as she gestured for Hugo to continue. 'Maybe you're right, Percy. Perhaps I am being too hard on him. But, honestly, why is he so badly behaved all the time? Is it us? Are we doing something wrong?'

Before I could answer, I saw Hugo had lost interest in the bone and was charging up and down the living room, wagging his tail, scampering through the boxes.

'Hugo!' I ordered. 'Calm down.'

Only my barks fell on deaf ears once more as Hugo darted over to Doreen, who had her hands full of teacups, and jumped up at her.

'Easy now, love.' She smiled down at my son. 'You nearly had me over.'

Hugo didn't reply. Instead, he charged away from Doreen and rushed over to Eric who was sitting in a chair by the windowsill trying to do the crossword he had found wrapped around a plate.

'Eric! Eric!' Hugo barked playfully, sitting at the older man's feet.

Eric lowered his paper and beamed at my son affectionately before scratching his ear. 'Hello, Hugo. Heard you ate some potpourri. Can't say I blame you, it's all it's good for.'

'That's what I thought!' Hugo replied, thwacking the floor with his little tail.

'Did us a favour, boy. Can't abide the stuff,' Eric grunted with alarming honesty, causing Simon to burst out laughing.

'What did I tell you?' he chuckled, turning to Gail. 'I said Eric wouldn't be interested in all that smelly nonsense!'

Jenny sighed and shook her head in mock-exasperation at her father. 'Dad! It is not nonsense, it's stuff to make your house pretty.'

'You tell him, Jen.' Gail giggled, as she sat cross-legged on the floor and bit into one of the cupcakes her mother had laid out on a plate.

'So did I really do you a favour, Eric?' Hugo barked, his eyes shining with pleasure at the thought of one of his actions doing someone a good turn.

'You can knock a bowl of potpourri over for me anytime.' He smiled and gave Hugo one last affectionate pat on the head, before turning back to his crossword.

Clearly moved, Hugo jumped up onto Eric's lap, determined to give Gail's dad a cuddle filled with gratitude. Yet the sudden movement left me wide-eyed with horror as, despite Hugo having the best of intentions, my boy had jumped on top of Eric's lap with such gusto he sent the vase filled with Gail's fresh flowers cascading all over Eric.

'Oh you dammed dog!' Eric howled, clearly soaked through. 'What were you doing?'

'Is it like the island?' Hugo barked excitedly. 'Will I need to swim?'

I rushed over to my son, determined to get to Eric's aid, but was beaten to it by Doreen, who handed her husband a towel.

'It was only an accident wasn't it, Hugo?' Doreen crooned, picking up the flowers that now littered their new living-room carpet.

'An accident that could have been avoided if Hugo hadn't been charging about the place,' Eric fumed, drying his navy chinos off. 'Honestly, this dog's a menace.'

'He's not that bad, Dad.' Gail bridled, as she, Sal and Jen helped Doreen replace the flowers in the vase.

In that moment I loved my owner more than I ever thought possible. Even after all Hugo had done today, she was still defending him.

'Hugo, come here now, please,' I ordered from my place next to Peg. 'Just stay out of the way while Doreen and Eric sort themselves out.'

Obediently, Hugo did just as I asked and, as I gave him a lick, I exchanged a worried glance with Peg. There was no way our son would find his forever home with behaviour like that.

Jenny sat next to Sal on the edge of Doreen's brown leather sofa and grinned at us. 'Don't feel too bad, you guys, it's hard being a parent.'

Doreen let out a low chuckle as Eric returned to his crossword and she took a seat next to her granddaughter. 'Know all about it do you, chicken?'

Jenny shrugged as she bent down to kiss my head. 'No,

'course not, but I know Mum and Dad had a pretty tough time when I was sick. It can't be easy raising a family, that's all I'm trying to say.'

'Oh bless you, child.' Doreen smiled, kissing Jenny's cheek. 'Why weren't you more enlightened at this age, Gail?'

Sal roared with laughter. 'Yes, Gail, why weren't you more enlightened?'

I looked up at Gail and watched as she spat her tea everywhere. 'What's that supposed to mean, Mum?'

'Nothing.' Doreen sniffed. 'Just our Jenny has a very wise head on very young shoulders.'

'You're not wrong there,' Sal agreed, smiling at Jenny.

'Very true,' I barked in agreement.

Gail raised an eyebrow. 'And while it might be true, Mum, if you want a hand getting these boxes unpacked I'd start singing my praises, and possibly Sal's as well as Jenny's if I were you.'

'Fair enough.' Doreen chuckled, her green eyes radiating the same kindness as her daughter's. 'You know I think the world of you, you're my favourite child!'

'I'm your only child,' Gail said, returning her grin. 'I'm so happy you've moved here, it'll be wonderful having you and Dad on the doorstep.'

Getting to her feet, she pulled her mother in for a hug.

Doreen returned her daughter's hug, and rubbed her back as if she were no more than Ben's age. 'And it'll be wonderful for us having you so close by. We've missed you.'

'And we've missed you,' Jenny cried.

She rushed towards her mum and gran and wrapped her arms around them. I gulped, I didn't want to miss out on a family hug. Together with Peg and Hugo, we bounded towards the women and pushed our noses into their laps and knees, much to their delight.

'They're everywhere.' Jenny giggled in delight.

'Oh you dogs are gorgeous.' Doreen smiled, bending down to smother us with kisses.

'And we think you're gorgeous,' Hugo barked, licking her hand.

'But not as gorgeous as Peg and Gail,' I barked loyally.

Gail beamed down at me, and planted a sloppy kiss on my snout. 'Percy, you're the best boy in the entire world.'

I howled in delight. There was nothing nicer than being surrounded by family.

As we broke apart, Sal glanced balefully at a box marked 'outdoors'. 'Shall I take this out to the garage?'

Doreen flashed her a grateful smile as she got to her feet. 'Thanks, love.'

'And I should get cracking as well.' Gail smiled, as she finished her second cupcake. 'Where do you want me?'

Doreen handed her daughter a pair of scissors and gestured to a box with black writing all over it. 'The pots and pans are in that one,' she explained. 'Can you give your father a hand with them in the kitchen. He knows where everything goes.'

Nodding, Gail picked up the box and turned to Eric who was still engrossed in the paper.

'Are you ready, Dad?' she asked.

Eric glanced up from the crossword in surprise. 'Ready for what?'

'To help me unpack the kitchen stuff,' Gail replied patiently.

Eric looked blank as he scratched the bald patch on top of his head. 'If you want, love, though I don't know where any of it goes.'

'You do,' sighed Doreen in exasperation. 'We discussed it not half an hour ago!'

'Did we?' Eric narrowed his blue eyes in confusion.

'Yes! What's wrong with you?' she grumbled. 'You're always forgetting things these days.'

'Am I?' Eric asked, his blue eyes rich with surprise.

'Yes!' Doreen sighed again.

Gail raised her hand in between the two of them.

'Come on, you two, there's no sense arguing now. Dad,' she said, turning to Eric, 'why don't you come and help me with all this. I'm sure that together we can work out where everything's meant to go.'

Eric put down the crossword and obediently got to his feet. 'All right, love.'

Together they trotted off to the kitchen leaving Doreen alone in the living room. As she set her teacup on the coffee table, she sank her head into her hands.

Watching the rise and fall of her shoulders, I suddenly realised she was crying. Turning to Peg, I gave a little bark of worry and we padded across to the elderly woman.

Getting nearer, I saw her body was wracked with sobs. I was dumbstruck. Doreen always put a brave face on things and I had rarely seen her cry, not even when Jenny was so poorly. She was known for her strength, something Gail had relied upon when they had faced difficult times.

Exchanging worried glances with Peg, we did the only thing we pugs can do in times of crisis. We used our tongues to mop up Doreen's salty tears, determined to be there for as long as she needed us.

'Do you think she's all right?' I whined quietly to Peg in between licks.

'Fine,' she yapped in reply. 'She's probably just upset because she's tired with the move. It's very distressing you know, upending your home.'

As Doreen's cries became quieter and she stroked each of us in turn, I moved my head and crawled onto her lap to show her how much I loved her. Breathing in her warm, homely scent, my doggy instinct fired on all cylinders as something told me there was something very wrong indeed.

Chapter Three

The next morning I woke to what I could only assume was all hell breaking loose. Opening my eyes and sitting bolt upright in my basket in the kitchen, I tried to make sense of the scene playing out in front of me.

Gail was standing at the stove, balancing a screaming baby Ben on one hip and heating his bottle with the other hand. At the table, Jenny was bellowing into her mobile phone, making plans to meet a friend at the cinema, while Simon was sat at the pine kitchen table engrossed in paperwork and furiously typing away at his laptop.

Blearily coming to, I looked around for Hugo, but he wasn't in his basket or in the garden. Anxiously, I padded out of the kitchen and into the sitting room. Even though it was the middle of summer Hugo loved nothing more than curling up on the sheepskin rug by the fire, but he wasn't there and neither was he anywhere upstairs.

Returning downstairs, anxiety gnawed away at me as I wondered where Hugo would go. He was still poorly, so he couldn't have gone as far as the park and, besides that, he knew never to go there alone. There was a chance he could have gone to see Peg, I thought, but again, he had never been there on his own, and I knew that the times we had visited he hadn't taken in the route as he had constantly yapped all the way there.

A creeping sense of horror coursed through my fur as I started to imagine all the places he could have gone and all the things that could have happened to him. Just as I was imagining Hugo being eaten by a hungry pack of wolves, or abducted by a Cruella De Vil type, the house phone rang, interrupting my nightmare.

'Oh you're kidding, Mum,' Gail gasped into the receiver, still jiggling Ben on her hip.

There was a pause before she spoke again. 'We'll be right over, and again I'm so sorry.'

I watched with interest as she hung up the phone and turned to Simon.

'You'll never guess what's happened.'

'I dread to think looking at the expression on your face.' Simon grimaced, glancing up from his computer.

'Hugo has just turned up at Mum and Dad's,' Gail explained with a sigh.

Simon raised an eyebrow. 'On his own?'

'On his own,' Gail confirmed.

The family fell into silence as they contemplated this news leaving me to consider what I had just heard. On the one paw, I felt a huge wave of relief crash over me as I realised my little boy was now safe. But on the other what was Hugo thinking of? Fury ate away at me as I realised how little he had learnt since being under my charge. I had told him repeatedly never to go anywhere alone, but here he was not only disappearing before my very eyes but bothering poor Gail's parents just as they had moved in.

'But how did he get there?' Jenny asked eventually, putting her phone down for the first time that morning.

Gail looked pointedly at Simon. 'I guess through that cat flap we've never got around to fixing.'

'Ah.' Simon winced. 'Sorry, I've been meaning to mend that for ages. I will get on to it, I promise.'

'It doesn't matter now. All that matters is Hugo is safe,' she sighed. 'I said I'd go and get him, but I've got to get Ben down for his nap and then I said I'd take Jenny into town, to buy her some new shoes.'

'That's OK, why don't I just go on my own?' Jenny suggested.

'Because you're fourteen, young lady, and I'm not letting you run amok with my money!' Gail admonished.

Simon stood up and shut the lid of his laptop. 'I'll go then. Me and Perce can pick up the whippersnapper and while I'm there I'll see if your parents need anything doing.'

The relief on Gail's face was palpable. 'Would you? Oh thanks, Si, that's such a help.'

Simon grinned, as he walked across to his wife and kissed her on the cheek. 'My pleasure,' he told her, before turning to me. 'Come on then, mate, let's rescue Hugo before he destroys Doreen and Eric's place like he does here.'

*

Simon had barely finished knocking on the door before Eric flung it open wearing a big grin, Hugo in his arms. I glanced in astonishment at them both, never before having seen one or the other quite so content.

'Hi, Eric,' Simon said evenly, stepping into the hallway. 'We're here on a rescue mission, heard Hugo had been bothering you.'

Eric chuckled and clutched Hugo tightly to his chest. 'Nonsense, it was a very pleasant surprise to see this one in the kitchen earlier. Little so-and-so must have got through the conservatory door.'

'I'm very sorry, Eric,' I barked seriously as I followed Simon inside. 'It won't happen again, will it, Hugo?'

As Eric set Hugo on the floor, my son hid behind the older man's trousers. 'Sorry, Dad, didn't mean to make you worry.'

'So why did you?' I barked grumpily, as we followed Eric down the long hallway and into the kitchen. There was still mess everywhere with half-unpacked boxes all over the place.

'Sorry the house is a bit of a tip,' Eric apologised, filling the kettle. 'We're still up to our eyeballs and Doreen's had enough so she's popped to the shops for a coffee and a break.'

Simon settled himself on one of the high chairs at Doreen's island while Hugo stood next to Eric, almost as if he was waiting for him to issue his next instruction. 'That's the other reason I thought I'd pop by, see if there's anything I can do.'

Eric smiled at his son-in-law as he reached for a pair of

mugs, tripping over Hugo in the process. 'Oh sorry, Hugo, didn't see you there.'

'That's OK, Eric,' my son barked, wagging his tail.

Turning back to face Simon, Eric scratched his head. 'Sorry, Simon, what were we saying? Honestly, I feel as if I can barely remember anything at the minute with this move.'

Simon chuckled, the frown lines on his face crinkling around his eyes. 'I can't say I'm surprised. Moving gets the best of all of us. No, I was just offering to lend a hand.'

'That's very good of you, Simon, but Hugo here has just been helping me sort through a load of boxes and we've got a lot done, haven't we?' Eric grinned, bending down and pulling a tomato from his pocket to give to Hugo.

I watched in amazement as Hugo ate the fruit greedily from Eric's palm.

'I didn't know you liked tomatoes,' I barked in astonishment from my position by the doorway.

'Oh yes!' Hugo yapped, licking his lips and looking up at Eric, clearly hoping for more. 'Eric gave me one from the greenhouse yesterday and it was delicious. Today, he found another handful had grown overnight and fed them to me.'

I was barkless and at a loss to know what to do. 'Just come over here,' I ordered, as Eric pushed a mug of tea in front of Simon.

'What is it, Dad?' Hugo asked, nearing my side.

'I want to know what possessed you to go running off like that,' I yapped quietly.

'I wanted to check on Eric and Doreen, Dad,' Hugo

barked. 'I heard you bark you were worried about Gail's parents. I thought I could come and help them for you.'

A rush of love surged through me, at my son's thoughtfulness. With each passing day, I was beginning to see glimpses of the dog I knew he could become. But, as always, he hadn't got it quite right. My mission to help him was far from over.

'You can't just dash off without barking something,' I told him gently. 'It was a lovely idea to help Gail's parents but you're too young to do these things on your own.'

Hugo hung his head in sorrow. 'Sorry, Dad. I was only trying to help. But listen, I've got to tell you something. I think you were right about something being wrong with Eric and Doreen. He keeps forgetting things, Dad. Earlier on he kept saying to Doreen that he was going to go bowling and she kept telling him that he couldn't do that any more as they didn't live in Barnstaple any longer. He got so cross, Dad, he went out into the garden for a walk around the tomatoes and then he gave me some and then he seemed OK again.'

I shook my head impatiently. I realised Hugo meant well but the fact was that running off, causing people to worry, was not what a forever family would be looking for in a dog.

'Hugo, I know that you acted with the best of intentions today so I don't want to go on at you too much. But dog obedience is so important and it's vital I start to see some from you. Do you understand?'

Hugo nodded. 'But didn't you hear what I said about

Eric and how he forgot where he lived? It was a good job I came, Dad. I made him remember I'm sure of it.'

I let out a sigh. 'Let's just drop it, OK. Now not another bark, do you hear me?'

'Yes, Dad,' Hugo yapped forlornly.

'Good, now let's get ready to get you home. You need to rest after all that rubbish you ate yesterday.'

'Yes, Dad.' Hugo sighed again.

I rubbed my nose against his to show he was forgiven and then watched him settle at Eric's feet. Surprise ebbed away at me that they had forged such a close bond already. Watching Eric reach down and fondle Hugo's ears I felt a pang of regret. The duo seemed so close. What a shame he couldn't do that with someone able to offer him a more permanent solution.

Chapter Four

The following morning I felt a surge of optimism that Hugo had got the message about his behaviour. Not only had he walked all the way home to heel but he appeared to have a spring in his step. I wondered if it had done him some good to spend some time with Eric, or perhaps Eric had slipped something in those tomatoes Hugo had apparently developed a bit of a taste for.

Only now, as I watched my son whine in the kitchen at the top of his lungs looking rather green, I wondered if it had been such a good idea.

'You all right, boy?' I asked, ignoring my breakfast as I got to my paws and walked towards him.

'Fine,' he yapped quietly. 'Just a feel a bit funny. I'm never eating feathers or candle wax again.'

'I'm very glad to hear it,' I told him, determined to remain cross.

Only looking at my son's mournful little face, it was hard to stay angry. No matter how badly behaved, Hugo was my gorgeous pup, and I loved him more than a bag full of chewy bones! Licking him gently on his cheek, I crooned into his ear.

'You'll feel better soon, I promise. The worst is over now. Give it a few hours and you'll be bounding about with your pals at the dog park just like before.'

Hugo brightened considerably at this news and scampered up and down on the floor to show his excitement.

'Will I, Dad? Do you think I'll be able to go to the dog park today? I want to see Bugsy. He promised to tell me all about the shadow monster today.'

I shook my head. Bugsy was a Border collie and together with Jake, an elderly cocker spaniel, and Heather, a mumsy German shepherd, was one of our best friends. However, the last thing Peg or I needed was Hugo listening to Bugsy's ridiculous theory on how shadows weren't really shadows, but were actually sinister monsters out to taunt and humiliate us dogs whenever the sun shone.

Still, now was not the time to dash his hopes. 'We'll see, maybe later.'

'This lad is definitely going to the park later,' Simon added, with a flash of understanding. 'If he feels ill he can be ill over there.'

Just then, Gail let out a massive squeal. I spun around from my position next to the fridge, only to see Ben had turned his bottle upside down, spilling the contents all over Gail.

'Are you all right?' I whined, trotting over to her.

'You look like a massive marshmallow.' Simon chuckled, looking up at the sight of his wife covered in milk.

34

Gail rolled her eyes. 'Thanks, love. Just what I needed to hear after a night of no sleep.'

I rubbed my head against her denim clad shins. Gail had been pacing up and down with a teething Ben most of the night. She had done her best to get him to sleep and had sung to him, read to him, offered him a bottle, her finger to chew, but nothing would quieten him down.

In the end I had got up with her and tried to sing him a song as well, but Ben hadn't approved of my attempts either and so Gail and I had both given up. Instead, we collapsed in a heap on the velvet sofa, urging sleep to find Ben and us.

'Not again, love,' Simon said sympathetically. 'I didn't hear anything.'

'No, I know,' Gail grumbled. 'I saw you were sound asleep.'

Simon looked shifty. 'It's not my fault I'm a sound sleeper.'

'No, but it is your fault you wear earplugs,' Gail replied, as she looked down and smiled at me. 'If it wasn't for Percy keeping me company last night, I'd have gone mad.'

I nuzzled my head against her legs once more, wishing there was more I could do.

'Well, like I said, I'm sorry, love.' Simon shrugged. 'I've a lot on at work at the minute, and I'd like it to stay that way with all these extra mouths to feed.'

Gail sighed as she glanced down at her sticky fleece. 'I know, I do understand. Look, just take Ben a minute can you, I need to get changed.'

'I can't, I've got to go to work. I'm late fixing Mrs

Gaston's boiler as it is,' Simon replied, already backing out of the door.

'Can't she wait a few minutes?' Gail hissed.

Sensing discord between his parents, Ben chose that exact moment to let his feelings on the matter be known. Opening his mouth, he let out another scream at the top of his lungs.

I looked up at him in horror. How could such a big noise come from such a tiny person? Simon wasted no time reaching for his van keys from the nook by the fridge.

'Sorry, love. I'll only be an hour. Call me if you need anything,' he insisted, making a phone gesture with his hands.

As the front door slammed shut, Gail looked helplessly at me, still drowning in milk.

'Can I help?' I barked helpfully. 'As Jenny doesn't have school, should I get her up perhaps to give you a hand?'

But Gail merely let out a sigh as she sat Ben in his high chair, and began mopping herself down with a tea towel.

With Gail temporarily engrossed, I wondered if this was the perfect time for a chat with the young fella. I padded across to his high chair and sat with my head cocked, gazing into his eyes. Mollified by a dummy Gail had just plonked in his mouth, I had to hand it to him, when he wasn't crying he wasn't bad. Like his mum he had blue eyes that sparkled when he gave off one of his trademark grins.

'Now, Ben, I know you're just a baby, but you need to give Gail, your mum, a break. She's tired, she's got a lot to do all said, and all this crying, well it's not the way,' I barked up at him.

I paused, allowing the suggestion to sink in, but judging from the way he banged his fists against his high chair it didn't look as though Ben had understood a bark I said.

With a sigh, I tried again. 'Look, Ben, you know how much everyone loves you, especially me. But do you think there's any way that you could think about easing up on the tears for just a little bit. I would be so grateful, I'll even let you pull my ears without fuss from time to time.'

The moment the bark left my lips, I regretted it. For a baby, Ben had a monstrously fierce grip, and allowing him free rein over my precious ears would be a sacrifice, and not one I was sure I would be willing to make.

Just then, Ben fixed me with what I called his excitable face and, as if by magic, he let out a happy gurgle. The sight of him looking so adorable left me feeling warm and fuzzy inside and I knew that I wouldn't just sacrifice my ears for peace and quiet but Hugo and Peg's too.

As Gail finished cleaning herself up, she bent down to tickle my chin.

'Look, you got him to stop crying! I don't know how you do it, Percy. You've got the magic touch.' She grinned.

'There's no magic to it, I've just bargained away my soul,' I barked in all seriousness.

Gail smiled, then stood up to plant a kiss on Ben's head. I looked at her as she bustled around the kitchen, appearing happy and content.

'So, Perce, I thought you and me could go to the shops

when Simon gets back. He can mind the kids and Hugo for a bit, what do you think?'

I thumped my tail on the floor to signal my delight. Talk about bliss! Gail and I hadn't spent time on our own together for what felt like months. It would be wonderful to be in her company without distraction even for just a few minutes.

*

Just as he promised, Simon returned an hour later, more than happy to look after the kids and Hugo, giving Gail and me some much needed time to ourselves. Eagerly, I followed my owner out into the hallway. Quickly, she slipped her trainers on and shoved a treat and my lead into the pocket of her wax jacket. I hadn't used a lead in over a year, but Gail always liked to tie me to a post outside the supermarket when she nipped in for groceries, just in case anyone stole me.

'Jen, we're off now. Any problems give me a ring, OK?' Gail called up the stairs.

'OK,' came Jenny's muffled voice.

Gail rolled her eyes as she opened the door and we stepped out into the fresh air.

'Teenagers eh, Perce?' she groaned. 'I remember when Jenny was Ben's age, she was such a sweet little thing. Now she spends all her time on her mobile phone playing games or chatting to her friends.'

'She still is sweet,' I yapped as we walked along Barksdale Way, the trees rustling in the wind. 'She's just making up for lost time. Don't forget she was sick for so long, you can't blame her for wanting to be a normal kid again.'

'You're so wise, Percy'– Gail smiled – 'I don't know what I'd do without you.'

'You'll never have to find out,' I told her seriously.

I meant it too. I would be with Gail until my dying day. She had showered me with love and kindness ever since the day she adopted me from the tails of the forgotten. I would never forget her loyalty.

As we turned the corner, I could see the shops up ahead and Gail and I quickened our pace.

'You were a big help at Mum and Dad's the other day,' she said suddenly. 'I just wanted to say thanks. All that fetching and carrying you were doing, dragging things from boxes, moving things out of the way with your snout, didn't go unnoticed, not to mention going to get Hugo as well yesterday.'

'It was nothing,' I barked in reply.

'Why do you think Hugo went off like that?' Gail mused. 'I thought we were making progress with his obedience, but after that and the potpourri I'm not so sure.'

My ears prickled with horror. Had Gail had enough of Hugo and his bad behaviour?

'We had a good chat,' I barked quickly. 'I think I got through to him, I think he just wanted to help your parents.'

'It's going to make such a difference having them around.' Gail sighed as we reached the supermarket entrance. 'I'd forgotten how much hard work babies are.'

'Not to mention an adorable, but still very naughty puppy,' I added.

'I know Mum's missed being around us all too. I think it will do her and Dad as much good as it will us,' she said warming to her theme. 'It will be great for us to keep an eye on them now they're getting older too. Of course I know that's a long way off,' Gail said, completely misunderstanding my last bark, 'but it's good for them to get settled in the area and make new friends before they start to need us. But for now it's just so perfect having them here! I couldn't be happier.'

Chapter Five

Returning to Barksdale Way we found the place in relative chaos. Poor Jenny was doing her best to quieten a fractious Ben who had apparently been screaming at the top of his lungs ever since we left. As for Hugo, he was clearly enjoying a surge of energy as he was now running up and down the hallway.

'The sterilising machine's broken and Dad's trying to repair it,' she wept as soon as we walked through the door. 'As for Ben, he just won't stop. I've tried everything. A bottle, changing his nappy, but he's not interested in any of it.'

'OK, love, give him to me,' Gail said, dumping the shopping bags on the floor and taking the baby from Jenny. 'Where did you say Dad was?'

'In the garage,' she said tearfully. 'I did my best, I'm sorry.'

'You've nothing to be sorry for.' Gail smiled soothingly as she tried to hush her son.Suddenly a loud tearing sound caught my attention and, as I looked at Jenny in alarm, the sound rang through the house again. It was coming from the living room, and together the four of us rushed to the front of the house to find Hugo swinging joyously from Gail's prized cream-and-blue Sanderson dandelion curtains.

'What the hell?' Gail blurted over the top of a still screaming Ben.

'Look at me! Look at me!' he barked excitedly. 'Look how high I can climb.'

'I'll deal with Hugo,' I barked angrily, taking in the scene. 'You've got enough on your hands with that young man.'

Gail didn't argue as she jiggled Ben in her arms to try to get him to stop crying. Taking a deep breath, she left the room with Jenny close behind and I continued to watch my son in annoyed astonishment as he carried on climbing up the curtains. I wasn't normally an angry dog, I never rose my bark or lost my temper. Yet since becoming a father I felt my patience increasingly wearing thin. Now, looking at my offspring running amok in my gorgeous owner's home, I felt fury rise. How ever would he find himself a forever home if he carried on like this?

I stood my black fur on end to make myself look big and scary, then growled loudly. 'Get down from there now!'

At the sound of my angry tones, Hugo's expression of jollity turned to fear. He was now nearly at the curtain pole, and turning to look down at me he realised my bark in this case was not worse than my bite. Immediately, he slid down the curtains and stood before me, his eyes wide and pleading.

'Sorry, Dad,' Hugo yapped. 'I didn't mean to make you cross.'

'It's not only me you should be apologising too though, is it?' I replied. 'It's time you grew up. Just look what you've done to poor Gail's curtains.'

Together, the two of us looked upwards towards the drapes and I shuddered at the sight. Not only were the cream curtains torn and frayed, but they were hanging by a thread from the pole. I knew Hugo was only a pup and bad behaviour was expected as he pushed boundaries, but I had never behaved like this.

'So how are you going to make it up to Gail?' I barked eventually. 'Don't you think she's got enough to deal with at the minute?'

Hugo yapped nothing in reply. Instead, he looked at the floor, unsure of what to bark. I knew how he felt. Just how could I get through to him that it wasn't acceptable to treat his home like a playground? A night in the tails of the forgotten would teach him how lucky he was to have a roof over his head as nice as this one, not to mention a family that adored him, I thought sagely.

Just then I had an idea. Seeing my boy was still excitable from his session with the curtains, I decided that what he needed most was some fresh air and a lesson in the importance of family.

Less than twenty minutes later and we had arrived at Doreen and Eric's and were creeping through the permanently open conservatory door and into their kitchen.

'Daddy, this is very nice,' Hugo barked as we stepped

into the kitchen, 'but I still don't know why you made us come here.'

I stopped by the mystery island and turned to face him.

'Because if you're well enough to run up and down curtains then you're well enough to help out here,' I growled before turning my back and walking towards the living room. 'You saw how much needed doing when you came of your own accord yesterday.'

It didn't take long to find Doreen. Sat on the sofa, she was busy polishing her china ornaments. Seeing the two of us pad into the lounge, she rewarded us with a big grin.

'Hello.' She beamed, putting her polishing cloth aside and getting up to greet us all with a tickle to our bellies. 'Gail just rang me, said you'd gone off wandering and thought you might fetch up here.'

'That's right,' I told her, 'thought we'd say hello.'

'Well, Eric's in the garden, didn't you see him on your way in?' she asked.

'Afraid not,' I replied, before turning to Hugo. 'Did you see Gail's father?'

'No, but I did see some tomatoes,' he barked hopefully.

I shook my head in despair, and beckoned him to follow me and Doreen out of the living room and outside. As soon as we set one paw onto the grass, it seemed the effort of being well behaved for five minutes had taken its toll and Hugo ran round and round Eric's shed, sending mud flying in the direction of Doreen's clean washing.

'Will you stop that?' I growled.

But Hugo took no notice of me as he continued to play chase with himself.

'Pay no attention, Perce.' Doreen sniffed as we walked across the garden to the shed. 'He's a child, it's his job to wind you up.'

I looked at her in confusion. 'What did she mean by wind me up? I knew some of Jenny's toys when she was smaller needed winding, and one of Simon's watches apparently always needed winding too, driving him 'up the bloody wall', but I had no idea why I needed winding or why Hugo would try to do it. I was just about to open my mouth and ask why when I caught sight of Doreen's face, it was the picture of concern.

'Eric was only here a moment ago,' she said to herself as we reached the open shed door. 'He wanted to propagate some lavender he said. So where's he gone?'

Quickly, she peered inside the wooden shed, which was filled with garden supplies, but it was clear to both of us that the empty structure contained no lavender and no Eric.

Just then, Gail appeared at the garden gate with Ben on one hip, Jenny and Simon just behind. Even though I'd only seen them less than an hour ago I still felt a pang of joy at the sight of my gorgeous family.

'Thought I'd come and take those dogs off your hands.' Gail grinned, her hair shimmering in the midday sunshine as it always did. 'And we fancied a bit of fresh air, didn't we?'

'Certainly did.' Simon nodded, looking up at the blue skies with a smile. 'Thought you might like me to have a look at those shelves in the kitchen you wanted putting up too.'

But Doreen merely nodded as Gail caught sight of her mother's worried expression.

'What is it, Mum?'

'It's your father,' she said quietly. 'He's disappeared.'

Gail narrowed her eyes in confusion. 'Are you sure?'

'He was just here a minute ago. And now he's gone.'

'Well, maybe he's nipped to the shops or something and you didn't hear him call to tell you that's where he's gone,' Gail suggested, adjusting Ben on her hip.

About to open her mouth to reply, Hugo rushed past Doreen, almost toppling her over with his speed.

'Will you stop it,' I yapped crossly. 'Go and lie under the tree in the shade and calm down.'

Looking contrite, Hugo retreated immediately while my eyes rested on the older woman. In that instant I saw that same look of fear that I had witnessed yesterday. There was clearly something very seriously wrong.

'It's not the first time he's done this,' Doreen admitted shakily, sinking onto the wooden bench that stood nearby. 'He vanished a few weeks back, turned up at Instow wandering the shoreline of all places.'

'You never said,' Gail exclaimed, taking a seat next to her mother.

'What happened, Doreen?' Simon asked, his voice rich with concern.

Doreen looked at the floor. 'Just that, love. I came home from line dancing, cross because he was supposed to have picked me up and he'd clean forgotten. Gone for a walk along the coast, he said, no apology nothing. Said I'd got confused! Me!'

'That's why you were so upset about him forgetting where the stuff in the kitchen went yesterday,' Jenny gasped.

'Yes, love. I thought a move up here might give him a change, refresh his energy levels a bit, you know.' Doreen sighed.

Gail smiled sympathetically at her mother as she jiggled Ben in her arms. 'Look, he's just getting a bit forgetful that's all. He's had a lot on his plate, you know what it's like when you're anxious about something.'

Silently, Doreen nodded.

'Well, that's it then.' Simon shrugged, stuffing his hands in his jeans pockets. 'He's just a bit overwrought with the move that's all. We'll keep an eye on him, but I'm sure there's nothing to worry about. Let's just think about where he might have gone now.'

Doreen rested her head in her hands as she obviously tried to think about where her husband could have gone.

'I just don't know,' Doreen said tearfully. 'We've only been here a few days and the only other place he knows is your house.'

'Right,' said Gail determinedly. 'Jenny, can you nip back and see if you can find Granddad at ours.'

'OK,' Jenny replied, before a flicker of confusion crossed her freckled features. 'Just one thing though – where's Hugo?'

Alarm shot through me as I glanced around the garden and saw that my son too had vanished. Frantically, I raced around the lawn, bypassing the rose bushes, dodging the pergola and checking the rockery to see if I hadn't somehow misplaced my son. But he was nowhere to be found. Panic washed over me and I slumped to the ground, the grass tickling my nose. Where on earth could Hugo be? Hadn't he listened to me yesterday when I drummed it into him that he was not to disappear? Panic coursed through my fur at the thought of my boy all alone, wandering the streets of London. Had he vanished because I lost my temper? Was it my fault he had disappeared? In that moment all I felt was guilt for every harsh bark I had ever uttered in his direction. He wasn't naughty, he was young and I would trade everything if Hugo was safe.

Chapter Six

As we all looked at each other wild-eyed, I knew this wasn't the time to panic and we had to keep calm. Eric was a grown man, he was perfectly entitled to go for a walk if he wanted to. As for Hugo, well he might be young, but he wasn't stupid, of that I was sure.

'OK,' said Gail, as if reading my mind. 'Let's try and think logically about where each of them could be. Is it possible they could be together?'

I glanced at Gail as if she were some kind of genius! Yes, of course, Hugo must have gone to find Eric. After all, they had appeared to have developed some sort of bond. Why hadn't I thought of that?

'So, Mum, you said Dad was in the shed right?' Gail continued.

Doreen gave a small nod of her head.

'So if gardening is on his mind, then he's likely nipped out to find a garden centre,' Gail reasoned.

'But Hugo doesn't know what a garden centre is,'

I whined. 'How will we even know they've ended up together?'

Gail handed Ben to her mother, and stroked my head, picking up on my worry. 'Don't worry, Percy. I've never lost one of my children yet, I'm not about to start with one of yours.'

I licked her hand, grateful she was trying to calm me down, but while we had come up with a plan to find Eric, would we find Hugo? All of a sudden, images of telling Peg I had mislaid one of her children flooded my mind. She wouldn't just be upset she would no doubt set the dogs on me at the news. I couldn't let her down.

'So,' Gail said looking at Doreen. 'Can you help Simon mind Ben while I nip to the High Street and see if any of our missing men are there?'

Simon raised an eyebrow. 'I don't need help, love, and surely it's best if I go?'

Gail shook her head. 'I'd rather you stayed here if that's all right. He's my dad, I feel responsible, as long as you and Mum don't mind?'

Doreen nodded, her face lined with worry. ''Course, love, thanks. Keep your phone on you, won't you? Then I can let you know if Jenny has any news or if they turn up.'

'OK,' she agreed. 'Let me just nip to the loo and I'll be off.'

As Gail went inside, I thought about what I could do. Perhaps the best thing would be to send out an alert on the dog telegraph appealing for help over Hugo's disappearance. The dog telegraph was a brilliant way of communicating with dogs all over the country, if not the world, and most of us were happy to while away an evening exchanging news with loved ones.

Glancing around the garden, I looked for a suitable spot. Finding a large cherry tree in full bloom at the end I made my way over there and got ready to bark for all I was worth and sound the alert.

Only I had scarcely made one woof, when a sudden shout from Jenny made me jump.

'Cooeee,' she called at the top of her lungs. 'Look who I found.'

Turning to look at my favourite little girl, wearing a smile a mile wide, joy washed over me. Because there, bold as brass, looking for all the world as if they had just been for a stroll in the park was Eric, walking side by side with Hugo. The two of them looked as if they were deep in conversation, never once giving a thought to us and how their disappearing acts had driven us around the bend with worry.

At the sight of them, Gail, Doreen and I flew at them, and wrapped our arms and paws around their necks.

'Where have you been?' I demanded, reluctantly breaking away from my son.

Hugo was just about to answer, when Eric beat us to it.

'I only popped to the High Street. I told you that's where I was going, love,' he said to a worried Doreen.

'Mum says you didn't,' Gail suggested gently, looking at her father with tenderness in her eyes.

A look of anger flashed across Eric's features for just a moment. 'Well, I did say. Your mother's got selective deafness.'

'Come on now, Eric, the girls are just worried about you, that's all,' Simon cautioned, holding Ben tightly against him.

Eric sighed in frustration and ran his hands through what was left of his hair. 'There was no need. I told you where I was going, and this one just fancied a walk, didn't you, boy?'

'Yes! Walk!' Hugo yapped happily, nuzzling his body against Eric's legs.

Doreen looked at the pair of them, ready to say something, before clearly changing her mind. 'Well, the good news is you're here now.' She smiled and turned to me and my son. 'And little Hugo's safe as well.'

I barked happily as Doreen, Gail, Jenny, Ben and Simon went inside. Hugo went to follow, but I stood in front of him blocking his path.

'Not so fast,' I barked quietly. 'Are you all right, boy?'

Hugo nodded. 'I just wanted to help, Dad. You said I needed to grow up. I thought rescuing Eric would make me a grown-up.'

'It does,' I yelped tenderly, rubbing my nose against Hugo's. 'But you can't just go off like that. Didn't you listen to a bark I had to say yesterday?'

Hugo looked contrite.

'Anything could have happened, and your mother would have made mincemeat of me,' I woofed, more gently now.

'Sorry, Daddy,' he replied softly.

I looked at Hugo and saw he did appear to be genuinely sorry he had caused us some worry and I didn't want to punish him further. 'Still it took a lot of guts to do what you did, Hugo. I'm proud of you.'

At the praise, Hugo beamed. It was true, I was proud of my boy. For once I felt he had been listening to the message I had been drumming into him. Humans first, dogs second.

'So was it like Eric said?' I asked gingerly. 'Did you find him in the High Street buying stuff for the garden?'

Hugo thought for a moment before answering. 'Yes. But he wasn't in a shop, he was just wandering about muttering something about the ever-changing face of Barnstaple.'

'That sounds strange,' I replied.

'It was a bit scary, Daddy,' Hugo admitted. 'Don't you remember I told you yesterday he seemed to have trouble remembering where he lived? Well today, Eric kept saying the same thing over and over. I know you had told us that Barnstaple was where they used to live and I tried to bark at him to tell him that he lived in London, but he didn't understand.'

I shook my head. I couldn't remember Hugo telling me a thing about Eric's forgetfulness but then it wasn't surprising, I'd had a lot on my mind.

'So then what did you do?' I asked, returning my focus to my son.

'Luckily he recognised me straightaway,' Hugo continued. 'And when I whined at him to follow me home, it was clear he didn't know what I was trying to bark, but he did it anyway.'

I nodded. This was good news, but it still didn't explain why Eric thought Perivale's high street was Barnstaple's.

I had no answers, but just for the moment I didn't need any. Everything I needed was right in front of me. Feeling a rush of love, I wrapped my paws around Hugo's neck once more and clung to him. There weren't enough barks in the world to tell him how proud I was of him for looking out for his family, but one thing was for sure, I didn't intend to let him out of my sight ever again.

*

I woke to a sharp citrus tang of what smelled suspiciously like oven cleaner and coughed, the noxious smell overpowering me. Opening my eyes, to my surprise, Jenny was standing with her head inside the oven and appeared to be furiously scrubbing the inside.

'What are you doing?' I whined, getting out of my basket and shaking the sleep from my eyes.

Jenny pulled her head from the oven, looked at me and smiled. 'Shhh, Percy! Don't wake everyone. I wanted to surprise Mum.'

At the sight of Jenny in her mother's apron and her rubber gloves, I felt a rush of love for the youngster. She was always helpful, even when she had been poorly, and now, sensing Gail needed an extra pair of hands, she had risen to the challenge.

Padding across to the little girl I loved so much, I rubbed my head against her shins causing her to smile and bend down. As she nudged my forehead with her nose, just as she always had, a small part of me wished I could time travel back to the times when it was just me and Jenny in the kitchen first thing in the morning.

When I had first arrived from the tails of the forgotten it had been Jenny who always let me out for a wee and gave me my breakfast first thing. Over time, Jenny had grown older, Ben and Hugo had arrived and we seemed to have less time together than before. Of course I knew it was only natural and right that she should want to be with her mates instead of her silly old dog, but at times I missed her dreadfully.

'So what's all this about then?' I barked, trying to change the subject.

'Well, a couple of things,' she admitted. 'Firstly, after everything that happened yesterday I want to give Mum a treat.'

'And the other reason you're keen to help your mum out?' I woofed.

Jenny grinned. 'Tonight's the Ed Sheeran gig at the arena across town. Mum's giving me and my friends a lift there and picking me up.'

'That is generous,' I barked.

'So I want to say thank you to her.' Jenny beamed. 'She's been under a lot of pressure lately, so I thought I could clean the oven. I know she's been meaning to get around to it for months.'

Just as Jenny stuck her head back in the oven, I felt a nose against my side.

'Morning, son,' I barked, licking him lovingly. 'Sleep well?'

Hugo blinked sleepily up at me. 'Need a wee, Daddy.'

'I'm sure Jen will get to it in a minute. Can you just wait?'

'I'm not sure, Daddy.' Hugo almost wept. 'After all the feathers I didn't need to wee for ages, but now I've needed to wee all night. I even dreamed about going for a wee.'

I gave him a lick once more and gave Jenny a little bark. Although she had always been able to understand what I was saying since the day Gail brought me home from the tails of the forgotten, Hugo's barks were something of a mystery to her, and the rest of the family come to that.

Nudging Jenny in the shin once more, she pulled her head out of the oven and looked at me.

'Everything all right, Perce?'

'Fine,' I yapped. 'Just Hugo needs a wee. Can you open the back door for him to have a tinkle in the garden, please?'

'OMG! Sorry, Hugo must be desperate!' Jenny exclaimed, ripping the rubber gloves from her hands. 'I'm so sorry, I should have opened it as soon as I got up. I didn't think.'

'Erm, Daddy,' Hugo interrupted.

I spun around as Jenny walked across the kitchen to the back door. 'What is it?'

'I just want to say I'm really sorry.'

'What for?' I barked, puzzled.

My son had only just got up. There hadn't been time for him to get up to mischief just yet.

'Sorry, Daddy,' Hugo whimpered. 'I couldn't hold it in any longer.'

I groaned as I caught sight of the little puddle of liquid

Hugo had obviously just created. 'We've been working so hard on toilet training, you haven't done this for ages.'

'I'm sorry,' Hugo whimpered again. 'It was an accident.'

Rather meanly, I rolled my eyes, despite the fact I knew it couldn't be helped. It just felt that Hugo's progress was a case of three steps forward and two steps back.

As Hugo jumped up and down with glee at the breakfast Jenny placed in front of him, I gritted my teeth, remembering how yesterday I had felt so guilty for any cross bark I had thrown in his direction after his disappearance. Who said fatherhood was easy? No pug I knew, that was for sure.

Chapter Seven

Together with Jenny we worked overtime to clean up the mess my boy had made. As Jenny ripped off several sheets of kitchen roll for me, I saw she had burst into fits of giggles. Suddenly feeling very tired, I looked across at my favourite teenager to find out the cause of all the hilarity. It didn't take long to see that although Hugo had tinkled all over the floor, he had managed to do it in the shape of a heart.

'Oh, Perce, you have to admit that's sort of adorable,' she whined, as Hugo walked back inside.

'I'll admit it's adorable when he can clean up after himself,' I yapped crossly.

'Come on, it's almost like art,' Jenny tried again.

'It would be better if Hugo did his art outside,' I barked, before turning back to face my son.

As Hugo silently scarpered towards his bowl, I carried on mopping the floor dry with my paws. I had no idea how Gail managed each day raising two humans, never mind all the other stuff she had to do.

As I dabbed the last of the floor dry, my thoughts

turned to Simon. I knew he thought that things were a lot easier now Jenny was strong enough to go to school and no longer needed teaching at home, but I still thought Gail was a marvel.

Right on cue, my owner appeared at the doorway, washed and dressed in leggings and a sweatshirt. Ben gurgled happily in her arms, and she kissed the top of his head as she placed him in his high chair. Looking at me and Jenny going about our various cleaning duties, she smiled at us questioningly.

'What's all this?'

'Just because we love you.' Jenny beamed, kissing her mum on the cheek as she returned to the oven and rinsed it for the final time.

'That's right,' I barked solemnly.

'And I love you too,' woofed Hugo, looking up from his breakfast.

Gail chuckled, as she flicked the kettle on and reached for a pair of mugs.

'Well, then it's a good job I love every single one of you as well,' she said, her voice full of warmth.

Quickly, I checked the floor. So far so good, it was all nice and dry and nobody would be any the wiser. I passed the used towels across the floor to Jenny with my front paws, who promptly bent down and stashed them in the bin. Standing up, she fixed me with her best, bark nothing look.

'So what are you all up to today?' Gail called over the whistle of the kettle.

'I'd like to go for a walk in the park and I'd like to see my family and friends,' I told Gail seriously.

'OK.' Gail nodded as I finished barking. 'Park for you, Perce. Sure we can manage that. And you, lovely daughter of mine?'

'Tonight's the concert.' Jenny grinned excitedly as Gail handed her a mug of tea.

Gail's hands flew to her mouth. 'Oh my God, I completely forgot. It's tonight?'

Jenny's face dropped like a stone. 'Mum! How could you forget? It's only like the most important night of my life!'

At the sight of Jenny's shocked face, Gail burst out laughing.

'Your face! Priceless! 'Course I didn't forget, love, it's written on the calendar in bright red pen, look.' She laughed, jabbing at the calendar hanging on the wall with her forefinger.

'Very funny!' Jenny grumbled, sitting at the table to drink her tea.

'I thought so.' Gail continued to chuckle.

Once Ben's breakfast had been heated, Gail sat at the table and spooned the purée into his open mouth. With Hugo still eating, I let Jenny scoop me up and I sat contentedly on her lap while she fondled my ears. As I basked in her attention, all thoughts of my troublesome start to the day were forgotten, until Gail opened her mouth to speak.

'So, are you all right if I take you along at about seven

tonight, Jen, after I've taken Hugo to the V-E-T for his check-up?' Gail quizzed.

At the mention of the dreaded word, both Jenny and I inhaled sharply. Just the hint of a trip to the vet's meant Hugo had a tendency to create havoc all day until his visit was over. He would hide under sofas or in cupboards, and lately had even taken to hiding in the garden shed when a visit to the vet's was imminent.

Hugo's ingenuity was impressive. Yet I knew it was vital Gemma examined him properly to make sure there was no lasting damage following the feathers, potpourri and candle wax incident.

'Yes, Mum, that's absolutely fine, thank you,' Jenny said quickly. 'What are you doing today?'

'The health visitor's popping over to give Ben his nine-month check this afternoon.'

Jenny raised her eyebrows as she leant over to pinch Ben's cheeks. 'How is this little monster nine months old already?'

Gail laughed. 'I say the same thing about you! How on earth are you fourteen all of a sudden? You were two weeks old yesterday.'

'I'm only just fourteen,' Jenny said helpfully, taking another slurp of her tea. 'If that makes you feel any better?'

'It really doesn't, and no doubt I'll be saying just the same thing about this little one when he's fourteen.' She smiled.

I looked at Ben sat in his high chair. He was happily eating his breakfast, purée all over his face as he gurgled and banged his fists on the little white table in front of him. Even though he was definitely wearing more of his breakfast than was in his mouth, he still looked strangely adorable and a part of me was as excited to see how Ben would turn out. I already knew I liked him. After all, he was fun most of the time, especially when he wasn't crying.

'And then this morning I'm going shopping with your granddad.' Gail continued, raising another spoonful of fruit purée into Ben's giggling mouth, 'he wants me to take him jewellery shopping. It's your grandparents' golden anniversary soon and he wants to get your gran something special.'

'Awww,' Jenny squealed. She clapped her hands excitedly, making baby Ben copy the move. 'I take it Gran has no idea then?'

Gail shook her head. 'No, she thinks we're going out together while she's at yoga this afternoon to get him some more crossword and Sudoku puzzle books or something, keep his mind active.'

'His mind is active.' Jenny frowned, her long fringe hiding her eyes. 'Granddad's always busy doing something. If he's not playing golf, he's in the allotment, volunteering in the homeless shelter or playing bowls or dominoes in the pub with his friends.

'But those were all things he did in Barnstaple, love. Your gran's worried that since the move he's getting forgetful. To be honest, what happened yesterday shows you she's probably got a reason to be.' Gail sighed.

'I don't see how Sudoku and crossword puzzles are

going to keep Granddad from forgetting his mates aren't around any more,' Jenny pointed out, not altogether unreasonably.

'You make a good point.' Gail smiled, spooning the last of Ben's breakfast into his mouth. 'But Mum's still worried about him. As if yesterday wasn't bad enough, she told me last night that he went out two days ago and left the kitchen tap running. She's still mopping up now, so if getting a few crossword puzzles for your granddad keeps her happy, I'm all for it.'

Jenny looked at her mother earnestly. 'Granddad is all right though, isn't he? I mean, if he's forgetting things like telling people he's going into town and leaving the tap on, shouldn't he go to the doctor's?'

Gail shook her head and smiled. 'Your grandfather's fine! You're as bad as your grandma worrying about things. I think it's just all the stress of moving house. It's difficult enough for anyone, never mind when you get to Mum and Dad's age. Dad'll be right as rain in a couple of weeks I'm sure, once everything settles down.'

I snuggled deeper into Jenny's lap, enjoying the warmth of her legs. I was about to shut my eyes and enjoy a snooze, when a sudden squeal from Gail made me jump out of my skin. Looking across at her, I saw she was staring in horror at Hugo.

'Tell me that's not what I think it is? It's bad enough changing nappies, never mind cleaning up after a pup as well,' she snapped.

A sense of cold dread enveloped my fur. Lifting my head, I saw that once again Hugo needed the loo. This time, despite the fact the back door was wide open he had still failed to make it outside.

'Why didn't you go in the garden?' I howled, taking in the pair of puddles next to his behind.

'I made Gail a present,' Hugo whined dejectedly. 'You and Jenny said a wee in the shape of a heart was adorable.'

I stared up at Gail's horrified face and saw she hadn't quite appreciated the love he had shown. A pang of sorrow flooded through my fur as I gave Hugo an affectionate lick on his ear. As he stood there, his eyes downcast, his bottom lip quivering, I knew he didn't mean to cause trouble, which was half the problem. Hugo often meant so well, but although good intentions were all very well, they wouldn't necessarily guarantee him a forever home if he continued with them.

Chapter Eight

After Gail took Ben shopping with Eric, Jenny and I set about clearing up Hugo's mess for the second time while he napped in his basket. Along with the heart shape, Hugo had also chosen to show his affection for Gail by running across her bed, getting muddy paws all over the sheets and upending the laundry basket in a game of chase with himself.

I looked helplessly at Jenny, wondering where to start. If anyone understood how much I needed Hugo to behave it was Jenny. When Gail had first adopted me, Simon had been hesitant to keep me, afraid I would be too much work with Jenny so poorly. However, thanks to Jenny, Gail and the love they had shown me, Simon had come around and realised I was their forever friend. With the threat of the tails of the forgotten looming large over Hugo's head, I desperately needed my son to stop being so naughty.

'He's just being a puppy, don't worry,' Jenny said soothingly, as if reading my mind.

'It's not sweet,' I whined. 'It means trouble, and not everyone wants trouble.'

'You didn't think Hugo was trouble yesterday when he went off to look for Granddad,' Jenny said accusingly. 'Then you thought Hugo was a hero.'

I barked nothing. Jenny was of course right. I had thought Hugo was a hero and when I fretted I would never see him again I knew I would trade my own life in a heartbeat to save his. Looking at him now, snoring away, head rested on the *101 Dalmatians* dog blanket Jenny had bought him, as though he didn't have a care in the world, I felt myself softening. Mouth open, head rested on paws, Hugo looked like a mini statue. I wasn't sure I had ever seen him so still. I saw Jenny also had a look of love in her eyes. I had to admit, she had a point. Hugo could be very cute at times. Watching him now, his little eyelids fluttering gently, it was hard to resist leaning over and giving him a huge cuddle. Reluctantly, I brought my attention to the here and now.

'So, shall I tug the sheets off the bed?' I barked in suggestion.

'I'll do the kitchen floor again,' Jenny sighed.

Together we raced off to our respective jobs and worked hard to make the place sparkling for Gail when she returned. I know many humans were surprised when they discovered I took on household chores, but when Jenny had been in hospital and Gail and Simon had been out of the house so much I wanted to ease the burden. So I learnt to dust what I could, as well as strip beds and clean the floor. I could even fold sheets at a push. I always thought that if things got really sticky for me in Barksdale Way I could become a service dog like one of those canine helpers that's trained to assist their lovely owners around the home.

I had always enjoyed helping others, especially the family I loved, and considered it my purpose as a dog. Whipping around the king-size bed, I tugged off the last of the Egyptian cotton sheets, and pushed them all into a ball in the corner of the room. Then I ran down the stairs to help Jenny. She had already cleared up enough of Hugo's mess today, without doing any more.

Finding her in the kitchen wiping up the last of the stains, my heart pounded with love for the little girl. With her ponytail swinging as she worked, she had a huge, sloppy smile on her face. Given the job she was doing, I thought this was unusual and told her so.

'It's just the concert tonight that's making me so happy.' She beamed.

'Is this Ed Sheeran good then?' I barked.

'Ed Sheeran is epic!' she exclaimed.

After balling up the dirty kitchen roll and throwing it out with the rubbish, she turned to me, her face thoughtful.

'But you know it's more that this will be my first ever concert, Perce,' Jenny said, quietly. 'There was a time I wondered if I would ever get to see a gig, and now look at me.'

As she stood there looking bashful, I rubbed my head against her legs. She picked me up and cuddled me to her chest. Just listening to her heart beat proud and strong made me dizzy with delight. Jenny had been through so much, had nearly lost her life. She was right to feel excited about her very first concert and I couldn't be happier for her. Something I told her with a gentle lick to the ear.

Just then the front door opened and Jenny and I exchanged looks of surprise.

'Mum? That you?' she called.

Gail appeared with Ben fast asleep in his carrycot. 'Who were you expecting? Father Christmas?' she replied sharply.

'Sorry.' Jenny raised her eyebrows in surprise at her mother's tone.

Gail held her daughter's gaze and sighed. 'No, I'm sorry, love, that was a stupid thing to say. Ignore me I've had a tough morning.'

'That's OK.' She shrugged, setting me down on the floor with a kiss to my head. 'What are you doing here though? I thought you were going shopping with Granddad.'

'I was,' Gail explained. 'But when I arrived Dad didn't know anything about it.'

I watched Jenny's brow crinkle with confusion. 'What do you mean? I thought Granddad asked you to go shopping with him? I thought it was his idea.'

Gail nodded, as she took off her cardigan and hung it from the back of a kitchen chair. 'Yes, it was. We talked about it only yesterday after his vanishing act. But when he opened the door, he seemed genuinely surprised to see me.'

'But didn't you tell him you were meant to be shopping,

that you'd sorted things out here so you could go into town together?' Jenny pressed.

Gail gently placed Ben's carrycot on the floor and sat down heavily in the wooden chair. Eager to give her a cuddle, I hopped up onto her lap. My lovely owner looked as though she had the weight of the world on her shoulders; the least I could do was offer her a bit of comfort.

'I tried.' Gail smiled, fondling my ears. 'But the more I talked about it the more distressed your granddad got, so I left it and made out it was all my fault and I'd got the wrong end of the stick.'

'Was Gran there?' Jenny asked, sitting opposite her mum.

Gail shook her head. 'She was at yoga and it was probably for the best. She would only have got upset if she'd seen him like that. Honestly, love, the way your granddad looked at me, it was frightening. He seemed so distressed when I implied he might have forgotten something. He insisted it was me who had got it wrong, that I was just like Mum and never listened to a word he had to say.'

'Do you think there's a chance that you might have got hold of the wrong end of the stick?' Jenny suggested gently.

Gail ran her hands through her chestnut hair and sighed. 'I've been wondering that all the way home. It seems unlikely after what happened yesterday, but it could be coincidence. I mean, maybe I did get it wrong, I've had a lot to juggle lately. Perhaps it is me that's having trouble keeping track of things.'

Jenny leant over to clasp her mother's hand. 'I mean maybe you could talk to Gran later, if you're worried.'

Gail smiled and stretched across the table to kiss Jenny's cheek. 'Yes, maybe I'll try to subtly mention something, without spoiling the anniversary surprise, of course. Now, just what did I do to deserve a daughter as wise as you eh?'

'Something pretty special.' Jenny chuckled. 'And to think, I don't ask for much in return, just a lift to the stadium later.'

'All right, all right.' Gail laughed, quickly getting to her feet, causing me to jump to the floor. 'Don't worry I haven't forgotten. Now let me get changed, and how about I take you two pugs to the park?'

At the sound of my favourite walk, my ears pricked up and unsurprisingly so did my son's. At breakneck speed Hugo got to his feet, drool hanging from his mouth and sleep crusted in the corners of his eyes.

'Walk! Did Gail say walk?' Hugo barked excitedly.

'Yes,' I yapped quickly. 'Now get ready, Gail will be ready to leave in a minute, and I'm not waiting for you.'

Hugo needed no further encouragement and after giving himself such a thorough shaking I thought his head might fall off, he walked briskly to the front door.

'Ready,' he barked, jumping up and down so excitedly he sent the little blue-and-white china bowl of potpourri Gail kept on the table by the door flying.

I stared in horror as the bowl crashed to the floor with a resounding thud, sending scented flowers and shards of china everywhere.

Rooted to the spot in horror, I gazed at Hugo as Gail's voice bellowed down the stairs.

'Percy! What's happened now?'

My eyes met Hugo's and he stared at me apologetically.

'Sorry, Dad,' he yelped forlornly.

As Gail and Jenny rushed to the scene, I let out a heavy sigh. Would my boy ever learn?

*

The midday sun beamed through the clouds, and I lay on my back, enjoying the warmth on my belly. There was nothing better than a trip to the park. But when the sun beat down like this it felt like a real treat and after the morning I'd had I felt I deserved it.

I had always loved this particular park and the fact it was so huge only made it all the more exciting. Although it was just a few minutes away, it was so big it felt as though you were in the middle of nowhere. All you could see for miles was greenery and trees, perfect for jumping and playing in. Yet it was the dedicated dog park right at the heart of the park that was my favourite place in all the world. Not only was it filled with trees and grass, there was plenty of shade and a proper drinking trough for us dogs to use when we needed to cool off in the summer.

I turned my head and felt a stab of delight as I saw Sal and Peg walk towards me, accompanied incredibly by Lily, Roscoe and Ralph.

Unable to believe my luck at seeing all of my children at once, I nudged Hugo who was napping next to me.

'Look, your mum and siblings are here,' I barked.

Excitedly, Hugo pushed past me and bounded towards his loved ones.

I had to admire his energy and followed as quickly as I could. Within seconds, I had reached Peg, and greeted her with a lick and nibble to the ear while Hugo, Lily, Roscoe and Ralph rolled around on the floor, each displaying their own particular puppy brand of affection. I chuckled. They were all an identical mass of blond and black fur, making it hard to tell where one pug ended and another began.

'Have you got a lick for your old dad then?' I barked with affection.

'Daddy!' Lily barked, throwing herself onto me.

'It's so good to see you, Dad,' Roscoe added, hurling his little body on top of Lily.

'I've missed you,' Ralph put in.

'We're all together, Daddy,' Hugo added warmly.

'Whatever are you all doing here?' I barked, detangling myself from my offspring.

'Sal offered to bring Hugo out for a walk,' Peg explained casually. 'You know what she's like.'

I knew just what Peg's owner Sal was like: big hearted and generous to a fault. Glancing across at Gail and Sal already engrossed in conversation on a park bench, I barked at her welcomingly. As soon as I finished, Sal smiled and blew me a kiss before turning back to Gail who chuckled with merriment.

Turning back to Peg, I saw our children had already disappeared, intent on a game of chase. I couldn't help

74

but watch with pride at the tremendous amount of energy they displayed. I wasn't known for my athletic prowess so they could only have got it from their mother, I thought admiringly.

A loud bark interrupted my reverie. Turning around, I saw my adorable friend Bugsy, bounding towards me while Heather and Jake brought up the rear. It was turning out to be a perfect day.

As Bugsy got nearer, I tried to avoid the onslaught of his enthusiasm and dodge out of his way. Only, despite my best efforts, I was too late and he greeted me with all the excitement of a dog that hasn't seen his owner after a week away and knocked me to the floor.

'Percy,' he yapped, licking me ferociously. 'It's so good to see you, so good.'

'Thanks, but I only saw you the other day,' I barked breathlessly in between licks.

Bugsy paused and let me get to my paws. 'But it feels like forever.'

'Don't mind him; he's been in a funny mood all week,' Heather yapped from behind us.

'It's true. Don't know what's up with the chap,' added Jake, slightly out of breath.

Bugsy looked at our friends balefully. 'You know what's wrong. Bella wants me to go to dog obedience school, but that just means she wants to send me to the tails of the forgotten doesn't it, Percy?'

I shook myself down, freshly mown grass flying everywhere, and fixed Bugsy with my sternest glare.

'Just because your owner wants you to go to training

classes, doesn't mean she wants to send you to the tails of the forgotten. It just means she wants you to behave a bit better that's all,' I yapped, thinking back to my own pup destroying Gail's home earlier.

'But I'm not bad, Percy; you of all dogs should know that,' Bugsy barked mournfully.

'Nobody thinks you're a bad dog, Bugsy,' Jake barked knowledgeably, looking to Heather for support.

She nodded her head in agreement with Jake. 'Exactly, lovey, it just means she needs you to stop being quite so barky.'

Bugsy looked indignant. 'I'm not barky.'

Jake, Heather and I exchanged knowing looks. Bugsy had always barked a lot, but lately he had become over-exuberant to say the least. The youngest in our little group aside from our pups, Bugsy still had a lot of growing up to do in my opinion, which was probably why Bella wanted to send him to doggy training school.

'It won't be as bad as you think,' Heather put in.

'That's right,' agreed Jake. 'It can be rather fun, lots of jumping through things, crawling through tunnels, rolling around in mud and playing with balls.'

Bugsy's eyes lit up at the thought of rolling around in mud, one of his favourite ways to spend an afternoon. 'That doesn't sound so bad, though not the tunnels. I hate tunnels.'

'What doesn't sound so bad?' Peg asked, joining us with our four pups in tow.

'Doggy training school,' Heather explained.

Peg nodded knowingly. 'After Hugo ran off by himself

on a rescue mission yesterday it sounds like something he could use.'

'I was just thinking the same thing myself,' I barked thoughtfully.

Lily, Hugo, Roscoe and Ralph eyed us in confusion.

'But not us though?' Lily yapped, almost daringly.

'Yeah,' Roscoe put in, glancing from me to her mother. 'Not us? We're good boys and girls.'

As if to demonstrate, Roscoe stood to attention, eyes forward, paws tucked in neatly together, closely followed by Lily and Ralph. Hugo, sadly, didn't get the hint and thought it was a game, preparing to leapfrog over his siblings.

Peg opened her mouth and bit Hugo by the scruff of his neck in warning. 'That is quite enough of that. You could hurt one of them. You just remember who's in charge here.'

'That's right,' I added. 'And, Hugo, you could do worse than follow your siblings' example. Look how well behaved they are now. That's how you find a forever home.'

Hugo let out a large sigh as Peg released him from her grip.

'It's true, love,' Heather barked helpfully. 'Humans don't like wilful dogs.'

'Sad but true,' Jake agreed.

We turned back to Hugo, who was looking at us with wide-eyed sorrow. Eyes big and mournful, he wagged his little tail on the floor.

'Sorry, Mum,' Hugo barked quietly.

Turning to Peg, I saw her shake her head. She was as powerless as me when Hugo was apologetic. She was especially susceptible to his wide-eyed look, as was I, which I suspect was why he had turned it on. Now, he was even rolling on his back, paws in the air to show us his tummy. My heart went out to him. Despite his naughtiness he was so little and sweet, something he wouldn't be forever. I had to stop comparing him to our other kids and finding fault. Just because it made me feel like a failure as a parent, it didn't mean that Hugo was a failure himself.

'Go on, you four, go play before Sal has to take you all back to your owners,' I barked warmly. 'Why don't you go and jump up and down in the fountain?'

Hugo looked at me in astonishment. 'Can we really, Dad?'

'Yes, really?' Ralph asked.

'You really can,' I yapped.

Rubbing my nose against each of theirs to bid them all farewell, I watched them scamper away.

Moments later, the sound of a woman shrieking up ahead made us all turn around. To my horror, I saw a young woman being chased around the fountain by a very excitable pup, namely Hugo.

'Not again,' Peg groaned. 'That's the fourth time this week.'

'What's he doing?' Jake asked in wonder.

'Every time he sees a woman out running in the park, he thinks it's a cue for him to join her,' I explained.

'Sounds quite a nice thing he's trying to do,' Bugsy barked.

'It does in theory,' Peg barked wearily. 'The only trouble is Hugo's idea of fun is to run and jump up at the poor runners.'

'Terrifying them out of their wits,' I finished.

'Poor runners,' Heather barked sympathetically. 'They have enough of a hard time dressed up in those ridiculous outfits, without some puppies going after them, thinking they're playing chase.'

'Leave it to me, I'll sort it out,' I barked, gearing myself up to it.

Running wasn't my strong suit, and I would have to work up to it if I had any chance of catching up with my pug, who was now terrorising the poor woman with his antics, while his brothers and sister looked on in astonishment.

'I'll go,' Heather said. 'Bark some sense into him.'

'I'll come with you,' Bugsy barked with enthusiasm, wagging his tail as if to demonstrate his delight.

'I'll stay here and watch.' Jake sighed.

For once I didn't argue, and as Jake slumped down a few metres away under the shady beech tree, I watched Heather and Bugsy galvanise into action. The two of them rounded on my son in seconds and barked gentle apologies at the poor runner. As my friends led Hugo and the rest of our pups across the park towards Peg and I, their faces full of joy, I sighed.

'We should appreciate Hugo more while he's so young,' I barked wisely. 'One day, he might not always be so close.'

Peg looked at me in surprise. 'Where's that come from?'

I said nothing. Despite his antics this morning, Hugo

had shown he had a responsible, caring streak yesterday and although I wanted nothing more than for him to behave and find his forever home, I had selfishly realised that it could happen a lot earlier than I anticipated.

'Percy, we need Hugo to find an owner. Gail can't handle him forever, she's got more than enough on her plate. We always knew this was temporary.' Peg sighed.

I nodded. 'I know, it's just at times I don't ever want him to leave. I'll miss him.'

'I will too, Percy,' Peg barked quietly. 'Despite his faults he's a sweetheart, but the best we can hope for is that he finds a human who he has an unshakeable bond with, like you have with Gail and I have with Sal. Why don't you just enjoy the here and now? We're all together, our pugs have great owners, and after yesterday Hugo has the makings of a wonderfully brave little dog, despite what he's just done to that poor runner. Isn't that enough?'

I barked nothing, I knew she was right. Whatever lay ahead for Peg, me, our pugs and our families, I just wanted to enjoy this perfect moment of joy while it lasted.

Chapter Nine

All too soon the park was a distant memory as Sal returned to her flat together with her brood, leaving the rest of us to troop home to deal with health visitors and vets. As Ben had been a little difficult lately I think we were all expecting him to be fractious when the health visitor arrived. Usually he spent the whole time crying as the poor man performed his various checks and measurements and I usually ended up feeling sorry for the little chap.

Today, strangely, and somewhat pleasingly, Ben was on his best behaviour as the health visitor arrived. Gail of course laid on the royal treatment complete with matching teacups, saucers and posh biscuits, specially purchased this very morning for the occasion.

Thankfully, the visit went well and both Gail and Ben seemed to let out a sigh of relief once it was over. With all the biscuits demolished, largely by Hugo I couldn't help notice, it was time to get him to the vet.

'Come on then, Hugo,' I barked from my position in

the hallway. 'Time for one last check-up with Gemma and then hopefully you can stay out of the vet's for a bit.'

For once there was silence.

'Hugo,' I called again.

Nothing.

I padded upstairs, walked up and down the hallway, poked my nose in Gail and Simon's room, Ben's room, formerly Simon's man cave, and even checked under Jenny's bed, a favourite hiding place of his, but Hugo couldn't be found.

'He's not in the loo is he?' Jenny asked desperately, spotting me peeking in her wardrobe.

I turned around and looked at her aghast. 'Why do you think he's in there?'

'I don't really. I just saw it in a film the other night; he was watching with me. A pair of dachshunds didn't want to go to the vet so they hid in the loo and got stuck.'

'Well, dachshunds can be particularly daft,' I barked loftily. 'But still, perhaps we'd better check just in case.'

Together, the two of us dashed to the bathroom and fearfully pushed open the heavy wooden door. Thankfully there wasn't a puppy in the loo, but there was an awful lot of rustling coming from the laundry basket.

Nodding at Jenny, she stood behind me and lifted the lid. Sure enough, an eager little pug face popped out of the basket, looking for all the world like an adorable meerkat. It was all I could do not to roar with laughter, particularly as my boy had his head firmly stuck in a pair of Simon's boxer shorts.

Jenny had no such manners and, at the sight of my son looking so disgusted by the pants stuck on his head, she burst into a fit of giggles.

As I swallowed my laughter, I shot Jenny a mock reproving look and she managed to recover enough to pluck Simon's underwear from Hugo. He was so excited to be rid of the offending pants that he bolted out, turning the basket upside down for the second time that day.

The relief on his wrinkly little face as he sat on the floor breathing in great lungfuls of air almost had me in stitches. Thankfully, I managed to restrain myself and instead concentrated on picking up the rest of the laundry. The last thing I wanted to do was encourage him to do this again by letting him know I secretly found it hysterical.

'The smell, Daddy, the smell,' Hugo whined between gulps of air. 'I thought I was going to die, Daddy.'

'Well you're perfectly safe now,' I barked.

'What were you doing in there anyway?' Jenny chuckled, as she helped me scoop the laundry back into the basket.

'I got stuck,' Hugo explained. 'I was just practising my climbing and jumping skills but ended up falling in.'

Jenny paused for a moment and looked at Hugo, clearly trying to decipher what he was barking. Although she usually understood me perfectly well, the puppies were a different matter. As he looked at Jenny, Hugo did the thing he knew always made her heart melt and slumped on the floor, head on top of his front paws, and looked up at her with big eyes.

'Oh, Hugo, we'll make sure you never end up in the washing basket again you poor thing,' she said, planting so many kisses on his face, he howled in delight.

I rolled my eyes. Hugo might not have been with us very long, but he had become a master manipulator when it came to human beings.

'Anyway,' I barked, moving things along. 'You're OK, that's the main thing.'

Hugo eyed me fearfully as Jenny got up to stand the washing basket back on the floor,

'You say that, Daddy, but I'm not sure. I think the smell might have damaged my little lungs. I feel ever so weak.'

With that he gave a little cough, before turning it into a full-on choking fit.

It was no good I had to turn away from him. There were times being a dad and setting a good example was the hardest job in the world, especially when all I wanted to do was join in the joke or smother Hugo with kisses. Even though I knew he was trying to do all he could to get out of going to the vet's, his performance was so good, I was almost tempted to let him off.

Almost but not quite. I managed to get myself under control and, without looking at Jenny, who I knew would set me off, cocked my head to one side and regarded him carefully.

I barked seriously. 'I'm sorry to hear that.'

Hugo met my eyes. 'That's OK, Daddy. It's not your fault.'

I licked his ear. 'That's sweet of you to yap. But I'm worried about you if you're feeling this poorly.'

Hugo nuzzled my nose. 'I'll be OK, Dad. You taught me to be a big strong boy so that's what I'll be.'

'I know,' I barked thoughtfully. 'But I think if you're ill, then it's even more important we take you to the vet's.'

As Hugo looked at me in alarm, I could almost see the cogs of his little brain cells working overtime as he tried to work out how his plan had backfired.

'You know,' Hugo ventured, 'I think I'm feeling better now and I don't want to waste Gemma's time.'

I glanced at him, pretending to give it some serious consideration before I shook my head.

'Sorry, think we'd better let Gemma check you out even though you have made a miraculous recovery.'

Growling under his breath, Hugo knew better than to argue and instead padded slowly out of the bathroom.

'What was all that about?' Jenny asked me as we followed Hugo downstairs.

'Woof syndrome,' I barked seriously. 'Frightened to death of the vet.'

*

Incredibly after the performance of a lifetime, Hugo had been well behaved from the moment we walked inside the practice. And even more amazingly had acted as though he was pleased to see Gemma, licking her cheeks and even rubbing noses with her.

There was a bit of a moment when the thermometer was produced, but a stern look from me and Hugo didn't utter another bark. Needless to say he was given the all-clear by Gemma who said that looking at him now it was hard to remember that the feather incident had ever happened. Gail and I exchanged knowing looks. We were still finding feathers all over the place and I had a feeling that we would for months to come.

After bundling Hugo into the back of Gail's silver car, I joined my owner in the front and nuzzled her hand before she started the engine.

'Thanks for bringing Hugo to the vet's. I know you've had a busy day,' I told her.

Gail rewarded me with a beaming smile and I lit up inside. 'You know how much I love having you all here, don't you? It's chaos but I love it. We won't let Hugo go before we find him the perfect owner, you know that, don't you?'

I barked gratefully. 'Hugo drives me up the wall, but I feel like we're making progress. I'm sure his perfect family is just around the corner.'

'Welcome to parenthood.' She smiled, starting the car.

Ten minutes later and we found ourselves stuck in a huge traffic jam. I craned my neck to peer out of the passenger window, but all I could see amongst the grey skies were cars and lorries stuck bumper to bumper. I turned around to look at Hugo in his puppy cage to see if he was upset but thankfully he was fast asleep, his trip to the vet's having worn him out.

Sighing, Gail fiddled with the radio and a traffic report burst into life alerting us to the fact there was heavy traffic in the area.

'I worked that one out myself, thank you,' Gail said irritably.

Switching off the radio, she rested her head on the steering wheel and closed her eyes.

'Gail,' I barked. 'You can't go to sleep here. It's a car, we'll be moving any minute.'

'Just for a moment,' she said wearily. 'As soon as we start to move, I'll be right on it.'

But there was no time for Gail to open her eyes as the next thing I knew the traffic started moving.

'Gail,' I barked anxiously.

Opening her eyes, she sat bolt upright and prepared to drive the car forwards. Only it was too little too late, as the bright red convertible that had been behind us since we joined the dual carriageway jolted straight into us causing the car to surge backwards and forwards. The bump was so strong I nearly rocketed out of my seat, but as I landed back on the seat unharmed I quickly checked the boy I loved.

'Hugo,' I barked, turning around to look at them. 'Are you all right?'

'Fine, Daddy,' he whimpered.

'Are you sure?' I barked again. 'Anything hurt, cut or broken?'

'No, Daddy,' he barked again.

I turned to look at Gail. She was shaking like a leaf and there was blood trickling down her forehead.

'Are you all right?' I asked.

'I'm fine, I'm fine,' she replied, her voice full of fear.

I turned around, to check on the state of the car

behind. The driver was a young man and on the surface he appeared to be all right. There were no cuts or bruises and so I expected him to get out of the car and talk to Gail. Only, watching him check his mirrors and place his hands back on the steering wheel, I realised that was the last thing he was going to do.

I stared at him in astonishment, as he roared straight past, the front of his car all bent and out of shape.

I turned to Gail to see if she was as shocked as me. Only, looking at her, I saw she was trembling so much she had barely registered the car behind, let alone the beeping horns and shouts from other frustrated drivers as she sat blocking the road.

'Gail,' I barked sharply, 'you need to move the car.'

Finally, she turned to me, her eyes large and scared. 'I can't move, Percy.'

'You have to,' I told her firmly. 'There will be another accident if you don't. Just pull over to the side and we'll look at the damage and then you can call Simon.'

I wasn't sure if Gail understood me but my barks seemed to have the desired effect as Gail sprang into life. After she inched the car onto the hard shoulder out of harm's way, I stepped outside with her to assess the damage.

Thankfully, it appeared to be only minor, with just a few scrapes and a dent to the rear, but Gail was a different story. She was still shaking badly, and the blood hadn't stopped running down her cheek. It was obvious she was in no fit state to drive.

'You need to call Simon,' I ordered. 'Tell him what's

happened and ask him to come and get you. You also need to call Jenny and tell her that she needs to find another way of getting to the concert.'

Nodding her head, Gail rallied. She pulled her phone out of her pocket as she stood on the grass verge. Meanwhile, I jumped back inside to check on Hugo. All curled up in a ball inside his cage, I felt a rush of love. Reaching inside, I stroked his precious head with my paw, just enjoying the touch of his velvety soft fur. A lump formed in my throat as I thought about how this accident could have been so much worse. Hugo was starting to grow up, but it would have been all for nothing if my lovely, but frazzled owner ended up killing us with one tiny mistake.

Chapter Ten

The following morning, Doreen arrived, her face grave as she rapped on the front door. At the sound of her telltale rat-a-tat-tat, I leapt up onto the windowsill together with Hugo and peered out of the window.

Not only was her expression serious, but the lines around her mouth seemed to have grown since the last time we saw her. Not for the first time I found myself worrying about Gail's lovely mum, as Jenny ushered her inside and greeted us all with a warm smile.

'Now there's a sight, the two of you up on that ledge peeping out at me. I ought to take a photo.'

We jumped down and rubbed our heads against her legs, enjoying the feel of her bare flesh against our snouts.

'Hello, stranger,' I barked.

'Hello, Doreen,' Hugo whined, jumping up to lick her hands.

Bending down, she stroked us both, and we revelled in her affection. Following Gail's accident last night, Doreen had become a bit of a hero. After Gail called Simon and assured him she was OK, he had dashed back to take Jenny to her concert, just in the nick of time. Doreen, however, had taken a taxi to our car then driven us all home.

The mood in the car had been particularly sombre. I stayed in the back with Hugo, eager to keep an eye on him while Gail sat in the passenger seat, weeping silently and sniffing into a hankie as Doreen occasionally took one hand off the wheel to pat her knee.

Looking at her now, simultaneously handing her cardigan to Jenny, and feeding Hugo a handful of treats, my heart went out to her. She was such a kind-hearted soul, I wasn't sure what we would do without Doreen.

'So where's my daughter this morning?' She beamed, getting to her feet.

'Right here, Mum,' Gail said, appearing in the living-room doorway, her usually rosy cheeks pale.

As the two women embraced, I let Jenny pick me up and together we walked into the kitchen. As Jenny set me on the floor and flicked the kettle on, Doreen, Gail and Hugo followed us inside.

'Well, you look better than you did last night at any rate,' Doreen said, as she pulled out a kitchen chair and sat at the table.

Gail did the same, sitting opposite her mother and letting out a noisy sigh. 'I could hardly look worse.'

'And that's just what I want to talk to you about,' Doreen said stiffly. 'I'm worried about you, love. You're taking on far too much.'

'I'm fine,' Gail said, raising a hand to bat her concerns away.

With that, Jenny placed a large mug of steaming hot tea in front of each of the women, then sat next to Gail with her own drink.

'You're not fine, Mum. You're doing too much as usual and it's showing,' Jenny said bossily.

Gail raised an eyebrow. 'Thank you very much.'

'I didn't mean it like that,' Jenny babbled, as she took a sip of tea. 'I just mean you need to take a back seat a bit more. Like there was no need to help out with my school bake sale last week, for example.'

'That was nothing. I only baked a few cupcakes and a Madeira,' Gail exclaimed, her eyes wide in protest.

Doreen looked down at me sitting between her and Gail. Bending down, she picked me up and placed me on her lap.

'You're a wise old thing,' she said, fondling my ears. 'Do you think Gail's doing too much?'

'Less of the old.' I sniffed, meeting her gaze. 'But yes I do.'

Doreen ruffled my fur. 'I've no idea what you just said, Percy, but I think you told me you agree.'

'That's exactly what he said,' Jenny said, matter-of-factly. 'And he also said "less of the old".'

'And how would you know, young lady?' Doreen asked in surprise.

'Because I speak almost fluent Percy. Mum does too. It took a while, but we understand nearly every bark and whine, don't we, boy?' Jenny crooned.

As she leant over to kiss my forehead, I pawed her arm affectionately. 'That's right,' I yapped.

Doreen raised an eyebrow in disbelief. 'And what about Hugo, do you know what he's saying?'

Jenny shook her head, her brown hair flying wildly around her. 'No, he takes a bit more understanding. But Percy usually helps us out.'

'I do my best,' I barked.

As I finished, I watched the three generations of women drink their tea in silence. Each one looked weighed down by their own worries and all I wanted to do was help them as best I could.

'So anyway, I think we need to have a think about how best to help you, Gail,' Doreen said.

Gail sighed. 'All right, I will admit to being a bit over-wrought.'

Jenny snorted. 'A bit! You were still shaking when I got home from the concert. And I heard that health visitor suggest you might be suffering from post-natal depression the other day.'

'Were you eavesdropping, young lady?' Gail's voice rose an octave. 'I brought you up to know better than that.'

'Is that true?' Doreen put in, ignoring Gail's protestations, her voice rich with concern. 'Are you suffering from post-natal depression love?'

'Mild,' Gail admitted, knitting her hands together. 'The health visitor suggested I might be suffering from very, and I do mean very, mild post-natal depression, but I think half of my problems would disappear if I could get a decent night's sleep. But honestly, Mum, it's not me we should be worrying about, it's Dad. I think it's him that needs a doctor. Did you know that he forgot to go shopping with me yesterday?'

Doreen patted her neat bob as if dismissing her daughter's concerns. 'Your father mentioned something to me when I got in last night, but, love, are you sure it wasn't you that got hold of the wrong end of the stick yesterday after all?'

Gail pinched the bridge of her nose. 'Maybe,' she whispered, 'I just thought . . .'

As her voice trailed off I looked down at Hugo, who had given up on our conversation and had now wandered off into his basket. Peering at him slumbering away peacefully in his bed – Hugo was even giving out little snores – I thought it was no wonder Gail and I were getting no sleep. Together with the baby, they were stealing all our allowance. Despite getting into bed nice and early last night, we had been up for most of the night thanks to Ben again. He had us rocking, singing and barking as we tried in vain to get him to fall asleep.

My heart had gone out to Gail. After the day she had endured, she really needed a good night's sleep, but Simon was dead to the world and couldn't help. I had wished there was something more I could do than stay up with her when the rest of the house was fast asleep. I had been wracking my brains for ways to help her and had so far come up with a big fat zero.

'What did the hospital say when you went last night?' Doreen pressed gently. 'You wouldn't tell me anything about it when they let you go.'

Gail looked uncomfortable. Doreen had insisted on taking her straight to Casualty for a check-up after dropping me and Hugo back at home. 'They said I had minor scrapes, and that I should talk to my GP about the possibility of taking a short course of antidepressants.'

'I think that's a very good idea,' Doreen ventured.

'I don't!' Gail fired, her cheeks pinking with fury. 'It's not tablets I need, just sleep.'

Jenny put an arm around her mother. 'But maybe the tablets, if it's just for a short while, will help you sleep and feel as though you're on top of things.'

'I don't know, love, I don't like the idea of putting things in my body,' Gail said, patting her daughter's arm.

'Nobody does, but we all need a bit of help every now and again and that's all these tablets would be: a little bit of help,' Doreen added, her tone gentle. 'I mean look at me, I took them when I lost my mother. They just helped me see a bit clearer, made me feel a bit less overwhelmed.'

I stared at Doreen in shock. She always seemed so capable and strong, I had never heard her admit to feeling vulnerable before. In an odd way it was nice. She seemed more human somehow, and, as a dog who adored humans, that was something I appreciated.

'Will you at least think about it?' Doreen persisted.

Gail nodded. 'I'll think about it. But honestly, a good night's sleep and I'll be fine.'

Doreen said nothing. Instead, she sipped her tea and looked down at me and then across at Hugo. I had the strangest feeling her little talk wasn't over yet, and that she had something else she wanted to say.

Sure enough, as Doreen cleared her throat and set her mug on the table, I noticed a look in the older woman's eye that told me two things. First, she meant business and, second, I wasn't about to like whatever she had to say.

'Me and your dad were talking last night, love,' Doreen began.

Gail raised a smile. 'Sounds ominous.'

'It's not, we want to help you and we were talking about the best way for us to do that,' Doreen explained.

'Just having you here is all the help I need. Knowing you're around the corner rather than a train or car ride away is wonderful. I mean look how good of you it was to take the car to the garage for repair last night. I really appreciate that,' Gail told her.

'Mum's right, Gran,' Jenny added, nodding. 'It's made all the difference, especially since Ben and Hugo have come along.'

I was keen to throw in my paw's worth of opinion so barked my agreement. Doreen looked down at me and kissed my head, before gazing back up at Jenny and Gail.

'And me and your dad are delighted to do what we can for you; it's the point of having us here. But we think we can do more and one of the ways we think we can do more is perhaps by taking Hugo off your hands for a little bit.'

I stood upright on Doreen's lap and barked in shock. 'What!'

Gail patted my head. 'It's all right, Perce, calm down.'

'What do you mean, Gran?' Jenny asked, confusion written across her face.

Doreen paused, and looked at each of us before kissing my forehead once again. 'I mean, that I know you're keeping hold of him until he's a bit bigger and you can find him a proper home, but in the meantime, pups are hard work. Remember when we had Bingo the labrador all those years ago?'

Gail nodded with affection, the memories of her childhood friend flooding back.

'Christ, there were times I could have torn my hair out with all the extra work he created.' Doreen rolled her eyes at the thought.

'But you loved him though' – Gail smiled – 'and we want to do our best for Hugo. I think Percy sees it as his own personal mission to mould his boy into shape and he's doing a good job.'

'Nobody is saying that he isn't. But Percy can only do so much and, unlike you, I only had one dog to look after. I didn't have a child not long out of hospital, a baby and two dogs as well. It's a lot for anyone, never mind someone suffering from mild post-natal depression.'

'What about Percy, Gran? He'll be heartbroken,' Jenny said quietly.

At the mention of my name, Doreen leant down and kissed my head again. I felt the trickle of a hot tear splash against my head, and I realised this was as hard for her to say as it would be for me to hear.

'The last thing I ever want to do is upset this little love, he's been a lifesaver to us all,' Doreen said quietly. 'And it doesn't have to be forever, just until you lot are a bit more sorted. A couple of months perhaps, and of course Percy is so close he can come around whenever he likes. That way he can keep moulding Hugo, or whatever it is he's been doing. I don't want to deprive him of time with his son.'

I allowed Doreen's words to sink in. As much as I hated to admit it, I knew she was right. It would be better for Gail and her health to have one less thing to worry about, and facts were facts, Hugo was a huge handful. Asking her to manage both of them, never mind a newborn baby, particularly when she wasn't very well, wasn't fair.

I lifted my head and gazed at her. She didn't just look tired and worn out, she looked frazzled and ashen. I hated to see my lovely owner that way and would do anything to help.

Looking back up at Doreen, I drank in every inch of her. She was a kind, loving woman who I knew would give my boy a good home. Hugo would have Doreen and Eric's undivided love and attention. Not only that, he would perhaps give Doreen some company if she was having problems with Eric, and perhaps Hugo would be a positive distraction for Eric if he was having trouble coping with the aftermath of the move. Most importantly, it would be one less thing for Gail to worry about. If this was the best way to help her then no matter how much it might hurt me I was all for it.

Chapter Eleven

There was no getting away from it, the first few days without Hugo were terrible and I felt a physical pain in my chest from missing him so much. Every time I walked into a room I had expected to see him getting up to mischief. Then I would remember with a sudden jolt that he no longer lived with me in Barksdale Way and my heart would shatter into a million pieces.

When I broke the news to Hugo that he was going to live with Doreen and Eric for a little while I had expected him to be a bit upset. But his response completely took my breath away.

'I will still see you though, won't I?' Hugo had asked hopefully.

'Of course, I'll be over every day,' I promised faithfully.

Hugo hung his head and pawed at the kitchen floor, before looking up at me and barking again. 'Is it because I'm bad?'

I widened my eyes in horror. 'What on earth do you mean, son?'

'Just that nobody wanted to take me when I was really tiny, even though Lily, Roscoe and Ralph were all chosen. Are you sending me away because you don't want me any more either? Are you tired of me not being able to find a forever home?' he yapped quietly, refusing to meet my eye.

A pang of guilt and shame had surged through me. Did Hugo really feel this bad about himself? How could I have done this to him? What sort of father was I? Immediately, I licked his ear and rubbed my snout affectionately against his.

'You're not bad, Hugo, you're a brilliant, funny, mischievous little pup. Yes, you've still got a lot to learn before you find your forever home, but that's not why I'm sending you to live with Eric and Doreen,' I explained kindly.

'Then why?' Hugo asked sadly.

'Because Eric and Doreen need you,' I told him, thinking that in a way that was almost true.

At that Hugo seemed to brighten. 'Is that true? Because I really like Eric, we just get on really well. He doesn't see me as a nuisance, he just sees me as a dog.'

I brightened at the thought as I realised Hugo was right. The rest of us all carried on as though Hugo was a problem we needed to solve, but Eric appeared to be genuinely fond of my little boy. Perhaps this was the best thing for him after all.

'I think Eric is very fond of you,' I barked. 'And remember it's not forever.'

He had seemed mollified then and began to bark about his new life with abandon, plotting his new adventures and all the fun he would have.

Gail had caught the dejected look on my face, and picked me up for a cuddle.

'Kids.' She smiled. 'They have you going out of your mind one minute then leaping about with joy the next.'

'I think you're right,' I barked.

'I'm always right.' Gail smiled and kissed the top of my head.

I leant into her kiss, and said nothing. I hoped my boy would find the same kind of connection with Doreen and Eric as I had been lucky enough to find with Gail. I knew that if he could even come within a paw of devotion and love like that, he would be a very blessed dog indeed.

Yet come the day it was time to say our goodbyes, I forgot all of that. And if it hadn't been for Peg, Lily and Roscoe, who were all there to wave Hugo off, I'm not sure I would have found the strength to have let him go.

As the last of Hugo's things were loaded into the car, Eric and Doreen came to find me. Unable to watch, I had hidden in the kitchen and pretended to be asleep in my basket. Hearing the sound of footsteps, I flung a paw over my eyes.

'We will take care of him you know, boy,' Eric said gently, stroking my ears with his soft hands.

'That's right, Perce,' Doreen crooned. 'And you know it's just for a little while until Gail gets herself sorted.'

'But you must come over any time you like,' Eric insisted. 'You're Hugo's father, he needs you.'

After that they had each bent down and kissed my head, and left me to it. I remember thinking it seemed a bit heartless at the time, but on reflection I needed a bit of time to myself and was grateful they had sensed that.

When I visited Hugo later, I felt ever so much better seeing him in his new environment and it was clear it hadn't taken him long to settle in. Doreen had arranged his bed in the kitchen just as he had it at Gail's, and Eric had even given him some of his precious tomatoes from the palm of his hand to help make him feel loved.

I was touched they would go to so much trouble, and resolved to do everything I could to make this move as easy on Hugo as I could. So I visited every day just as I promised, but I always agreed with Doreen and Eric about what he should eat, how he should be disciplined and trained.

It seemed to work, as Hugo, who had already developed a bond with Eric after he went missing, seemed even fonder of Gail's dad.

And now, as I met Hugo, together with Eric and Doreen, at the dog park, it was obvious those ties were becoming stronger by the day.

Sitting next to Peg under the shade of a cedar tree, the late July heat scorching my fur, I watched Hugo as Doreen and Eric chatted with Sal outside the coffee shop, while Eric absent-mindedly fondled Hugo's ears.

'He looks like he's settled in well,' Peg barked, observing our son.

'Yes, he does,' I admitted. 'And I suppose I'm pleased. I still wish it hadn't happened this way though. I still think Hugo should be with me until we find him his forever family.'

Peg rested her paw on mine and licked my ear tenderly.

'You know it's for the best, don't you? Doreen and Eric are able to give him the love and attention Gail and Simon just can't right now.'

'I know.' I nodded. 'I can see how much happier he is already at Doreen and Eric's. I don't know if that makes it worse not better. I feel like I let him down.'

'Percy! Stop being so hard on yourself,' Peg admonished with a small bark.

'Sorry,' I yelped. 'I'm getting there, I promise. Each day without him doesn't feel quite so bad any more, and of course it helps that Gail's improving all the time.'

Peg visibly brightened at the news. 'Is she? That's great to hear.'

I woofed in agreement. 'I think so. The doctor says she's doing really well on the tablets and can perhaps think about coming off them shortly.'

'Oh good. So you see, it's all worked out for the best,' Peg finished.

We turned our attentions back to Hugo who had now been joined by Bugsy in a game of chase.

'Hello, Percy! Hello, Peg,' our friend barked, as he caught sight of us and abandoned Hugo to come and say hello.

Peg stood up to greet him. 'Hello, Bugsy, didn't know you were coming down here this afternoon.'

'Yes, Bella said she needed to get out of the house for five minutes as Jasper's new game was doing her head in,' Bugsy explained, coming to an abrupt standstill under the tree.

'What's the new game?' I asked.

Bugsy's expression was grave. 'It's called the why game.

And it means that Jasper asks why every time Bella opens her mouth to speak.'

'Why?' Peg asked, clearly puzzled.

Bugsy whumped his tail against the ground, the action making a satisfying thwacking sound. 'Ha-ha, very funny, Peg.'

Peg gave the Border collie an earnest look. 'I'm serious, Bugsy, why?'

Bugsy looked confused by the question. Then, realising he knew the answer, he gave the ground another thwack with his tail. 'It's something kids do apparently. They ask why until it's not possible to ask why any more. It seems to make Bella very cross, at least.'

We all looked over at Bugsy's owner and saw the dark-skinned woman with kindly eyes was sitting on a bench near Doreen, Eric and Sal, furiously puffing on a cigarette as though her life depended it.

'I'm not sure I'll ever understand children.' I sighed, resting my head against my paws. 'They seem to go out of their way to make things difficult for their parents.'

'Do you think if you'd been stricter with Hugo, he might still be living with you now?' Bugsy asked, sitting on the floor next to me.

I was surprised at the perceptiveness of his question but didn't let it show. 'No, I don't think it would have made any difference,' I barked.

'It wouldn't,' Peg put in. 'Gail hadn't been coping for a long time before the accident and Hugo's behaviour had nothing to do with the way she was driving. You said that he really behaved himself in the car after their trip to the vet.'

'For once,' I barked teasingly.

'You may not like it, Percy, but Hugo living with Doreen and Eric is better in the long run,' Peg barked authoritatively.

'But are Doreen and Eric better off?' Bugsy asked, once again surprising me with his perception.

I was just about to answer and say that I thought they probably were, when Hugo came running up to me. Watching him race across the park, I tried to swallow my feelings of worry. It wasn't good for pugs to tear about the place and get hot. Not only was it unattractive, but it was dangerous because of our short noses and breathing difficulties, something I had lectured my four about over and over again.

'Eric and Doreen were just discussing having a barbecue tonight. Do you want to come too?' he barked excitedly.

'Oh! Oh! I want to go to the barbecue,' Bugsy whined in delight.

I swallowed another laugh. How had I somehow become a parent to Bugsy as well as my own brood? Thankfully, Peg spotted my mirth and came to my rescue.

'We would love to come,' she barked. 'And I'm sure you can come as well, Bugsy.'

As I finished, everyone's faces brightened and they all leapt up and down in the air.

'OK, OK, now do Doreen and Eric need any help with anything?' I asked over Hugo and Bugsy's woofs.

Hugo shook his head.

'Are you sure?' I asked, crinkling my wrinkles.

'Yes, Eric said he looked at the weather report yesterday

and it said it would be a perfect day for a barbecue. Then he said he was going to the butcher's to buy all the meat so we could have a huge grill-off!'

'A grill-off?' Bugsy asked, looking perplexed.

Hugo rolled his eyes. 'Yeah! Don't you know anything? It's a massive cooking thing with loads of meat.'

'Hugo, don't be rude,' I barked. 'Apologise to Bugsy immediately or no sausages for you.'

The look of fear in his eyes told me he knew I was serious.

'Sorry, Bugsy,' he yapped urgently.

'That's OK,' Bugsy replied good-naturedly, 'I know a few things but not very many things and this was one of the things I didn't know, so thank you for telling me.'

I rested my paw on Bugsy's black-and-white one. Sometimes his sweetness left me dumbstruck. He really was the gentlest and kindest of dogs.

'So do Gail and Simon know about the barbecue?' I asked.

Hugo nodded. 'Doreen was just ringing them about it on her mobile. And Sal's asking Bella now, look.'

Immediately, we all turned to see Bugsy's owner and Sal knee-deep in conversation. From Bella's expression it looked like she was more than happy to go to Doreen and Eric's barbecue and the thought gladdened me. After so much heartache it would be nice to have a celebration, and a barbecue in the summer sunshine surrounded by friends and loved ones seemed the perfect way to unwind.

Chapter Twelve

It was turning out to be one of those lovely summers humans wax lyrical about. The sun shone every day, and a gentle breeze rippled through the evening air, ensuring people and dogs, especially us pugs, always managed to keep their temperature just right.

Now, as I walked in between Gail and Simon up the path to Doreen and Eric's bungalow, I wagged my tail with excitement at the evening that lay ahead. I loved a good family get-together and a barbecue in Eric and Doreen's new home promised to be a treat. As we rounded the corner and turned into the leafy lane filled with bungalows, otherwise known as Yappersley Road, I ran ahead, eager to reach the blue front door I recognised as belonging to Gail's parents. Sure enough, as Gail rang the bell, I saw a familiar snout pressed against the glass, and then suddenly we were inside.

Immediately, Hugo fell on me, pawing at my ears and licking my nose as though he hadn't seen me for days rather than a couple of hours since we said goodbye at the park.

'Hello, boy,' I barked, rubbing my snout against Hugo's.

'Daddy! Daddy,' he barked in excitement, as the smell of meat wafted from the garden through the house.

'It smells wonderful, Mum.' Gail smiled, then kissed Doreen's cheek and simultaneously handed her a bottle of wine.

'Thanks, love,' she said, taking the bottle. 'Shall I open this? I feel like I need a drink.'

'What's Eric done this time?' Simon chuckled, as we followed her into the kitchen.

'Don't get me started,' Doreen grumbled, as she reached into a cupboard for her best glasses.

'Gran! He can't be that bad.' Jenny giggled, taking a seat at the pine kitchen table.

I caught Doreen's expression, and saw that it was that bad. Alarm pulsed through me. What on earth had happened now? There had been no more talk of vanishing acts or Eric forgetting things and I had hoped that having Hugo around seemed to have solved everyone's problems. I looked across at my son who was sitting by the fridge, hoping for a titbit to see if he could shed any light but he looked at me blankly. With a sigh, I held my breath and waited for Doreen to explain.

'That bad!' she gasped, pouring everyone a large glass of Chardonnay. 'Your father forgot all the bloody meat, didn't he? So muggins here had to troop to Sainsbury's and pick up whatever I could lay my hands on. And on a sunny day like this one, well, you can imagine it was slim pickings I can tell you, so I had to trudge to Tesco as well.'

Gail frowned, and reached for her mum's hand. 'You should have said, I'd have done it.'

'Don't be ridiculous,' Doreen snapped, taking a good gulp of her wine. 'I've two arms and two legs, I'm more than capable. All I will say is it's a good job London's a twenty-four-hour city.'

'Poor Granddad,' Jenny said, peering out of the window and watching him get everything ready on the grill.

'Poor Granddad nothing!' Doreen sniffed, taking another sip of her drink. 'It's me that wants the sympathy, having to go to two supermarkets on a hot summer evening like this at my time of life.'

Simon picked his glass up from the table and took a large slug. 'Best go and say hello to the poor old sod then if he's in the doghouse.'

'We'll all go,' Gail said quickly.

'Go on then,' Doreen sighed. 'And take him a beer, no doubt he's drunk the last one I gave him, rotting more of his brain cells.'

With that we all went out into the garden and greeted Eric. For a man in the doghouse as Simon had so helpfully put it, he was looking remarkably chipper in his checked shirt and jeans standing at the new barbecue Simon had given him just last week.

'What's all this about you forgetting the meat then, Eric?' Simon chuckled, presenting his father-in-law with a bottle of beer.

Eric accepted the drink gratefully. 'Oh that, yes,

Doreen's not let me hear the end of it. It was silly of me really. I thought I'd got it yesterday after I'd been up to the library and it must have slipped my mind.'

'Women!' Simon said helpfully, earning himself a stern glare from both Jenny and Gail.

'Ah, it's all right, my own fault,' Eric sighed, flipping the burgers.

Gail put her arm around his shoulders. 'Everything is all right though, isn't it?' she asked, her voice rich with concern.

''Course it is.' Eric smiled, patting her hand. 'You know how your mother gets, don't read too much into it.'

'Sorry.' Gail smiled, taking a sip of her wine. 'I just want you two to be happy here. This move to London was a big one and you should enjoy it.'

Eric frowned. 'Who's moved to London?'

Jenny burst out laughing. 'You're so funny, Granddad! You crack me up.'

Glancing at Jenny's face crinkled up with laughter, Eric pulled his granddaughter in for a cuddle.

'Isn't that what granddads are for?' He chuckled, kissing the top of her head.

Just then, I smelled yet more familiar scents behind me. Turning around, I was delighted to see Bella and Sal, together with Bugsy, Peg and, surprisingly, Jake and Heather.

After rushing towards Peg, I greeted her warmly with lots of licks before turning to my friends.

'Bella asked Giles if she could bring Jake,' Peg explained

helpfully. 'And Heather heard about it on the dog telegraph so here they are.'

I thumped my tiny tail on the floor in approval. Since Bella and Johnny had helped Jake's elderly owner, Giles, out with his care, Jake had been a lot happier, as had Giles thanks to some meals on wheels the couple also helped organise. As a result, Jake had felt able to relax a bit more about his owner, leaving him with a little more free time to spend with the love of his life, Heather.

'It's lovely to see you two,' I barked warmly.

Jake looked bashful. 'Well, old boy, the two of us are inseparable these days. I don't like to go anywhere without Heather by my side.'

Heather shot him a look of pure love. 'Oh, Jakey, you bark the sweetest things.'

Jake looked bashfully at the ground. 'All true, my dear.'

'Percy, Percy, I'm here, where's the sausages?' Bugsy asked, tongue lolling out of the side of his mouth.

I rolled my eyes. 'Long story, but the fact of the matter is, Bugsy, there may not be any sausages.'

Watching his face fall like a stone, I didn't know whether to laugh or cry.

'I'm not saying there's no food, just that there may not be enough sausages. It might be chicken or burgers or something.'

At that Bugsy brightened considerably, while Heather shot me a worried glance.

'What happened?' she asked.

Quickly, I filled them in, leaving nothing out, including

the detail that Eric had seemed confused about the fact he had moved to London.

'And you're worried about what this means,' Heather put in as I finished.

I nodded. 'Something isn't right.'

'I still think he's a bit stressed out after such a big move,' Peg suggested.

'Peg's right, old thing,' Jake agreed. 'After a lifetime in Devon, uprooting to a new city can be very challenging, never mind the fact that, like the best of us, Eric's getting on a bit.'

I let out a little sigh, feeling reassured. 'You're right, I hadn't thought of it like that. I must try to be more supportive of Eric, help make him feel more settled.'

'Exactly,' Peg yapped. 'They only moved up here a couple of months ago don't forget, it's early days.'

'And we'll do all we can, lovey,' barked Heather. 'Perhaps it's a blessing Hugo has moved in with Doreen and Eric, give them a bit of company like.'

I looked across at my boy playing next to Eric's feet and felt a swell of love. Perhaps it was a good thing he was living here for a bit. I watched keenly as Hugo tucked into a tomato from Eric's outstretched hand and then sat back down right by his side. A heady mixture of pain and pride ebbed away at me. On the one paw, I was delighted to see Eric and Doreen had bonded so well with Hugo, but selfishly I realised there was every chance I would never be able to finish training Hugo up to being the pup I needed him to be if he remained here for too long. As Hugo gave Eric's hand one final lick, he got up and wandered into the house, leaving me to play the perfect pug host to my friends.

'Let's find you some sausages then, Bugsy,' I barked, turning back to my friends.

'Well, it's about time,' Bugsy grumbled. 'My tummy's been rumbling and rumbling and I've been ever so patient.'

'All right, all right,' I replied good-naturedly, 'let's see what Eric can offer us.'

Incredibly, Doreen did us proud. Not only had she managed to get her hands on burgers, chicken and sausages but she had also got some bones especially for us.

'They're in the kitchen, loves. I got extras because I had a feeling all your friends would come, as well as Hugo of course,' she explained.

'I think I love Doreen,' Bugsy said happily as we followed her inside.

'I know I do,' Peg yapped, walking alongside the Border collie.

Only, reaching inside the special cupboard I knew Doreen kept all our treats in, she appeared to have trouble finding what she was looking for.

'These were bought just yesterday I know it,' she said, shuffling tubs and containers around to get a better view.

'What are you looking for, love?' Eric asked, appearing at the doorway, his apron covered in grease.

'Those bones I got yesterday, they're all gone.'

'Ha! Maybe you didn't buy them, like I didn't buy the meat,' he said triumphantly.

Doreen shook her head. 'I know I bought them, I

remember paying for them at the till. The lady at the checkout remarked on how many bones I'd bought, and I told her I knew a lot of lovely dogs.'

Just then, a noise made me prick up my ears. It sounded like a groaning sound coming from the living room. Exchanging worried glances with my friends, we rushed to the front of the bungalow and immediately solved the riddle of the missing bones. There on the living room floor, slobbering all over Doreen's new rug, was Hugo, eating not just his own bone but everyone else's.

Fury rose, but my love beat me to it.

'What on earth do you think you're doing?' Peg barked angrily, rushing towards him and kicking the bone away from his paws.

Hugo looked up, guilt written large across his features.

'Sorry, Mummy, sorry, Daddy. But it's not like they weren't meant for me,' Hugo barked, looking longingly at the bone Peg had kicked to the other side of the room.

I shook my head in disgust. Where had I gone so wrong? I was so furious I was trembling. Not only had Hugo proved he had no manners at all, but he had deprived my friends of the treats they had been promised. Rage coursed through me as I charged over to him.

'Just who the hell do you think you are?' I barked angrily. 'Taking things that don't belong to you, causing trouble whenever me or your mother's back is turned. You're lucky not to be at the tails of the forgotten, because any more nonsense from you and that's where you'll be. There'll be no more me, no more Mummy, no Doreen, Eric or Sal, and definitely no bones, so think about that.'

As I finished my outburst, Hugo looked at me as if he was about to perform the human equivalent of bursting into tears, a loud round of whines. Sure enough, he opened his little mouth and wailed at the tops of his lungs.

'Tell me you don't mean it, Daddy,' Hugo yelped. 'I don't want to go to the tails of the forgotten.'

But this time his tears had no effect and I walked out of the door. There was no denying I adored Hugo, but there were times he left me reeling. The worst thing was I knew Hugo could be good, caring and responsible, something he had proved . But consistency was everything and how could I rely on him to not only help the family I adored but become a pup people would want to take home and become part of their own family? I needed to get this pup in line, but how?

Chapter Thirteen

I spent most of the night talking on the dog telegraph to Peg, along with a little help from Bugsy, Heather and Jake. As parents, Peg and I wanted to do something to instil discipline in our pup, not just for ourselves but because I wanted him to be a help not a hindrance to Eric and Doreen.

After I had hightailed it out of the living room, Doreen had found Hugo and been just as cross as me. Discovering later she had ticked Hugo off, I felt a pang of guilt he was adding to her burden and went out into the garden where she was enjoying a glass of wine on the decking to apologise.

'I've no idea what you just barked at me, Percy,' she had chuckled, bending down to fondle my ears, 'but knowing you as I do, I can only imagine you feel bad about your boy's behaviour, and you mustn't.'

'Yes I should,' I had told her, 'he is my responsibility.'

'It was my fault,' Doreen said softly. 'I should have put the bones away. How could I expect a pup to leave them alone until they were told? It'd be like leaving a kid in a sweetshop and telling them not to touch. Don't you give it another thought, Percy.'

But I had given it another thought. In fact, I had spent most of the night giving it plenty of thought, and today Peg and I had decided to go and talk to Hugo and explain to him once and for all that he had to start behaving, not just for our family but for himself. If he ever wanted the chance of finding a forever home, this was not the way, and Hugo needed to understand that – and fast.

After Jenny gave me my breakfast, I slipped out of the cat flap undetected and ran around the corner to Sal's flat. Giving three barks on the corner, Peg appeared right on time.

'You were quick,' I told her, greeting her with a lick.

'Sal left the back door open again,' Peg explained, slightly out of breath. 'She's up to her neck in VAT returns so she won't notice we're gone for hours. Did you tell Gail you were going to see Hugo?'

I shuffled my paws uncomfortably on the ground. Usually I told Gail everything but I didn't want to let on just how worried I was about Hugo. Gail had enough to cope with. I didn't want to add to her concerns.

'Didn't get a chance,' I barked swiftly. 'Come on, let's go.'

Together the two of us ran the short distance to Yappersley Road and within minutes arrived at Doreen and Eric's conservatory door.

'Are you all right?' I barked quickly, turning to check on my love as we stood outside the glass door.

'Fine, Perce,' Peggy replied, hardly having broken into a sweat. 'But I'm just wondering how we're going to get in. The door is shut.'

I realised with a stab of horror that Peg was absolutely right. How could I have been so foolish. I pressed my snout up against the glass, searching for signs of life, but couldn't see a soul. With a sigh, I knew we would have to resort to more usual doggy tactics.

'I think we might have to bark quite loudly,' I suggested.

Peg nodded her agreement. 'Fair enough.'

Only just as she opened her mouth the door swung open and there stood Gail, looking lovely in a navy-and-white striped summer dress, amusement crinkling in her eyes.

'Whatever are you two doing here?' she asked.

It was my turn to look sheepish. 'Visiting,' I put in quickly.

'Well, then you had better come in.' She beamed. 'Mum's popped out with Ben, so Dad and I have been putting the world to rights.'

'OK,' I said, following her inside, and beckoning Peg to do the same.

Reaching the kitchen, I saw Hugo, fast asleep in his basket, his little blanket pushed to the tiled floor. I groaned inwardly. There would be no talking to him while he was comatose and I was reluctant to wake him and start things off on a bad bark. Reluctantly, Peg and I went outside to join Gail and Eric, who were about to go into the garden. Once again, the sun was shining and, after saying a warm hello to Eric, we sat under the shade of the garden awning. The scent in the garden was glorious. It was hard to believe Gail's dad had only been here a couple of months as everywhere I looked plants and flowers were blooming, giving off a beautiful aroma. Not only were there brightly coloured tea roses in the borders and a rockery that Eric had lined with pretty bedding plants, but he had even planted some echinacea in the corner by the sundial, which we pugs loved to chew on. It was such a thoughtful gesture to think of us in that way that I couldn't resist rubbing my head against his shin to say thank you.

'Oh, Perce, whatever was that for?' Eric asked warmly, bending down to stroke my head.

'Just for being you,' I told him happily.

But Eric, like Doreen, didn't understand my barks.

'Well, whatever it's for, I rather like you nuzzling my leg, boy, you're such a lovely dog,' he told me.

I basked in his praise and turned my face towards his hand. I was enjoying the feel of his absent-minded strokes and, catching Gail's eye, I could tell she found my love of affection amusing.

'So where were we, Dad?' I heard her say.

Eric laughed as he continued to rub my head. 'You're getting as forgetful as me. Did I tell you the other day I went out and left my keys in the door? It was lucky we weren't burgled!'

'Dad!' Gail gasped. 'You've got to be more careful. Anything could have happened.'

'You sound like your mother. My brain's just a bit overworked at the minute,' Eric replied sagely.

There was a brief pause as they sipped their tea, the wind gently rustling in the trees behind them as they remained lost in their own thoughts.

'Are you forgetting things a lot then, Dad?' Gail asked gently, looking her father squarely in the eye.

'No more than usual,' Eric snapped, his cheeks pink with frustration. 'Sorry, love, your mother means well, but she's convinced there's something wrong with me, and I've had about enough to be honest.'

'And you don't think there is?'

''Course not,' Eric sighed, leaning back in his chair and knitting his hands together. 'I'm eighty next year, aren't I entitled to forget a few things? Besides, your mother's not a walking advert for a good memory either. Did she tell you she drove the car back the other day with a bag full of shopping on top of the roof?'

Gail roared with laughter, delight lighting up her entire face. 'No, she didn't mention that. When did she realise?'

'When a bottle of tomato ketchup fell out of the bag and smashed onto the windscreen. Your mother thought she'd killed someone.' Eric chuckled ruefully.

'She didn't.' Gail shook her head. 'Well, she kept that very quiet, I must say. Still I can't say I'm surprised if she thought she was an extra in *Reservoir Dogs*!'

'*Reservoir* what?' Eric asked.

'Nothing, Dad.' Gail smiled, waving his confusion away. 'It's a film, but no, never mind, the important thing is you really feel you're all right.'

There was another pause as I saw Eric lean over the little metal table and clasp Gail's hand.

'I'm fine, love. The only thing that's wrong is your mother's worrying too much about me. Trust me, it's just a case of me getting on a bit and getting confused in the new house. I'll get there,' he assured her.

'And you will go to the doctor's if you think there's ever something wrong, won't you?' Gail urged.

Eric sighed. 'I'm a grown man, love, and I'm not stupid. Trust me, if I thought there was something wrong I'd be up the quacks like a shot. I like my life thank you very much and I'm very keen on making the most of this new start up here. I was only saying to your mother last night after everyone had gone home how it feels like we've got a new lease of life now with the move.'

'I'm very glad to hear that, Dad,' Gail said, treating her father to a small smile 'I'll stop worrying.'

'If you could,' Eric said, scraping his chair back and getting to his feet. 'And if you could also have a word with your mother and get her to stop worrying I'd appreciate that too. Now, as we've all convinced ourselves I'm not going senile, can I make you another cup of tea?'

Gail stood up to join him. 'That would be great, thanks, Dad, but I'll help. I'm going to the loo anyway before you ask, it's not because I think you can't lift a kettle.'

'As long as that's all it is,' he said warningly.

Looking at the two of them walking across the gravel path, their footsteps crunching noisily as they made their way inside, I felt myself relax.

'So, what did you make of all that then?' Peg asked from her position in the corner of the decking.

'I thought Eric made a good point,' I barked. 'Perhaps

like Doreen I've been worrying about his forgetfulness a bit too much. Maybe Eric just needs time to adjust to his new home, and perhaps he's right, if you can't forget a few things when you're almost eighty then I don't know when you can.'

Peg padded across to me under the table and nibbled my ear. 'I think that's exactly what you've been doing, and that is exactly why I love you so much.'

I felt myself colour with embarrassment underneath my black fur. Peg was the most gorgeous girl in the world and there were times I still couldn't believe how lucky I was that she picked me.

'You know I love you too, Peg,' I whined in her ear.

'Which is precisely why I know you'll be my perfect partner in crime to read the Riot Act to our son about his behaviour last night,' she barked, getting to her paws.

I grumbled. 'Do you honestly think it will do any good?'

'We have to try,' Peg barked seriously. 'We cannot allow Hugo to live here and mess Eric and Doreen about like he did last night. It's not fair on them and it's not fair on Hugo either. We want him to grow up to be a lovely, happy adult dog with a forever home. We're doing him a disservice to let him carry on with behaviour like last night.'

'You're right,' I told her, getting up and giving myself a shake.

'I'm always right,' she barked cheekily. 'Besides, Hugo was so frightened of you after you roared at him last night, we have to make the most of that.'

I frowned, causing my little wrinkled face to wrinkle even more. I had not enjoyed shouting at Hugo and in truth felt more than a little guilty about it. Before Hugo and the pups were born I had promised myself I wouldn't be one of those dads that barked and whined, and yet that was exactly what I had done last night. I disliked the pug I was becoming, and the last thing I wanted to do was tell my son off yet again. Frankly, what I felt like I really ought to be doing was giving him a great big cuddle and apologising but I knew that wasn't an option.

'It's all about the greater good, Perce,' Peg barked, reading my mind. 'Sometimes you have to be cruel to be kind, and that's what we're doing now.'

'All right,' I woofed with a sigh, following her across the gravel path towards the house. I knew she was right. Still, the sooner we got this over with the better. With every paw strike I practised the little speech Peg and I had promised to give our boy today. We wanted to sound both firm and loving but I also didn't want my son to think I was picking on him.

We were just a metre or so away from the house when the sound of a loud thud followed by an ear-piercing scream rang out across the garden. Peg and I looked at each other in alarm, then raced inside. There was clearly something very wrong now.

Chapter Fourteen

Reaching the kitchen, I stopped dead in my tracks as I took in the sight before my eyes. There on the cool tiled floor was Eric, lying on his back groaning softly, while Gail crouched over him and whispered soothingly into his ear.

Anxiously, I ran to her side and pushed my snout into her hand, doing my best to ignore the waves of fear that pulsed through my fur.

'What's happened? Is Eric OK?' I asked.

But Gail was too busy trying to talk to her dad to answer my barks.

'Dad, you're going to be fine,' she said, her voice shaky. 'I'm calling an ambulance.'

As she reached into her pocket for her phone, I raced around to the other side of Eric's head and leant over him. His eyes were glazed and all the colour had vanished from his cheeks. His grey hair seemed lifeless and, worryingly, I could see a pool of blood trickling from under his skull.

I gave his nose a tender lick. The only small comfort I

could glean from this action was that I could tell he was still alive, as I felt his breath tickle my snout.

'Ambulance, please,' Gail said hurriedly into her mobile. 'It's my dad, I think he's fallen. I don't think he's conscious.'

As she ended the call, I thumped my tail anxiously against the ground.

'Gail, Gail,' I barked. 'Are you all right? What's happened.'

But again it was as if I wasn't there as she ignored me and continued to crouch over her father, her chestnut mane falling into her eyes. But I couldn't miss the tears that were streaming down her face as she held her dad's hand and peppered it with kisses.

Just then, Peg appeared at my side, and licked my ear.

'Percy, I'm going to take Hugo back to Sal's. We'll bark later. In the meantime you stay here and be with Gail,' she yapped, taking control of the situation.

'OK,' I replied, feeling unsure and afraid. 'Eric will be OK, won't he?'

Peg nibbled my ear reassuringly. 'Of course. Doctors do marvellous things nowadays. You only have to look at Jenny to see how miraculous medicine can be.'

With that, she rubbed her snout against mine, and wandered off into the living room to get our son. Quickly, she roused him from his bed and waltzed him silently out of the front door and I somehow found myself saying a silent prayer to whoever was listening that I had found a pug partner as loving and capable as Peg.

She had only been gone a minute or so when the sound of the front door went.

'I'm back,' Doreen called. 'Cooee, Eric.'

Gail got to her feet. 'In here, Mum.'

'Oh Gail, I didn't know you were coming ov—' she began.

Doreen's hands flew to her throat as she dropped the supermarket bags she was holding, and caught sight of her husband of fifty years lying on the floor.

'Oh, Eric, oh my love.'

She rushed towards him, sank to the floor and tenderly kissed his forehead. Then, holding his hands, she glanced up at Gail. 'What's happened?'

Gail pushed her hair back from her face and across at her mother.

'I don't know. I'd just gone to the loo, Dad had come in to make us a cup of tea. Suddenly there was a loud crash and I rushed out of the bathroom and found him here like this. I'm so sorry, Mummy.'

Doreen's face softened as she launched into practical, motherly mode. 'Sweetheart, this isn't your fault. This is just an accident. Now, have you called an ambulance?'

Gail nodded, and I noticed that she seemed to have reverted into childhood, looking to her mother to give her guidance. But, watching Doreen, and seeing the colour had drained from her face, I realised she needed someone to be there for her.

Quickly, I went up to her and pushed my face in her lap. I wanted her to know how very sorry I was, and that

I would do anything I could for her, even if it was just letting her cry big fat tears into my fur.

'Oh, Percy.' She beamed, tickling my ears. 'How lovely it is to see you.'

'And you,' I whined softly. 'I'm here for you.'

Just then, there was a loud rap at the door and a man's voice boomed through the door. 'London Ambulance. Someone at this address called us.'

'Coming,' Gail shouted.

After she raced to the front door to let the paramedics in, everything seemed to happen so quickly. Memories of the time I had seen Jenny collapse flashed before me and I remembered how frightened I had been as the paramedics ran various tests before bundling her into the back of a big van.

Standing in between Gail and Doreen as we moved back to allow the man and the woman dressed in green outfits do very similar things, I tried to swallow the fear I felt. Instead, I tried to remember how Jenny had been fine, that she had pulled through and Eric most likely would too.

'What's wrong with him?' Doreen asked quietly.

'He's concussed and bruised, but we want to take him in to hospital to check it's nothing more serious,' the male paramedic explained.

'You're more than welcome to come with us or follow with your daughter?' The woman smiled. 'Don't worry, he's going to be OK.'

In seconds, the paramedics had bundled Eric onto a long portable type of bed, and whisked him out into the waiting van.

As I stood at the front door watching Doreen clamber into the back of the ambulance, clutching her husband's hand, I found myself shivering. Suddenly the temperature had taken a dramatic dip and the weather no longer seemed summery with dark grey clouds looming threateningly in the sky.

'Gail, will you follow on behind?' Doreen called, just as the paramedic shut the doors.

'Yes, I'll be right behind you.'

As the ambulance roared off, Gail looked down at me. 'I'll drop you home, Perce. We don't want a repeat performance of the last time we took you into hospital, do we?'

'OK,' I barked, trying not to feel disappointed as I followed her out to the car.

It was, after all, a fair point. The last time I had sneaked into hospital to see Jenny when she was poorly, all hell had broken loose when I was discovered. At the time I wasn't sure what was worse, being accused of smelling by a doctor or having to be smuggled out in Simon's coat. Either way it was a humiliating experience for all concerned, yet I would do it again in a heartbeat if I thought that's what Gail needed.

Only looking at her now, her expression grave, I got the impression she was frightened. As Gail went to turn the key in the ignition, I placed my paw on her hand.

'Just breathe, Gail. Everything is going to be OK.'

Gail turned to look at me, her eyes shining with tears. 'He's my dad, Perce. He's the best dad in the world, and I'm not ready to lose him. I can't lose him,' she wept.

I stroked her hand with my paw, and tried to comfort my owner.

'Of course you're not going to lose him,' I whined. 'Eric's tough, he'll get through this and so will you. You've already been through so much, Gail. This is just another little thing.'

With that, Gail picked me up from the passenger seat and held me to her chest. As she gave in to the sobs she had been trying to keep at bay in front of her mother, I allowed the tears to fall into my fur, happy at last to give Gail what she needed.

*

Once Gail dropped me at home, she quickly broke the news to Jenny and Simon. Naturally, they insisted on going with her to the hospital, which meant I was alone in the house, something that hadn't happened since Jenny had been in hospital all that time ago.

As I wandered up the stairs, I couldn't help admiring the family portraits that hung from the hallway wall. They had changed an awful lot since I had been adopted and I was now proud and delighted to see that me, Peg and our wonderful pups were in a fair few of them too.

Looking at them, I felt a warm glow. It was a lovely thing to be part of a family and I could understand why Gail was so pleased when her mum and dad decided to move up to London to be closer to her. It wasn't just about helping out with the family, it was about being with people who really understood and loved you. In that moment, I felt a sudden stabbing pain to my heart and I realised just how much I missed my own family and how I would give anything to be amongst them right now.

I thought for a moment; there was nothing to stay in Barksdale Way for. And before I could change my mind, I raced down the stairs, through the hallway, into the kitchen and out through the cat flap into the stormy afternoon.

I arrived at Sal's in minutes, breathless and panting and announced myself with three barks as always. Immediately, the door opened.

'Oh, Perce, we were just on our way to see you.' Sal beamed, scooping me up and smiling at me as she gave me a cuddle. 'Gail rang me on her way to the hospital and told me what had happened. I said I'd go and get you straightaway but look, here you are, showing initiative as always.'

I barked nothing. Sal never understood what I had to tell her. In fact, she barely understood Peg half the time and she was her owner! Instead, I licked her cheek to show her I appreciated what she was telling me. Then she set me on the floor and I wandered through to the living room where I found my family watching TV.

'This is what you get up to when I'm not here, is it?' I teased. 'What sort of an example is TV to set to our kids? No wonder our son is turning into a hooligan!'

At the sound of my yelps, Peg and Hugo got up from the rug and covered me with licks and nibbles.

'OK, OK,' I barked, pulling myself free. 'I'm very happy to see you too.'

'I just want you to know we love you, Daddy,' Hugo barked earnestly. 'And I'm so sorry about Eric. Is he going to be OK, Daddy?'

I nodded reassuringly. 'He's going to be fine, but, Hugo, we really need to have a serious bark about the other night.'

At that, Hugo's face fell. He glanced at the floor, refusing to look anywhere but at me.

'He's embarrassed about his behaviour,' Peg explained, giving Hugo a sideways glance. 'We had quite an important bark on the way home, where I explained how he had let us down, and that he really needs to think before he acts sometimes.'

I licked Peg's nose gratefully, as not for the first time I wondered what my life would be like without her in it.

'Your mother's right,' I told him.

'I know,' Hugo yelped. 'I didn't think. It was stupid. That isn't why Eric got sick, is it? Because I ate all the bones without asking?'

In that moment my heart went out to my boisterous pup. Had he really been sat here blaming himself all morning? I looked into his eyes, trying to convey how much I adored him.

'No, that had nothing to do with it. This was just an accident, nobody's fault,' I barked quietly, echoing what Doreen had told Gail hours earlier. 'But listen, we really do need to bark about this properly, because what has happened today has serious consequences for everyone, and it's up to us now to try and take care of our family. Are you ready to rise to the challenge?'

As I stopped barking, I looked down and saw my son's eager little face. He nodded his head at me. A rush of love for my child ebbed and flowed through my veins as I realised he was finally doing what I had longed for – growing up.

Chapter Fifteen

It was yet another warm, sunny morning in late July when Gail received a phone call from Doreen letting her know that Eric was due to be discharged later that day. He had been in the North London Royal for just two days, but it had felt like a lifetime as we all fretted over his health.

Each day, Gail and Simon returned from the hospital, I would wait anxiously in the house, or would pace up and down the kitchen, holding my breath until I learnt the news. It seemed that other than a mild concussion and a few bruises he was fine. They had wanted to keep him in because of his age, much to Eric's dismay, but thankfully he hadn't grumbled too much and was expected to make a full and speedy recovery.

Of course it helped I had Hugo to look after. As Doreen was with Eric round the clock, I cared for him here. It was like old times having him with me twenty-four hours a day.

Since Peg and I had given Hugo a bit of a barking-to,

he had completely calmed down, and did what he was told immediately. The transformation was amazing, and I was grateful he had recognised that the situation with Eric was grave and his antics would not be tolerated.

Now, as Gail put the phone down, her face was a funny mix of happiness and fear. Her mouth seemed to be turned upright, but her eyes didn't follow.

'So the hospital is sure Granddad's ready to come home today?' Jenny asked, pouncing on her mother the moment she replaced the receiver.

Simon turned away from his laptop and glanced at Gail, concern etched in his eyes. 'That's great news, can't have been much wrong with him then, if he's out so quickly.'

'No,' Gail said absent-mindedly. She moved across the kitchen, her long legs moving fluidly towards the table.

I watched as she sat down and drummed her fingers against the side of her mug of tea. Gail only did that when she was nervous or worried about something, and I was pleased to see the action wasn't lost on Simon, who got up to join her.

'What is it?' he asked gently, putting an arm around her.

Gail lifted her chin and gave him a weak smile. 'Oh, I'm probably being silly but Mum says the doctors would like to talk to us before we take him home.'

'Well, that doesn't necessarily sound like anything to worry about,' Simon pointed out reasonably. 'I mean, they probably just want to go through the tests they've run, and check he won't do it again.'

'I suppose so,' Gail replied, not sounding convinced.

Simon pulled her towards him 'Hey, come on, this is good news. Don't worry about things that haven't happened yet.'

Gail chuckled and kissed his cheek, her lips brushing against his day-old stubble. 'You're right, I'm being daft as ever. I'll go and shower then I'll go and get Mum. Are you all right to look after Ben today or have you got a lot on at work?'

'No, I'm a free man today. No boilers or loos require my attention, so you can leave the children to me,' Simon said adjusting his dressing gown.

'Thanks, love,' Gail replied, kissing him again, this time on the lips.

Simon grinned as she pulled away. 'Hey, if I can have another one of those, I'll even throw in dinner as well tonight.'

'Make it your special spag bol, and I'll give you two.' Gail laughed, kissing him lovingly again on the lips.

Watching them smile and laugh together made me feel all warm and cosy inside, and I danced a little jig in excitement, shuffling my paws up and down, much to Hugo's delight.

'Daddy, what are we celebrating?' Hugo called, running across the kitchen floor towards me.

'Eric's coming home today,' I told him, my bark full of delight.

'Oh yes!' Hugo barked excitedly. 'I've missed Eric so much. Does that mean I can go home today too?'

I stopped dancing immediately. With that one innocent bark, I felt as though I had been stabbed in the heart a million times over. Deep down I knew it was a good thing Hugo now considered Yappersley Road his home. After all, I had seen the way Hugo had bonded with Eric and was delighted he loved and adored Gail's parents as much as I did. Yet I knew there was so much more work to do with Hugo before he was ready to find his forever home, and it hurt he would rather be there than with me. Clearing my throat, I looked down at Hugo. This wasn't about me, it was about him, and I owed it to my boy to be positive.

'Yes, I very much expect you can go home today,' I barked.

As soon as I finished my yapping, Hugo jumped up and down in the air in excitement while I tried to push away the pain tearing me apart inside.

*

Just as promised, Eric was discharged before dinner and Simon took Jenny, Ben and us pugs over to Yappersley Road. All the way there, Hugo was so excited he raced up ahead, and I grew sick of the sound of my own bark as I told him to wait for the rest of us and watch the roads.

Thankfully we all made it there in one piece and, as we rapped on the door and waited for it to open, I tried to get Hugo under control. After a few minutes, Gail opened the door, but, as I looked up at her, I saw her hair was sticking out all over the place and her face was red raw from crying.

I wasn't the only one, as Simon, clearly shocked at the state of his wife, glanced at Jenny to see if she had noticed. Thankfully, she was so busy fiddling with her phone, she was the only one who appeared not to have noticed her mother's distress.

'Jen,' he called, tugging at the sleeve of her Ed Sheeran T-shirt to distract her.

Pulling her face from her phone, she shot her dad her usual easy smile. 'What is it?'

'Can you take the baby inside, please. I just want a quick word with your mum.'

'Oh yeah, OK, I just need to send a text,' she replied with a shrug.

I glanced at the phone in her hands. On the screen seemed to be a picture of a boy I had never seen before. He had his arm around Jenny and the two of them were beaming into the camera for what I knew to be a selfie, having posed for so many with Jenny in the park lately.

Simon narrowed his eyes warningly. 'Now, please, Jenny.'

Thankfully, she got the hint and reached for the pram. 'OK, don't bite my head off.'

As Jenny pushed the buggy inside, I realised whatever was going on I wanted to be here for Gail without distraction. I looked down at Hugo and licked his head. 'Go with Jenny,' I barked quietly.

He followed the little girl inside and I stayed with Simon as he pulled Gail into his arms. They must have stayed like that for several minutes, before eventually pulling apart so Simon could look into his wife's eyes.

'So what's happened?' Simon asked gently.

Gail rubbed her hands over her face, as if she couldn't

quite believe what she was about to say. 'Dad's ill,' she said tearfully.

I stared at Gail in surprise. Of course Eric was ill, he had just got out of hospital. That didn't mean it was something to get upset over. Surely this was a good thing. I pressed myself against her legs and whined supportively. At the feel of my weight against her body, Gail looked down at me and smiled.

'Oh, Percy.' She beamed. 'I need a cuddle from you right now.'

She scooped me up in her arms and I leant my head against her chest. Usually, I found the soft rhythmic lull of her heartbeat a comfort but today it was pounding as quickly as a heavy metal drummer.

Alarmed, I looked up at her. 'What is it?' I barked.

'Come on, love, what do you mean?' Simon asked, echoing my thoughts.

Gail took a deep breath and looked tearfully from me to Simon. 'There's no easy way to say this, but you know how I said the doctors wanted to talk to me and Mum ...'

'Go on,' Simon coaxed.

'What I didn't know was that they wanted to talk to us without Dad being there,' she said, her voice trembling with emotion.

Simon furrowed his brow in confusion. 'Why?'

'They needed to talk to us about some concerns they had which led to them running some tests.'

'What kind of tests, love?' Simon gripped Gail's shoulders in support.

'Well, first of all they checked his liver and kidneys,

that sort of thing,' Gail explained. 'But then they asked Dad lots of questions about his life and stuff, and there were things he couldn't remember, stupid things that anyone would forget like the day of the week and the year. I mean there are days I'd struggle to tell you what day of the week it is myself, something I tried to tell the doctors.'

'What were the other tests, Gail?' Simon asked again.

'Oh, they did a brain mapping thing or something. Apparently, the answers he gave to some of the questions gave them cause for concern.' Gail sighed.

'And?' Simon pressed again, this time rubbing his hand along Gail's arm supportively.

Gail's eyes stemmed with tears as she steeled herself to say whatever she needed to. 'They say Dad has Alzheimer's.'

Simon let out a gasp of shock. 'Oh no! Oh, love, I'm so sorry.'

'It's all such a shock,' Gail wept. 'I just don't know what to think.'

'Are they sure? I mean he seems fine to me,' Simon exclaimed.

'They're sure,' Gail whimpered. 'They've given us a load of pamphlets and Dad's got to see a specialist next week once he's recovered from his fall.'

'But is all this just because he's been a bit forgetful? I mean I'm forgetful but I don't think I've got Alzheimer's,' Simon said, shaking his head, trying to make sense of it all.

'There are other things too,' Gail sighed. 'Apparently he

told the doctors that he had been having trouble sleeping and often felt tired.'

'But isn't all that just because of the move? It was a big step for them at their time of life,' Simon put in.

Gail shook her head. 'Apparently not. Dad told them about the move, but his answers were enough to trigger the doctors to run more tests, and they seem fairly convinced that he has Alzheimer's.'

'How's he taken it?' Simon asked.

Gail sighed. 'Badly. He and Mum both have, although she's trying to put on a brave face of course, just as she always does. I told her after we came out of the doctor's office that it was OK to cry, shout, scream but she said there was no point. That you just have to keep putting one foot in front of the other no matter what life throws at you.'

Simon raised his eyebrows. 'She's right, of course, but I'm not sure I'd see it that way so soon.'

Gail shook her head. 'I'm not sure it's all sunk in properly to be honest. It will probably hit her a lot later. She keeps coming out with how people with Alzheimer's have a lot of help these days, that there's more support out there than you think there is and that there are things the doctors can do.'

'Are there things the doctors can do?' Simon asked bluntly. 'I thought there was no cure for Alzheimer's.'

'There isn't.' Gail sighed. 'But there are treatments and drugs that can lessen the symptoms. Apparently these are all things that can be discussed with the consultant next week and we'll find out a bit more then.'

As Gail tailed off, she rested her head against my own and I felt the wet tears run down her chin and drip onto my head. I wasn't sure what this Alzheimer's was but if there was no cure then I knew it couldn't be good. I tried to make sense of what this could all mean and how I could help. I was under the impression that doctors and science could treat anything these days. That the thing the humans relied upon, the NHS, was a fantastic, wonderful place where miracles happened. But now it seemed that wasn't the case.

My heart went out to Eric and to Doreen. All of us, Hugo included, would have to go out of our way to offer them all the love and support they would need to get through the weeks and months ahead.

Chapter Sixteen

The visit to the consultant the following week went well. He suggested that Eric's symptoms could be managed with medication, at least for the moment, which seemed like good news to everyone. Eric, however, had other ideas, and in no uncertain terms told the doctor what he could do with his tablets and refused point blank to take them, insisting there was nothing wrong with him, apart from the fact he was getting older.

Both Doreen and Gail had tried to get through to him, but their words had fallen on deaf ears. And, as Gail and I joined Hugo and Eric who were sitting together in the garden the following day, we were both hoping to drum some sense into him.

'The garden's looking good, Dad,' Gail told him brightly, the early August sunshine peeping through the clouds.

Eric grunted. 'Is it? Can't say I'd noticed. Looks a bloody mess to me.'

Gail leant her hand towards the newly trimmed laurel

bush and ran her fingers across it. 'It looks wonderful. Look at all you've done since you moved in.'

'Pah!' Eric grumbled. 'If it was down to your mother she'd have me wrapped in cotton wool sitting in a bath chair waiting to die.'

'Don't say that, Dad.' Gail sighed, picking me up from my position next to her feet and settling me onto her lap. 'Where is Mum anyway?'

Eric shrugged as he reached for his tea on the grass. 'Christ if I know. She'll probably swear later that she told me, but that I've forgotten.'

Gail squeezed his hand. 'You've got to stop this. We're all here for you, Dad. We just want the best for you.'

'Best for me?' Eric suddenly roared, making me jump in fright. 'Your mother's been looking at specialist care homes, did she tell you that? It comes to something when your own wife wants to put you in a home for the bewildered just because you've got a few memory problems.'

I looked up at Gail and saw she appeared to be as shocked as me at her dad's outburst. 'I'm sure it's not like that, Dad,' she said gently. 'You've probably got confused.'

The moment she said the words I could see the regret in her eyes as her father coloured red with anger.

'Confused am I now, Gail? Is that right? Well, here's what I'm not confused about: I'm not going in a bloody home and I'm not losing my bloody marbles.'

Just then I heard the sound of footsteps behind me. Whipping my head around, I saw Doreen at the top of the garden.

'Oh calm down, Eric, for God's sake,' Doreen called. 'That's no way to speak to Gail or anyone else.'

As Doreen approached us, she bent down and gave Eric a kiss before fondling my ears and squeezing Gail's shoulder.

'Take no notice of your father, love,' she continued. 'He's been like a bear with a sore head all week.'

'Only because you want to ship me off to the nearest funny farm,' Eric grumbled. 'I won't have it.'

Doreen's nostrils flared with annoyance as she sat in the empty chair between Gail and her father. 'And I won't have you talking to your family that way either.'

'Gah.' Eric got to his feet. 'I'm going in the greenhouse, get a bit of peace. Come on, Hugo, let's get away from these interfering women.'

As Hugo followed him down to the bottom of the garden, I leant over towards Doreen and licked her face.

'Thank you, Perce.' She smiled.

'You're welcome,' I told her.

'Sorry about your dad, love.' Doreen sighed as Eric disappeared out of view.

'Does he always talk to you like that?' Gail asked quietly.

Doreen nodded. 'Usually. He must be feeling bad though if he's talking to you that way. You know he doesn't mean it, don't you? You're the apple of his eye. He loves the bones of you.'

Gail gave her mother a watery smile. 'I know. It must be hard for him.'

'It is,' Doreen agreed. 'He's always been a man who

knows his own mind you know, won't take orders from anyone, and now suddenly he feels out of control, lashing out is his way. It won't last forever though, it never does.'

'He still thinks the doctors are wrong though, doesn't he, and that he doesn't have Alzheimer's?' Gail put in.

'He does. Apparently the consultant says it's quite common for those who are diagnosed to enter a period of denial,' Doreen explained. 'He'll come around. But I do wish he would come around while taking the tablets. It would make life ever so much easier for everyone including himself.'

As Doreen trailed off, I watched Gail briefly observe her mother before she spoke.

'And what about you, Mum? Are you all right?' she asked gently.

Doreen laughed. 'Me? I'm always all right.'

'So why were you looking at homes for Dad?' Gail pressed again.

Doreen sighed and crossed her long legs out in front of her. 'Because I like to have all the information I can get my hands on. It's not that I want to put your father in a home, far from it. The idea of it terrifies me. Mind you, if he carries on biting my head off like this I might just do that. No, it's just that I like to know what options are available to us if we need them. Your father wasn't supposed to find out but of course he caught me on the computer last night and tore strips off me.'

'Ah.' Gail nodded in understanding. 'That explains why he's in such a bad mood today then.'

'It does.' Doreen sighed, leaning back in her chair.

From my vantage point on Gail's lap, I managed to look at Doreen properly. In the last two weeks, she appeared to have aged about ten years. Her face was lined, and her grey hair had lost its lustre. But it was the bags under her eyes and ashen look she seemed to permanently wear that told me how much strain she was under. It was such a shame things had turned out this way, after their move held so much promise for all the family. Life really was hard sometimes, I mused, just as a sudden shout from the greenhouse caught my attention.

Looking around, I saw Hugo racing out of the door, with Eric chasing after him, shaking his fist in the air.

'If I catch you doing that again, you'll be down the dogs' home,' Eric snarled.

'Love, what's happened?' Doreen shouted anxiously as she got to her feet.

'Hugo!' Eric shouted. 'He ate two of my tomatoes clean off the tree. I wouldn't mind but they were the only two left.'

I looked down at Hugo who was cowering behind my chair. He didn't look as though he knew he had been naughty, then he tended to have a defiant look in his eye. Now, he looked scared and even surprised by Eric's outburst.

'What happened?' I asked gently.

Hugo slumped to the floor, looking reproachful. 'I'm sorry, I didn't mean to cause trouble. I don't know what I did wrong. Eric always lets me take tomatoes from the plants when they're ripe. He says it's my own special plant grown for me. When I saw two ripe ones I just took them like I usually do, but today he told me off. I don't understand, Dad.'

I jumped down from Gail's lap and licked my son's ear affectionately. For once he hadn't done anything wrong, and I didn't want to chastise him any more than I had to. Hugo was entering a confusing new world, one that I didn't understand any more than he did. For now, my fatherly love would have to be enough.

*

When Gail took Ben to a mum and baby club, and with Simon at work, I decided to keep Jenny company that afternoon. It felt like ages since we had spent some quality time together and, once Gail left, I ventured upstairs, and brushed her closed bedroom door with my paw.

'Percy!' she cried, recognising my knock immediately.

I pushed the door open and took in the huge Ed Sheeran poster that lined the wall above her bed. On the floor was a fluffy sheepskin rug and the stuffed toys that had once stood proudly on her shelves had been replaced with an impressive array of photos of her friends from school. I swallowed a pang of nostalgia. Not so long ago this room had been full of One Direction goodies and pictures, while the cuddly toys had pride of place – everything was changing.

'Are you busy?' I asked, taking in the school books that were splayed out all over her bed.

'I'm never too busy for you,' she said, picking me up

and pushing the books out of the way in one impressive move.

'How are you?' I woofed.

'OK.' She smiled. 'Busy with school stuff.'

'And boys?' I asked cheekily.

Her eyes lit up. 'I have got a bit of a secret. I've got a boyfriend, Percy! Can you believe it? His name's Jamie and he's in the year above me. But don't tell Mum and Dad though, they'll only go on at me.'

Ha! So I had been right after all.

'I promise I won't,' I barked seriously. 'He'd better be looking after you though.'

'He's amazing,' she replied, a faraway look in her eye. 'And also, he's helping me take my mind off all this stuff with Granddad.'

I nodded sagely. Anything that helped get her thinking more positively had to be a good thing. Jenny had already been through so much in her short life, it seemed unfair that she should have to deal with her grandfather's illness so soon after making such a good recovery herself.

'I've been trying to read about it on the internet,' she said, picking up her laptop and opening a page. 'I've found all this stuff about Alzheimer's, but it says there's no cure. Is that really true do you think, Percy?'

'Apparently not,' I barked mournfully. 'There are pills that your granddad's been given, but he won't take them.'

Jenny sighed as she scrolled down the page. 'I just wish there was more we could do for him. I hate thinking of him suffering like this.'

I laid a paw on top of her hand, and looked at her

lovingly. She was such a sweet, thoughtful girl, she should be enjoying her life like any normal teenager, not fretting about her grandfather's health.

'Try not to worry,' I yapped soothingly. 'Your mum and gran are doing all they can.'

'There was something I found though,' Jenny said, ignoring my barks. 'I wondered what you think.'

'What is it?' I asked, peering over her forearm as she opened another webpage.

Not being able to read English, or any other human language come to that, I couldn't tell what Jenny was trying to show me. All I could make out were a handful of pictures with dogs dotted all over the page.

'This is a special doggy training school for people with Alzheimer's,' she said excitedly.

I barked in surprise. I had heard of special training schools for dogs that helped those who were blind, deaf or needed support because of disability, but this was new.

'How can dogs help?' I asked.

'Basically, they make sure the person with dementia manages to stick to their normal life and they give them confidence as they're a familiar face at all times when they get confused,' she finished triumphantly. 'What do you think?'

I thought for a moment. It sounded good, but I wasn't sure what Jenny was getting at. Did she think we ought to get Eric another dog to help him?

'What do you think about sending Hugo to this doggy training school?' she asked, when it was obvious the penny hadn't dropped. 'That way he could assist Granddad when he starts to get worse.'

I looked at her in surprise. It was a wonderful idea. And of course Hugo was incredibly intelligent, he would pick the training up immediately. But this wasn't what any of us had planned for Hugo. All we wanted for him was to become well behaved enough to find a forever family. The idea of him becoming a service dog to Gail's mum and dad would mean a serious rethink. The big question was, could Hugo rise to the challenge?

Chapter Seventeen

After Jenny looked at the website a little more thoroughly we discovered the dog training centre was based in north Cornwall, just a stone's throw from Doreen and Eric's old home. It was bright, spacious and full of home comforts. Visits were encouraged by owners and family, and it seemed like a lovely, supportive place filled with staff that reminded me of Kelly, the lady who had taken such good care of me when I had been at the tails of the forgotten.

Even though I wasn't sure Hugo was ready to be a service dog, I thought it best to keep my opinions to myself for now. At this moment it felt as though Jenny and I had stumbled across a practical solution to help Eric, but, naturally, there were a couple of obstacles to overcome, the biggest one being money. Closer inspection told us that if you wanted to send your dog to the centre for special training then they would need to spend at least two weeks with their experts, which naturally didn't come cheap.

'We'll never find that kind of cash,' Jenny wailed, her eyes out on stalks as she took in the figure.

'It does seem a lot,' I agreed.

Jenny peered at the screen in desperation, hoping to find some loophole. 'It even says that you can't pay a bit now and a bit later, it all needs to be upfront. We would need to find thousands.'

I flopped onto the bed, head resting on my paws. It seemed impossible. Closing my eyes, I felt an unexpected surge of pride as I imagined a future where Hugo helped Eric around the house. But then an image of him destroying Eric and Doreen's garden, devouring a meal that Doreen had lovingly prepared or causing some other catastrophe around their home appeared. Even if by some miracle we could find the money, what were the chances of getting Hugo to behave long enough at doggy training school for him to learn anything of any use to Gail's parents? Would it be better to stick to the original plan of getting him to learn how to behave well enough for a normal family to take him in? Would we be placing too much pressure on the boy?

'I feel depressed,' I barked mournfully.

'I do too,' Jenny said, lying down on her bed and pulling me in towards her for a hug.

As I stretched out my body along her paisley duvet and soaked up the warmth of Jenny's tummy, my mind began working overtime. We needed to seek advice and the best place to find it was amongst friends. After all, with good teamwork there wasn't a problem on earth that couldn't be solved and I had a feeling my closest canine pals would know just what to do.

Excited, I wriggled free from Jenny's embrace and got to my paws.

'Come on,' I barked gently. 'We're going to the park and putting this plan into action.'

*

Just twenty minutes later, Jenny and I had arrived. Quickly, we made our way to the dog track where I was delighted to find Jake, Heather and Bugsy already waiting for me. Flopped onto the lush green grass, Jake had one paw over Heather's as they lay under the shade, leaving Bugsy to chase his own shadow once more.

'You got my message through the telegraph then,' I barked, bounding towards them.

'Certainly did, old boy,' Jake barked, getting up to greet me.

'Yes, we were just outside in Giles' garden when we heard,' Heather put in, welcoming me with a lick to my forehead.

'So what's this about then, old thing?' Jake asked, getting to the point.

I looked around anxiously. 'Well, I would really like to wait for Peg if that's all right. I hope she heard the message as well.'

Heather patted my paw comfortingly. 'I'm sure she did, Perce. She'll be here in a minute.'

'Didn't you bring Hugo?' Jake asked.

I shook my head. 'It's him I want to talk about and I thought it might be easier without him here.'

'Oooh intriguing,' Heather yapped, just as Bugsy came up behind her.

'Hi, Percy!' Bugsy barked excitedly. 'Have you seen the monster? I just lost him, but I know he came this way, now he's disappeared.'

I exchanged frustrated glances with Heather and Jake. No matter how many times we explained to Bugsy that he didn't have his own personal monster, it was just a shadow, he didn't understand. Every summer he proceeded to leap, chase and occasionally even hurt himself as he raced after his own tail in a bid to catch the monster he insisted was after him.

'No, sorry, Bugs,' I barked. 'He disappeared around the same time as you got to the tree. I don't know where he could be.'

Bugsy shuffled his paws on the ground excitedly. 'I'll get him when he comes out. He can't hide from me forever —ooh here's Peg,' he barked, changing the subject.

Turning around, I did my own little paw shuffle of excitement as I saw my love bound towards me. She looked as beautiful as ever, the yellow sunshine making her fur look even more golden.

'Hello,' she barked, reaching my side and giving me a lick. 'How are we all today?'

'All the better for seeing you, my dear,' barked Jake warmly.

'So now Peg's arrived, what is all this about?' Heather asked impatiently. 'Come on, me and Jake have been on tenterhooks all the way here.'

I took a deep breath and looked at each of them, keen to convey the seriousness of the situation.

'Well, it's about Eric and Doreen. Jenny may have found a solution that will help Eric,' I barked carefully.

'How's the old thing doing now?' Jake asked worriedly.

'Not brilliantly,' I replied with a long sigh. 'He's still in denial about having Alzheimer's, says he's just getting old and there's nothing wrong with him.'

Jake looked sadly at the ground. 'Unfortunately it happens to the best of us. It's rather a shame for Eric. I imagine that admitting something is wrong is terrifying for him.'

I felt a pang of sympathy for Eric. Jake had managed, as always, to sum up the situation perfectly. Even more reason for our plan to work.

'Well come on then, Perce. Out with it,' Peg coaxed.

'Jenny has been doing some research on her computer and found a school that trains dogs especially to help those with Alzheimer's.'

'Oh that sounds brilliant,' Heather barked excitedly. 'Were you thinking you could get Eric one of those dogs that has already been trained straight from the school.'

'Er no,' I barked, looking pleadingly at Peg.

Catching my gaze, Peg shook her head in alarm. 'Oh no, I know where this is going. You're not serious, are you?'

'I'm very serious. Have you seen the way Hugo follows Eric around everywhere? And the way Eric lights up whenever Hugo is in the same room? Despite the bad behaviour, they think the world of each other. If anyone can help Eric, it's Hugo,' I barked earnestly.

Nobody barked for a while. Instead the dogs looked at me with a mixture of confusion and fear in their eyes.

'Well, I think it's a good idea,' put in Bugsy eventually. 'Hugo is very bright and very clever. He can do anything he wants to.'

'And usually does,' Peggy barked drily.

'Oh, he's not that bad,' Heather barked. 'Just a bit wilful. His heart's in the right place. Look what he did when Eric went missing that time – that was instinctive protection on his part. Now then, Perce, what is it you want us to do? Help you explain to Hugo what you need him to do and why he needs to help?'

'That would be good,' I replied slowly, 'but my question really is do you think he's up to this challenge? As the boy's dad all I've ever wanted for him is to find a forever family. Is he ready to become a service dog or should we go back to the original plan and focus on getting him to behave long enough for a family to take him on?'

Peg let out a large sigh. 'Much as I recognise Hugo's faults, I think you're underestimating him, Perce. I know you're his dad and I know you felt responsible for him when we couldn't find him an owner, but Hugo's changed a lot over the last few months, especially since he's moved in with Eric.'

I looked into her eyes pleadingly. 'Do you really think so?'

Peg nodded. 'He's become a lot more thoughtful and

responsible and he and Eric have a real bond. That's half the battle of a dog finding a forever home right there.'

'But Eric's illness is very challenging,' I put in. 'Is he ready for that kind of commitment?'

'I think we owe it to him to give him the chance to try,' Peg replied.

'I agree,' Heather barked.

'Me too,' barked Bugsy.

'As do I, old thing,' Jake added. 'They always say you can't teach an old dog new tricks, well Hugo's a young dog and it's been rather marvellous to see him mature a little these past few weeks.'

I felt a rush of relief. I hadn't realised until that moment how much I wanted my friends to say they thought it was a good idea. As ever, they were right of course, I knew in an instant that it was time to let Hugo grow and at least give him the opportunity to help the man he very clearly adored.

'There is one other problem,' I barked.

'How can there be another problem?' Peg scoffed.

'Well, there's the money side of things to consider,' I began. 'It's quite a lot of money to send a dog to this school for training.'

'How much does it cost?' Jake asked.

As I barked an eye-wateringly large sum, the dogs looked at me in despair.

'Now you're really asking for the impossible,' Peg barked. 'Where are we going to come up with that sort of money?'

Feeling dejected, I glanced around at everyone else. Did

they all feel the same way? Their faces suggested they did. Forlorn, I looked back at Jenny who was standing under a tree laughing. I saw now she had been joined by a boy and, on closer inspection, it looked as though it was the same boy from the photo on her phone. With his floppy brown hair, matching brown eyes and cheeky grin I realised this must be her boyfriend, Jamie. Watching the two of them together, I saw happiness flood Jenny's face in a way I had never seen before. Although they were together laughing at something on Jamie's phone, this time, she looked at peace. This was more than anyone could have hoped for when she had been so poorly less than eighteen months ago. If anyone was proof no task was insurmountable it had to be Jenny. Look at all she had achieved in such a short amount of time. If she could accomplish so much, we could certainly do a lot less. Inspired, I turned back to my flock and looked at them excitedly.

'Yes, it is a lot of money, but we've managed to pull off an awful lot as a team in the past. We can do this! I know we can!' I encouraged, thumping my tail on the floor for good measure.

As I finished barking, the others all looked at one another still a bit unsure, until Bugsy started barking like a mad thing and jumping up and down on the spot.

'Yes, Percy, yes, we can do this! We're going to make a dog out of that pup and we're going to find the money to send Hugo to dog school! Yes!'

His enthusiasm was infectious as Peg, Heather and Jake looked with affection from me to Bugsy.

'Go on then, we'll give it a go,' Peg barked.

'Of course we will, wouldn't let you down, old chum,' Jake added.

''Course, lovey, you just let us know what you need help with,' Heather yapped.

I thought for a moment. The thing that would probably take most time would be getting the funding together to send Hugo to the centre.

'Fundraising ideas seem the best place to start,' Peg barked, reading my mind. 'Anyone got any ideas?'

'Bring and buy sale?' Heather suggested.

'Egg and spoon race?' barked Jake.

'What about a jumble sale?' Peg barked.

I shook my head. They were all good suggestions but we needed something a bit more dynamic if we were going to make the money we needed to send Hugo to school.

Just then I saw Jenny race towards me. With her long hair flying behind her, and her beaming grin, I knew she had to have something good to tell me.

'I know how we can make the money for the training,' she babbled, before turning to a boy standing next to her, wearing a broad grin. 'Me and Jamie have just thought of it!'

There was a ripple of curiosity as we all looked at each other, waiting for Jenny to do her big reveal.

'Perivale Animals With Skill, or PAWS for short!' Jenny beamed. 'We'll get the community involved, and get everyone's animals to perform their best talent in front of a panel of judges. I mean you all have one. Percy, yours could be mind-reading, dusting or even cuddling, you're so gifted!'

I felt myself blush under the weight of so much praise.

'You're all talented, though that's the thing,' Jenny continued breathlessly. 'And here's the best bit, Jamie's aunt is Tanya Herring, you know, the host of that singing competition we love on Saturday nights, Percy?'

I nodded in awe, thinking of the talent show we all enjoyed as a family in front of the telly with a curry as Jenny carried on, her excitement reaching a crescendo.

'Anyway, oh you tell them, Jamie,' she said, giving the boy a little push towards us.

Shuffling from foot to foot, I saw Jamie looked a bit reluctant to address a group of dogs so I gave him a gentle bark of encouragement.

'Well, Aunt Tanya has got three pugs of her own. She's always getting involved in dog and charity stuff, I texted her already and she said she'd love to help get things off the ground,' he finished.

'So what do you think?' Jenny asked, crouching down to tickle my chin.

'What I think is that you're brilliant,' I yapped, gently licking her hand in appreciation.

Trust Jenny to think up something so perfect. With a plan like this, we were guaranteed success.

Chapter Eighteen

Of course having come up with a plan, we wanted to sound Gail out about it before yapping it over with anyone else, particularly Hugo. Luckily, Jenny knew the best way of dealing with it. Once we got home from the park, she set about making her mum a cup of tea and a lemon drizzle cake, which looked and smelled so good it could have easily rivalled anything off the *Great British Bake Off*.

Needless to say, the smell alone brought a smile to Gail's face as she walked through the door after a day with her parents.

'My goodness, what have I done to deserve all of this?' Gail gasped at the sight of the zesty delight sitting on the kitchen table complete with a pot of tea.

'Nothing,' said Jenny,' I just think you've been under a lot of strain lately and I wanted to do something to show you how much we love you and appreciate you.'

'I second that,' I barked.

'Well, I don't know what to say,' she exclaimed, pulling out a chair and scraping it noisily across the floor.

'Say you'll have a huge slice.' Jenny grinned, cutting her a big wedge and placing it on a plate in front of her.

As Gail took a bite, a huge smile spread across her face. 'That is delicious, love, but why do I get the feeling I'm being buttered up for something?'

I thumped my tail against the floor. There was no pulling the wool over Gail's eyes. She had a knack for spotting when someone was up to something and nothing ever got past her.

Jenny cut herself a slice and sat opposite her mum. 'Well, I wouldn't say we were up to something, would you, Perce?'

'No,' I replied, jumping up onto Gail's lap for a cuddle.

'Exactly.' Jenny smiled, taking a bite.

'I would say we definitely weren't up to anything,' I continued. 'What I would say is we are trying to be helpful.'

'Yes, that's right,' Jenny put in. 'We're trying to be helpful.'

Gail looked from me to Jenny and back again before she spoke. 'All right, out with it.' She sighed, pushing the cake away, clearly signalling she wouldn't be bought with a slice of lemon drizzle.

'I've been doing some thinking,' Jenny explained.

'Go on.' Gail sighed, a ghost of a smile playing on her lips.

'Well, I know Granddad's been having a really hard time with all this Alzheimer's stuff,' she began.

Gail cocked her head to one side and arranged her features into a look of concern. 'Jenny, you mustn't worry about that, honestly. This is for me, your dad and your grandparents to worry about. Please don't give it another thought.'

'Thing is I will give this another thought, Mum,' Jenny said firmly. 'I've only got one Granddad and I love him so much I hate to think of him suffering like this. I know how hard it is when you're in hospital and faced with lots of treatments and tests you don't understand. Everything feels so frightening, as though you're not in control of your own life or body any more.'

There was a pause as Gail and I took in the enormity of what Jenny was saying. Of course she understood better than anyone what Eric was going through. After all the years of tests, prodding and poking and of course surgeries she had endured, Jenny had a first-hand knowledge of the NHS and how difficult it could be when you were faced with a life-threatening illness. She was the one that would probably understand best out of all of us just how wretched Eric was feeling. I felt a stab of guilt – perhaps we should have listened to her earlier.

Gail smiled at her daughter. 'You're right, of course you're right, sweetheart. I'm sorry. OK, so what's this brilliant idea?'

Jenny cleared her throat as Gail looked at her expectantly. 'Well, Percy and I have put our heads together.'

'I might have known you'd be involved in all of this.' Gail chuckled, rubbing her nose against mine.

'Only trying to help,' I woofed.

'Anyway,' Jenny continued, 'we think the answer might lie with Hugo as he's latched on to Granddad.'

'Yes, they have taken rather a shine to each other.' Gail smiled. 'OK, so how does Hugo come into all of this?'

'Well, I know the plan was for Hugo to stay with us until we could find him a family all of his own,' Jenny began earnestly.

Gail nodded. 'That's true, I know Percy has been working hard to encourage Hugo to behave and I get the feeling that he's been worried he can't help Hugo more with him living with Mum and Dad at the minute.'

'What would you think about Gran and Granddad becoming his forever family?' Jenny asked.

'Oh, love, I don't think so,' Gail gasped. 'Mum and Dad have never wanted another dog after Bingo and Hugo wouldn't be suitable. No, they're just doing us a favour. We'll sort Hugo out with another family as soon as we've got things straightened out with Dad.'

Jenny and I exchanged glances. We had already recognised that Hugo wasn't just a favour to Doreen and particularly Eric. In fact, Hugo had fast become a welcome addition to their home. It seemed a logical next step, now I had thought about it, for Hugo to help with Eric's care, particularly given their strong bond.

'The thing is, Mum, there's a special training school for dogs to help those with Alzheimer's,' Jenny explained quickly before Gail could interrupt her again. 'It's down in Cornwall, not far from Gran and Granddad's old house actually. Anyway we thought we could send Hugo there to train so he could help Granddad when he needed a bit more assistance. You have to admit, Mum, that even though Gran and Granddad might not want another dog,

Hugo and Granddad are inseparable these days. Where there's one you'll generally find the other, and look how happy Granddad is when Hugo's around.'

'That's very true,' Gail conceded. 'Even when Dad's told Hugo off, Hugo stays by his side. It's sweet actually.'

'So you think it's a good idea then?' Jenny beamed.

Gail smiled at her daughter's enthusiasm and patted her hand. 'I'll admit I've got my reservations but you're right, Hugo and Eric do adore one another. Perhaps there was a reason we couldn't find a home for Hugo after all. Maybe he is meant to be Dad's dog.'

As Gail finished, I did a little dance on the spot with my front paws to show my pleasure, causing Gail and Jenny to giggle with delight.

'You mad thing.' Gail smiled, scooping me up into her arms.

'So do you think Granddad will go for it?' Jenny asked.

Gail wrinkled her nose. 'To be honest, I'm not sure. But I'm fairly confident that even if we can't talk him into it, your gran can. The bigger question really is do you think Hugo will be keen? I mean he has been a bit naughty lately.'

'I know,' I grumbled. 'But it could be just the challenge Hugo needs. Peg and I are going to have another bark with him later. And we also think that the fundraising idea we've got might be just the thing to encourage him to behave as well.'

Gail looked at me blankly. 'Percy, I've got pretty good at understanding what you're saying to me lately, but even I struggled with that one.'

Luckily, Jenny leapt to my rescue. 'The other stumbling block, Mum, is, erm, money.'

'What do you mean? How much is this place?' she asked, a note of hesitation creeping into her voice.

As Jenny said a figure, Gail physically jumped with shock and it was all I could do to remain balanced on her lap.

'My word!' she gasped. 'If we decide to send Hugo then it had better all work out.'

'It will,' Jenny replied confidently. 'And it would be so worth it. Look, here's the school.' Reaching for her laptop, Jenny quickly typed the address and brought up the school's website.

'Well, it looks very nice I have to admit, and you're right, it could be just what Dad needs. But we don't have that kind of money,' Gail said with a sigh, closing the laptop lid down.

'No, we haven't but we can raise it,' I barked.

Gail looked at me quizzically. 'Again, Percy, I'm sorry, I think I'm just tired or something, but I really have no idea what you're trying to tell me.'

'You don't have to worry about the money, Mum. This is the best bit, we've got a plan to fundraise.' Jenny grinned. 'We're going to hold a competition, for dogs. A bit like doggy Crufts. My friend Jamie's asked his aunt, who is Tanya Herring, to get involved and she's said yes.'

'You know someone who knows Tanya Herring?' Gail gasped.

Jenny nodded happily. 'And she's already agreed to get involved. We just need to take care of the rest.'

Gail thought for a moment and then smiled. 'You really are the nicest, kindest daughter a mother could wish for.'

Jenny coloured at the praise. 'It was Percy too.'

'I did nothing,' I barked. 'This was all Jenny.'

'You're too modest, Percy,' Jenny told me, wrapping her arms around Gail and me. 'Well, there's still lots to organise, so I guess we'd better get a committee together. Do you think Sal will help?'

'I'm sure she will,' Gail said, returning to her cake and taking another bite. 'And Mum will want to help too, though I don't think Dad will be up for it. We'll also have to convince him that this isn't charity as he'll never go for it if he thinks that's what this is.'

'You did once tell me Doreen could sell ice to the Eskimos,' I barked, eyeing the last of the crumbs on Gail's plate.

Gail chuckled. 'Very nicely put, Percy. Yes, she does have a certain way about her. I'll ask some of the mums at the school as well and a couple of the others at Ben's baby group. Maybe we should extend the contest out to people with other animals too. That way we might get a bit more interest.'

'That's a great idea, Mum.' Jenny beamed, feeding me the scraps from her plate.

'As long as I don't have to have anything to do with the cats!' I barked through a mouthful of crumbs 'They don't like me and I don't like them.'

'Percy, you know that's not true.' Jenny chuckled, tickling my chin. 'What about Mr Wiggles next door? You're always playing with him.'

'That's not playing. He's always trying to annoy me by sticking his paw under the fence,' I barked in annoyance, thinking of the large ginger moggy who routinely tried to make my life a misery.

'Well anyway, it sounds as though things are coming together quite nicely.' Gail smiled. 'I'll give Sal a ring now, see if she's free tonight. I'll get her to bring Peg over. You'd like that wouldn't you, Perce?'

'Always,' I yapped happily at the thought of seeing my love twice in the same day.

Rubbing her hands together delightedly, Jenny smiled at us both. 'So that's settled then. I love it when a plan comes together.'

Just then Gail put me down on the floor, and reached into her saddle bag for her mobile. Before pressing call, a look of merriment flickered across Gail's features as she paused.

'Just one thing, before I call Sal, Jen, do you mind telling me who Jamie is?'

At the mention of her boyfriend, Jenny's mouth fell open as she tried desperately to think of what to say. I shot her a flash of sympathy. She didn't deserve to be teased by anyone after all she had done today.

'You know very well he's her boyfriend,' I barked. 'I caught you going through her Facebook page the other day so you're just being mean.'

Gail looked at me fondly and gave me a smile. 'Sorry, Jen,' she said looking at her daughter. 'I didn't mean it. I think it's great you've found someone who makes you happy. You'll have to bring him over for his tea one night.'

'Erm OK,' Jenny stammered.

Giggling at Jenny's obvious embarrassment, Gail brought her laughter under control. 'We'll meet him anyway if his aunt's Tanya Herring and she's going to be involved in the show. You might as well make it sooner rather than later.'

'OK,' she mumbled again, her cheeks still crimson as Gail turned away and punched in Sal's number.

As the two of them started discussing our brilliant idea, a wave of happiness flowed through me. It finally felt as though we were doing something practical to help Eric and Doreen and I couldn't be more pleased. This show would be the talk of Perivale and I knew me and my pals would do all we could to ensure it was a success.

Chapter Nineteen

The excitement surrounding Perivale Animals With Skill had a positive effect on everyone. Firstly and most importantly, it seemed as though Eric had begun to make positive steps in coming to terms with his diagnosis. Left to his own devices, he was taking the drugs doctors had recommended to slow down the progression of the disease.

Gail, Jenny and I were all over at Doreen and Eric's having a cup of tea in the garden. Well, everyone else was having tea, me and Hugo had water. Anyway, I was lying at Gail's feet, grass tickling my nose, and followed her astonished gaze as she watched her dad pull out a blister pack of tablets and pop one in his mouth.

'What are they?' Gail demanded.

'Just some old timers' tablets.' Eric shrugged, shoving the packet back in his pocket. 'No big deal.'

Gail got to her feet in shock, causing me to stir. 'No big deal! We've been on at you to take those tablets for weeks, what made you change your mind? And don't say "old timers'", it's disrespectful.'

'My disease, I'll call it what I like,' he said gruffly, taking a gulp of water.

'Granddad!' Jenny scolded, folding her arms crossly.

Doreen shot her daughter and granddaughter a warning glance. 'Don't get him started for heaven's sake. You know what he's like. Just be glad he's taking them, I am.'

'Did you know?' Gail asked, switching her attentions to her mother.

Taking a sip of tea, Doreen paused. 'Yes, I did. But it was up to your father to tell you not me. We've had quite a few conversations over the last few days and it's important to Eric to feel in control.'

'At least while I still can. It's bad enough this dog here has started to predict my every move,' Eric grumbled half-heartedly as he stroked Hugo's head.

My eyes roamed over my son who was lying at Eric's feet, head resting on his toes.

'What have you done?' I asked automatically.

Hugo gave me his wide-eyed look. 'Nothing, Daddy. Just tried to be a bit more helpful, like you said. I get Eric his slippers in the morning and his paper with breakfast.'

Now it was my turn to be astonished. Peg and I had discussed Eric's condition with Hugo straight after Gail had agreed to the fundraiser last week. We knew it was important we told him the truth as quickly as possible and explained as much as we knew about Eric's condition. We told him that because Eric was facing a very difficult health battle it was vital he helped out more, and that if Hugo was willing we were hoping to send him to a special training school. To be honest, I had been unsure how he would react, but, as ever, my son continued to surprise me.

'I get to be Eric's special carer then?' he had barked in amazement.

'Sort of, love,' Peg had explained gently. 'You get to help Eric the most as he's your best friend.'

'And I really get to go away for two weeks? On my own?' Hugo had yapped in excitement.

I nodded. 'That's right. We're placing a lot of trust in you because we believe in you, Hugo.'

At that, my beloved son fell silent. Peg and I glanced at each other, worried Hugo was finding this level of responsibility a bit much to cope with.

'So you think Eric and Doreen are my forever family?' he barked quietly. 'Does that mean we can stop looking for a new owner for me now?'

I felt a pang of guilt as I stared into Hugo's eyes that were filled with hope. Had he realised just how worried we had been about finding him a permanent family? Did he know we secretly fretted he would end up at the tails of the forgotten because we panicked he was untrainable? My heart went out to my son. I hoped he hadn't ever felt like a burden.

'We hope so, son, yes. You love Eric, don't you?' I barked eventually.

Hugo nodded eagerly. 'He's the bestest, kindest man in the whole world. I love him, Dad, and would do anything for him.'

'Even behave at school and learn things when me and your dad aren't there to keep you on the straight and narrow?' Peg whined, her face grave.

'Yes, Mummy,' he barked quietly. 'I know I can do it.'

He had then slumped onto his paws, digesting his new future. And a week on, as my eyes roamed over Hugo, I had to admit I liked what I saw. This new attitude of taking his responsibilities seriously was very much a breath of fresh air, I only hoped it would continue.

'So, has this Tanya woman said yes or what then?' Doreen asked, interrupting my train of thought.

'She's a definite. And apparently she's speaking to Rik and Lee today,' Gail explained, draining her cup dry and setting it on the table in front of her.

Doreen let out a low whistle. 'Fancy! Imagine if we can get Rik and Lee to be the judges. That'll be one in the eye for Mrs Bevan at number sixteen, old cow!'

Jenny raised an eyebrow, the midday sunshine having already caught her nose, causing her to break out in a handful of freckles. 'You haven't been causing trouble already have you, Gran?'

'Yes, please try and get on with the neighbours, Mum. You haven't been here five minutes.' Gail groaned.

'It's not me, it's her.' Doreen's voice rose an octave in protest. 'She told me I couldn't possibly organise a talent show as I hadn't been here very long and knew nobody. Took the flyer we'd made right out of my hands. Well, I showed her.'

'I'm almost frightened to ask, but what did you do?' Gail asked, wincing.

'She wanted a flyer, so I stapled half a dozen to her front door.' Doreen sniffed, before taking another sip of tea.

'Half a dozen?' Eric roared, his eyebrows almost reaching his hairline. 'More like fifty. It was a nightmare, your mother and Mrs Bevan had to be physically restrained by me. Not an easy thing when you've got old timers'.'

'Dad!' Gail hissed, a twinkle in her eye before she turned to her mother. 'Well, you're not going to be winning any popularity contests with that attitude.'

Doreen sniffed again, before bending down to fondle my ears. 'Don't care.'

'Don't care was made to care.' Jenny giggled.

At that the three women burst out laughing, while Eric looked on in despair.

'And they say I'm the one that needs help, eh, boy,' he said softly, tickling Hugo's ears before he walked off into the greenhouse.

'Nothing wrong with you, Eric,' my boy barked gently, following him.

I was touched at the special moment between owner and dog. It was one of the most beautiful relationships in the world, and I was so pleased my son was getting to experience it first-paw.

'So, what else is there to organise?' Doreen asked again.

'I'm not sure. Sal said she would be here in a minute to talk through the finer details,' Gail explained.

At the sound of my love's owner coming along my ears pricked up. It would be wonderful to be with all my family again. Right on cue, the doorbell sounded and Gail leapt up to answer it. As Gail brought Sal and Peg out into the garden, I greeted them both with a rub of my snout. If Eric's diagnosis had taught me one thing it was that time with your loved ones was precious and should be enjoyed and treasured at every moment.

'Hello, all. I brought refreshments,' she said, waving around two bottles of Prosecco.

Doreen brightened immediately. 'I knew I liked you, Sal. And there was me about to put the kettle on again. Let me get some glasses.'

As Doreen bustled out of the room, Sal bent down to scratch my chin. 'How are you, Percy? I feel like I've not seen you in ages.'

'Fine,' I barked gratefully. 'Thank you for getting involved in all of this. I do appreciate it ever so much.'

Sal looked at me blankly but continued to rub my chin. In the end it was Jenny who put her out of her misery.

'He says he's grateful for everything you're doing.'

'You got all that from one bark?' Sal replied, her eyes crinkling with laughter. 'I don't know how you do it. I've still not got a clue what Peg's saying to me half the time.'

Peg head butted her owner affectionately. 'That's because you never listen, you daft mare.'

Sal dropped a kiss on her pug's head before sitting on the leather armchair opposite the girls.

'My own fault really,' she said, taking the glass Doreen offered her. 'I just don't listen. Anyway, cheers.'

'Er, I haven't got anything to have a cheers with,' Jenny pointed out, her ponytail swinging defiantly.

'That's because you're not eighteen,' Gail said pointedly.

Doreen rolled her eyes. 'Give over, Gail. She's fourteen now, she can have half a glass.'

Jenny's eyes lit up at her grandmother's suggestion. 'Can I, Mum? Please?'

'All right,' Gail groaned as Doreen quickly poured her some fizz.

'Anyway, as I was saying, cheers,' Sal said, raising her glass. 'So what's left to organise?'

'Well, we were hoping you could tell us,' Gail put in.

Doreen raised a hand. 'That's all very well. But if I can ask a stupid question I still don't really understand how we're going to make money out of this event, let alone enough to send our Hugo to doggy training school.'

Gail shook her head then pinched the bridge of her nose in despair. 'We've been through this a thousand times, Mum.'

'But I still don't get it.' Doreen shrugged.

'It's simple, Doreen,' Sal began patiently. 'We charge the entrants, and then a smaller portion of that money is offered as a competition prize. Then we also make money from sponsors who advertise on the back of the programme. Speaking of which, I am delighted to say I have got all of our slots filled.'

'Have you?' Gail gasped.

Sal smiled as she delved into her handbag for a leather notebook. Rifling through the pages she soon found what she was looking for. 'Yes, we've got almost all the independent local businesses pledging their support.'

'That's just wonderful.' Doreen smiled, tears pooling in her eyes.

'I always say people are inherently good. We just hear about the bad stuff.' Sal smiled. 'Anyway, the council said we can use the community centre next month so we have a date at the beginning of September, just before the kids go back to school so there should be loads of people about and the weather should be good as well. We've also got security sorted thanks to a couple of my neighbours.'

'Security?' Doreen looked puzzled. 'It's a talent show.'

'Yes, but have you seen how many nutters are out there? They don't take it well when they don't get through,' Sal pointed out reasonably. 'You only have to look at that talent show Tanya Herring fronts.'

'But this is a local event, for charity,' Doreen gasped.

Sal took another slug of her drink. 'My point exactly. Now what about food and drink?'

'Sanjay, who runs the corner shop, said he'd be more than happy to help,' Gail explained.

'Oh bless him.' Doreen smiled.

'And Simon's sourcing more chairs,' Gail added.

'Brilliant,' replied Sal, crossing something off her list. 'Do we know who's doing programme printing and admin?'

'A mate of Simon's said he'll do us a deal on the printing but we still need someone to organise the contestants on the day.' Gail sighed.

'Well, surely we can do that, can't we?' Doreen suggested. 'How hard can it be?'

Gail raised an eyebrow. 'For us, no problem, but you have a tendency to get a bit upset.'

'I do not!' Doreen protested.

'Let's ask Mrs Bevan about that, shall we?' Gail teased.

Doreen narrowed her eyes. 'We still need judges. We can't have a flaming talent show without judges.'

Sal whipped her head around to face Jenny. 'Any news on Rik and Lee, Jen? Otherwise we might have to rope your gran in after all!'

Jenny fished out her mobile from the pocket of her hoodie and flicked through her messages. 'OMG! Jamie's just messaged me! They'll do it!'

'Are you serious?' Sal shrieked, dropping her pad and pen with excitement.

'Yes!' Jenny squealed, peering at her phone again. 'They said they can think of nothing they would like more.'

At this the girls got to their feet and hugged each other in delight while Peg and I looked at each other in amusement.

'Do you know who Rik and Lee are?' I asked above the din.

Peg shook her head. 'Not really. Some TV presenters that always win things apparently. Sal has a huge crush on one of them.'

I nodded in understanding, yet not really understanding anything. Still, Gail, Sal and Jenny seemed pleased so that was all that mattered.

'Looks like our fundraiser's all in paw then,' I barked softly.

Peg nodded and leant her head against me. 'Looks like it. Well done, Perce.'

'I haven't done anything,' I told her. 'It's the girls that have sorted this one.'

'Well, they've got the boring human bit sorted. What we need to make sure we have now are brilliant acts, and I think that's where you come in,' Peg barked knowingly.

'Me? I don't know anyone,' I barked anxiously. 'It's you, Jake, Heather and Bugsy that have been here longer than me.'

'That's as maybe,' Peg put in, 'but we don't have your charm. You're always so persuasive. I have a feeling you'll need to tap into that to get the humans and animals we need to make this thing a huge success.'

I gave Peg a lick as I considered her yelps. I hadn't thought that me and my pals could be so involved in the contest, but now I realised the future and success of this talent show could lie in our paws. With my friends' help we had the power to turn this event into a huge success that could not only benefit Eric, Doreen, Hugo and Ralph but the community as well. With the thought of such greatness ahead, I felt a sudden pulse of excitement. The show must and would go on!

Chapter Twenty

The sights and sounds of the dog park never failed to excite me, and arriving at the grassy playpen together with Jenny, I couldn't wait to see my friends. We had spent much of the previous night barking on the dog telegraph, making arrangements and I was delighted to find they were already there waiting for me.

Bugsy was busy running around the tree, while Heather and Jake were knee-deep in barks on the other side. As for Hugo, he was nowhere to be seen, and greeting Peg with the warmest of licks I wondered if she might know where he was.

'Sitting with Eric,' she barked in reply. 'Hasn't left his side all morning.'

I glanced across to the bench where Eric was sitting reading the paper while Sal and Jenny nattered away beside him. On the floor, faithfully beside his master was my Hugo, head resting on Eric's shoes, one eye closed and another flickering with interest, as if on high alert.

Feeling a flash of pride, I turned to Peg. 'What's brought this on with Hugo?'

Peg gave me another lick in reply. 'I don't know. I've tried to ask him about it, but he won't leave Eric long enough for me to get a straight answer.'

I observed him carefully. It looked to me as though he was a dog merely looking after his owner and barked as much to Peg.

Peg rested her paw on mine and gave out a little sigh. 'It does seem that way, but I'll confess I'm worried. I adore all of my children, but I've been doing some thinking and I'm worried this good behaviour of Hugo's won't last. He means well, I'll give him that, but I think it's going to be a struggle for him to keep it up.'

'You need more faith in our boy,' I admonished. 'I'm sure you were right before. I think he's finally turned a corner.'

'Really?' Peg barked knowingly. 'Then why has he just started to chew Eric's shoe?'

Horrified, I glanced across at Hugo once more and saw to my surprise that Peg was right. I shook my head in despair. How did she know our children better than I did?

'Don't feel too bad, Perce,' Peg barked as if reading my mind. 'I heard Doreen tell Sal earlier that she had already told Hugo off for chewing Eric's slippers last night while he was sleeping.'

I let out a low growl. Was there any getting through to that boy?

'Hugo,' I barked, causing him to look up immediately. 'Leave Eric's shoe alone, and get over here now.'

To my surprise, Hugo stopped immediately and raced towards me.

'Daddy!' he barked, greeting me by rubbing his wet snout against mine. 'I'm so pleased to see you.'

'Don't think you can try and get around me that easily, my boy,' I barked crossly. 'You know it's naughty to chew shoes.'

'Especially while humans are wearing them,' Peg put in.

Hugo hung his head in shame. 'I'm sorry, Daddy and Mummy. I can't help it, it's just Eric's shoes are so tasty.'

I rolled my eyes. I had thought that the one advantage to Hugo no longer living with me was the fact I wouldn't have to tell him off quite so often. Yet it felt as though all I ever did when I saw him now was criticise.

Glancing across at Eric, I swallowed a wave of disappointment as I saw the sole of his sandal was hanging on by just a thread.

'They might well be tasty, son, but look at poor Eric's shoe. You can't destroy people's things. How would you like it if Doreen ripped one of your toys in half?'

'I'd hate it, Daddy. Is that what Doreen's going to do?' he barked in alarm.

'No of course not,' Peg replied. 'Dad's just trying to get you to see what it would be like if a human destroyed one of your things.'

Hugo slumped to the floor, his eyes wide. 'OK. I get it. I won't do it again.'

'Good, now if everyone's here, how about we get down to business. We need some talent for our show,' I barked, keen to change the subject. 'How about we split up into groups and try to spread the word to as many animals as we can.'

'Even cats?' Bugsy barked doubtfully.

'And what about horses?' Heather put in. 'They're huge.'

'All the animals,' I barked firmly. 'We're open to everyone. The more animals, and the more acts, means the more money we raise.'

'And what about a prize, old thing? Jake barked. 'What does the winner get?'

'I think Sal and Gail have sorted out some vouchers for the High Street,' I barked.

'Yes, but while they're very nice for the owners, they're not a lot of good for the winning pet are they?' Heather replied.

The penny chew dropped. How could I have been so foolish as to forget about a prize for the animals?

'Surely, whichever pet wins they'll be happy with the glory of winning?' I barked desperately.

Heather looked at me as if I was mad. 'You can't honestly believe that, Percy?'

I groaned. 'You're right, I'll try and speak to Jenny later. I can't believe I've been so stupid.'

'Don't be so hard on yourself, Percy,' Bugsy barked soothingly. 'I would be happy just to have the glory if I ever won anything like that.'

I woofed at him gratefully. 'Thanks, Bugsy. If only all pets were like you.'

'Oh don't look like that, Percy,' Peg yapped. 'We'll sort something out, don't worry.'

'Yes, lovey, don't worry. These things always work out in the end. Now then, let's get going. If anyone asks us about the prize, we'll say it's a surprise,' Heather woofed.

'Good thinking,' I barked, impressed at Heather's ingenuity. 'Now are we all ready?'

Jake nudged me with his paw. 'Just one thing, old boy, are you honestly sure about inviting cats to participate? They're mighty tricky blighters.'

'Now, now, Jake,' Heather barked soothingly. 'As Perce said, we want all animals at this event. There's no reason to discriminate. Just because they're another breed of animal doesn't mean they don't have feelings too.'

'I'm not sure cats do,' put in Bugsy mournfully. 'One jumped right on my head the other day in the garden.'

'Look, that's enough,' Peg barked wearily. 'This event should bring all humans and animals together not drive us apart. Now come on, everyone. Heather, Jake and I will take one side of the park. Percy and Bugsy, you take the other.'

'What about me, Mummy?' Hugo yapped, his bark full of hurt. 'You forgot about me.'

Peg let out a low whine. 'So I did. I'm sorry, Hugo. OK, why don't you go with Daddy.'

'All right,' Hugo agreed, mollified.

'We'll meet back here when the sun reaches that cloud,' I woofed, peering up at the sky. 'Now remember, spread the bark, far and wide.'

'Will do, old chap. Even to cats.' Jake chuckled, as he bid us farewell.

*

An hour later and Bugsy, Hugo and I had worn our barks out telling everyone and anyone who would listen. We had barked at horses, dogs, cats, pigeons and even mentioned something to a llama we saw loitering at the corner of the field near the city farm. All the animals we encountered were full of enthusiasm and promised to tell their owners as well as their friends.

'Can we go now, Perce?' Bugsy groaned. 'My legs are so tired.'

'Yes please, Daddy,' Hugo whined. 'I don't think my little paws have got any flesh left on them, we've walked so far.'

'All right,' I sighed, peering up at the sun and seeing it was almost time to get back to meet the others. 'Let's turn around.'

Only just as I put one paw in front of the other I crashed head first into a stately looking Westie.

Head throbbing, I murmured my apologies. 'I'm so sorry, I should have been looking where I was going.'

'Percy!' the Westie barked joyfully.

'Boris?' I yapped, lifting my aching head with a sudden jerk as I recognised the woof.

Seeing my old pal from the tails of the forgotten, I forgot my aches and pains and jumped up and down in delight. I hadn't seen Boris since we bumped into one another one Christmas Eve.

'How are you, mate?' Boris yapped excitedly.

'Really well. I'm a married man now, Boris,' I told him.

'You and Peg got together?' he woofed with affection.

I nodded. 'We certainly did. And this is my son.'

Turning to Hugo, who was watching eagle-eyed, I pushed him forwards with my snout. 'Say hello to a very old friend of mine.'

'Hello,' he barked obediently.

'Nice to meet you,' Boris barked, shaking Hugo's paws solemnly. 'I hope you know how lucky you are to have a dad like yours, he's wonderful.'

Hugo nodded seriously. 'I do, my daddy's the best daddy in the world.'

At the unexpected praise, I felt myself blush and changed the subject. 'How are you, Boris?'

'Good,' Boris replied. 'Just out for a walk with my owner, Zoe.'

'Ah the nurse,' I yapped. 'Things still going well then?'

Boris looked across at the woman sitting on a nearby bench with love in his eyes. 'Very well. She's engaged to a lovely bloke and the pair of them treat me like royalty. I'm a very happy Westie.'

'That's lovely news, Boris,' I barked warmly. 'I always told you that the perfect family were out there waiting for you, didn't I?'

'That you did.' Boris nodded wisely. 'Best of all, Matt's a TV vet, so I get lots of presents. Honestly, we never have to pay for dog food, and I've even been invited to go on a luxury doggy escape with Zoe.'

I stared at him in surprise. 'Not Matt McDonald? He's that super vet! Gail loves that show.'

Bugsy shook his head, despair looming large in his brown eyes. 'I can't watch it. It makes me so sad when they can't cure the little doggies. You see all the hope on their faces, and then they die. And then what about the owners? They get really, really, really sad and don't stop crying. It's too traumatic for me.'

I stared at him in horror as Hugo started barking mournfully up at me. 'Is that true, Daddy? You always say that's the happiest show on the TV because there's nothing the super vet can't cure and that everyone that sees him is always saved.'

Giving Bugsy an almighty kick to the shin with my paw, I turned to my boy. 'Of course that's true. Bugsy's got muddled again, haven't you, Bugsy?' I barked through gritted teeth.

'Yes,' he howled in pain. 'I've got muddled again.'

'Anyway,' I barked turning to Boris. 'Have you heard about our charity pet talent contest, PAWS? I've been telling everyone.'

Boris raised an eyebrow. 'Is that your idea then, Perce? I did hear something about it, yes. So Eric's the one with the Alzheimer's, is he?'

I nodded sadly. 'It's early days now, but we want to send our son Hugo to dog training school to help him.'

'A brilliant cause, mate,' Boris barked. 'Listen, Zoe wanted to sign me up but I wasn't keen. Now I know it's you that's doing it I'll get her to put my name down straightaway. What's the prize?'

I hung my head in shame. 'That's the thing, Boris, I haven't sorted that out yet.'

Looking at me thoughtfully, Boris turned back to look at Matt. 'How about I ask the super vet for some help?'

'Really?' I yelped gratefully. 'Would you mind?'

'For you, mate? Not at all,' he barked cheerfully. 'Leave it with me. Matt's a smashing fella. When I tell him what it's for, he'll be only too happy. I'll get details to you over the telegraph, if that's all right?'

I did a little jig on the grass with my paws. 'That's more than all right, that's brilliant, thank you.'

Boris thumped his tail on the floor. 'What are mates for? It's no problem.'

Watching him walk away, I felt excitement flood through me. Thanks to Boris it looked as though we were going to pull off this talent show and make it a huge success. With pets, celebrities and now a top prize from the super vet himself, what could possibly go wrong?

Chapter Twenty-One

Show day arrived in the blink of an eye and I was delighted to find the weather had been kind to us, with a cloudless, sunshine-filled sky. I had woken early with excitement and now Gail was up and about making tea for the family I rushed to greet her, rubbing my snout against her legs.

'Big day today then, Perce,' she whispered, running her hands through my fur.

I pushed my snout into her hand then glanced upwards and met her worried eyes. 'The biggest. But we can do this. The show will be a huge success and we'll raise more than enough money to send Hugo to doggy training school so Eric will be looked after.'

She smiled and leant down to kiss my forehead. 'I don't know what I would do without you, Percy. You do such a good job of holding me together sometimes, I'm sure it's down to you I've been strong enough to come off these tablets now.'

'No, Gail, we hold each other up,' I barked seriously before licking her cheek. 'It's called being a family.'

With that, my lovely owner held my gaze, and was just about to say something in reply when the doorbell went.

'I'll get it,' Jenny shouted down the stairs.

Hearing the heavy tread of a teenager throw herself down the stairs in a bid to answer the door, Gail and I both grimaced until she reached the bottom and pulled it open.

'Gran, Granddad,' she said excitedly.

As she walked towards the kitchen I could not only hear the sound of human footsteps but doggy ones too. Realising it had to be my beloved son, I raced towards him.

Seeing his little pink tongue hanging out as he trotted obediently behind Eric and Doreen, I felt a lurch of joy. After today, if all went well, Hugo would be off to school, returned to me when he was a man. His days of being my pup were short-lived and I wanted to make the most of it.

The moment he walked into the kitchen and sat before me, I greeted him with a lick in each ear, then rubbed my snout against his delicate little nose. Fixing my eyes on him with my best fatherly look, I felt a pang of sadness.

'I love you so much that sometimes it hurts,' I barked seriously. 'You four pups are the best things in my life and I want you to know how proud I am of you all, but, Hugo, well, for stepping up and giving your family what they need, I love you.'

Hugo flew at me, knocking me to the ground, covering me in licks, nibbles and whimpers, declaring his love.

Emotion coursed through my fur as I felt the weight of my son on top of me, bursting with love. How lucky I was to have such a wonderful human and family around me.

'I love you too, Daddy,' Hugo whimpered, giving my ear a furious lick and wrapping his paws tightly around my neck.

'What's up with him?' I heard Doreen exclaim as I tried to unsuccessfully extricate myself from Hugo's grip.

Gail glanced over and caught my eye. 'I think Hugo is trying to show Percy how much he loves him, but in actual fact he's on the verge of strangling him instead.'

Rushing towards me, she pulled Hugo from around my neck, and helped me up.

'Everyone all right now?' she asked kindly.

'Yes, thank you, Gail,' I croaked.

'Good.' She smiled, giving each of us a pat before she turned to Hugo. 'Be gentle with Daddy, he's not indestructible.'

Hugo thumped his tail on the floor. 'Sorry, Daddy.'

I gave him a lick. 'That's fine. You won't see off your old dad with too much love, that I can promise you. Anyway, what are you doing here?'

'Doreen wanted to see if she could do anything to help the show and Eric has a present for Gail,' Hugo told me eagerly.

I turned to look at Eric who was about to hand his daughter the largest bouquet of flowers I had ever seen.

'Whatever are these for?' she gasped as Eric handed her the blooms.

'It's a thank you really,' he said quietly. 'For all you've done for me.'

Gail waved away his comments with her hand. 'Don't be daft. I haven't done anything,'

'You've done more than you know,' he said clasping her hand. 'I know I haven't taken this diagnosis very well. And I have made both of your lives a misery at times,' he continued, turning to Doreen who smiled sadly at Eric, 'but I want you to know I appreciate every little thing you have done for me.'

'Oh, Dad,' Gail gasped, her eyes shining with tears. 'It's nothing. Honestly, I know it can't have been easy for you. I don't know how I would ever have coped if I discovered I had Alzheimer's.'

Eric nodded. 'I won't lie to you, Gail. It's been tough. For a man like me, who hates being told what to do—'

'You can say that again,' Doreen interrupted as Eric patted his wife's arm with affection.

'As I was saying,' he continued, 'I've always been in control of life and to suddenly know that control has been taken away, well, that's no easy thing. But the fact that Hugo here is prepared to go to school and learn things so he can help me when this disease really takes hold, well, that's quite something, and honestly I'm lost for words. I don't like charity but knowing that any money leftover will help other good causes, well, that's what sold all of this to me.'

'Dad, you know we would do anything to help you,'

Gail babbled. 'I just wish there was more we could do. I really wish we could find a cure for this horrible disease that's going to rob me of my daddy.'

Eric pulled his daughter into his arms and held her as if she were no more than a little girl. 'We all wish that love, but facts are facts, we have to recognise that's never going to happen. I've faced up to it, and you must too.'

'I know.' She wept silently into his shoulder.

Watching the two of them cocooned in love, I felt a lump form in my throat at the sight of father and daughter together. Anxiously, I reached for my own son by placing a paw on his shoulder for him to respond in kind and rest his head against mine. There was nothing like the power of family and knowing we were doing all we could to help Eric cope with whatever lay in his future gave me comfort.

'Come on now, you lot,' Doreen called tearfully, breaking the spell. 'That's enough of all that, we've a show to get on with today.'

Reluctantly, Gail and Eric broke apart. Shooting her dad a sheepish smile, Gail went to put the flowers in water, while Eric sat opposite his wife and clasped her hand. I could see from my own vantage point on the floor that Eric's eyes were brimming with tears, a fact that wasn't lost on Hugo who immediately went to sit by Eric's feet.

It was the perfect spectacle and for once I didn't feel jealous. That simple moment in the kitchen had told me there was more than enough love to go around between us. I knew it was love that bound a family together and there could never be too much.

*

We soon arrived at the community centre ready to set up. Sal had suggested we start the event at three, which would give everyone more than enough time to see the acts, and then if they wanted to carry on the party there would be plenty of beer tents ready to take their money, and help us with our proceeds for doggy training school and more.

Simon had done us proud by organising not just extra chairs, but little trestle tables that volunteers had offered to fill with refreshments for the audience and the acts. I was delighted to see that the pets hadn't been forgotten, as thanks to Boris and his super vet there were several dedicated stalls full of treats, grooming and feeding products, along with clothes. I shuddered at the sight of a doggy Batman costume. Why did humans want to dress up their animals in clothes? It wasn't remotely dignified for the animal or even the human. Outside, a team of volunteers, ably assisted by Gemma, our lovely vet, had set up the dog agility course which would start off the event. With the cones, ramps, tunnels and even mini rope ladders it looked every bit as good as something from Crufts, and I couldn't wait to watch all my doggy pals take part.

'It's like a mini-festival, isn't it?' Jenny said, interrupting my thoughts.

Gail raised an eyebrow. 'And what would you know about festivals, young lady?'

'Nothing!' Jenny coloured. 'Just saying it's what I think it would be like.'

I watched Gail suppress a smile. For a woman so full of love she could be very wicked at times.

As Sal arrived through the double doors, arms laden with notepads, clipboards, forms and pens, I did a double take. She was carrying so much stuff I could barely see her face. Looking behind her, I saw she had even enlisted the dogs' help, as Peg had her mouth stuffed with what looked like Post-it notes and sticky tape, while Hugo was dragging what appeared to be bunting across the floor. Together with Jenny, I rushed towards them, and helped them all with their load. 'Why are you carrying all this?' I barked at Peg.

My love rolled her eyes as she gave me some of her Post-its. 'Silly mare forgot a bag didn't she. So rather than go back, she piled it all on us. I said we're dogs not packhorses, Sal, but she still didn't understand a bark I said.'

I stifled my own version of a doggy giggle. 'Well, you made it, that's all that matters.'

'Too true. I saw Jake, Heather and Bugsy in the car park with their owners so no doubt they'll be able to lend a paw in a minute.

'Oh good,' I barked anxiously. 'There's still so much to do.'

Peg surveyed the scene. 'I don't know, looks like every-thing's all under control.'

I peered around the room, and saw to my delight that Peg was right. The stalls were up, the chairs were laid out in rows, the banners and posters lined the walls and Simon was busy putting the finishing touches to the stage and the judging area.

A warm glow coursed through my fur. Me, my friends and my lovely family had achieved all this. And if we could pull it off, then we would not only be the talk of Perivale, but we would have done something wonderful for our family.

Spotting Jamie walk through the room, surrounded by what I guessed were his family, I barked at Jenny to let her know.

'Jamie.' She smiled, rushing towards him, and greeted him with a hug. 'How are you?'

'Really well.' He beamed. 'We're all so excited to be here.'

Turning to the people that surrounded him, I watched with interest as Jenny greeted his mum, dad and brothers.

'And of course this is my Auntie Tanya,' he said, pushing a very small, but very glamorous woman, with long dark hair and bright red lips, to the front.

'Hello, Joanna,' the woman said in a very high voice. 'It's so nice to meet you, you're all Jay talks about.'

'Er, Auntie, it's Jenny,' Jamie said quietly, clearly embarrassed.

Tanya clamped her hands to her mouth. 'I'm so sorry, darlin', I don't know where my head's at some of the time. It's like I always say to the producers, don't give me no lines or nothing to learn, cos I'll only get muddled. Always best off with an autocue.'

With that, she erupted into a tinny raucous laugh that was so high-pitched it hurt my ears.

'Anyway.' Tanya smiled, as she caught sight of me, Peg and Hugo. 'Are these the dogs we're raising money for? Aren't they gorgeous?'

Without waiting for an answer, she rushed towards us, and bent down to tickle each of us under the chin. When it came to my turn, I couldn't help but let out a whimper as her long fake nails scratched my flesh.

'You're all so precious, you shouldn't be put down,' she cooed.

I felt my fur bristle with anxiety, a fact that wasn't lost on Hugo.

'Who's being put down, Daddy?' Hugo whined. 'I promise I'll behave.'

'Nobody's being put down,' I barked angrily, something I was grateful Jamie backed me up on.

'Tanya, we're raising money to send Hugo to training school not save dogs from death,' Jamie said to his aunt in an exasperated tone.

'Oh course!' she trilled, getting to her feet. 'Take no notice of me, loves, it's all a worthy cause whatever it is in aid of, the precious, gorgeous animals! Oh look, there's Rik and Lee.'

As she pushed her way through the family, arms outstretched, she air-kissed the two men and I breathed a shaky sigh of relief she had gone. Turning to Peg, I fixed her with my best 'what do you think' look.

'I think she's an idiot,' she yapped, getting to the point. 'But the humans love her, and that's all that matters. They're the ones putting their hands in their pockets, Perce. You've got to think of the bigger picture.'

'You're right,' I barked in reply. 'I just hope she knows what she's doing.'

'I doubt it,' Peg barked sagely. 'But whatever happens there's no going back now.'

I barked nothing, and ignored the beginnings of a knot of worry forming in my tummy. We had done all we could, now it was show time.

Chapter Twenty-Two

As Tanya walked on stage, clutching a wad of cards, she was greeted by a huge round of applause and cacophony of cheers. Waving and smiling as though her life depended on it, Tanya beamed at the crowd.

With no autocue, whatever that was, Jamie had gone to huge trouble to write a script for Tanya to read from. I had no idea presenters had things written down for them and had always assumed when I watched TV they made things up as they went along. However, Jamie had told me that wasn't the case. Most presenters needed words put into their mouths and I was delighted Jamie had stepped in at the last minute to help us out, and rewarded him with a huge lick as I sat in the front row between him and Gail.

'Welcome, everyone, to Perivale Animals With Skill,' Tanya called as the applause died down. 'I'm so excited to welcome you all here today to raise money for a truly special cause close to my heart.' Tanya paused for a moment as she bent down to read her cards. 'Yes, we're raising money today to send a little dog to training school so he can learn how to help his owner with Alzheimer's, so please step forward, Hugo.'

As Jenny carried my boy on stage, I felt a surge of joy. Hugo might have had his moments in the past, but here he was, stepping up, ready to face responsibility and I couldn't be prouder. Clearly the crowd agreed as they burst into another round of applause, much to Hugo's delight. He lapped up the applause, getting on his hind legs and walking up and down the stage, which caused even more cheers.

'Oh wow! Hugo can moonwalk, I never knew that,' Jamie laughed.

I looked up at him blankly. What was moonwalking? As far as I was aware all of my children had stayed firmly on planet Earth and I had no intention of sending Hugo any further than Cornwall for a doggy training course.

All around me, the crowd continued to laugh, and Hugo ate it up, clearly enjoying the attention. I shook my head. I hoped this competition wasn't going to turn his head. As well as this moonwalk he had so expertly mastered, he was now jumping up and down from one end of the stage to the other. His actions were so energetic he reminded me of a kangaroo never mind a pug, and I found myself wishing he would calm down and stop showing off. We were here to raise money for Eric not send Hugo to circus training camp.

As Jenny met my gaze, something in my eyes must have told her of my concern. Gently, she called Hugo to heel and rewarded him with a treat.

'Well, I think we can see who the winner is.' Tanya grinned. 'Shall we all go home now? Call it an early night?'

As the audience laughed once more, Tanya faced the crowd and continued her speech. 'Without further ado, I think we should get the competition started, but first, I would like to welcome two very old friends of mine, Rik and Lee.'

Once again the audience erupted into a round of applause as the two men who were seated right at the front of the stage stood up, turned around and waved.

'Howay, are we all excited?' one of them with short, spiky brown hair and large blue eyes called.

'I know I am, Rik,' the other one I now guessed was Lee replied. 'I canny wait to see some fine pets performin' here today.'

'I've heard Perivale is the place for talented pets, Lee,' Rik replied as the audience cheered again.

Lee, half the size of his friend Rik, but just as handsome with a head full of long blond hair and sparkling green eyes, laughed. 'Heard it? I've seen it! Me and that pug are goin' on the hoy later, I tell you. I'll not need to buy a drink all night with him by my side.'

The audience erupted into laughter once more and Hugo sat back down, leaving Tanya to address the room.

'And now, ladies and gentlemen, boys and girls, dogs, cats, horses, parrots, rabbits and budgies, I'd like to ask you all to follow me outside where we'll begin the dog agility section.'

Obediently, everyone trooped out of the room, and I

was grateful Gail scooped me up and helped me through the crowds. There were so many people I was terrified of getting squashed and, looking around, I was pleased to see Sal carrying Peg, with Jenny taking charge of Hugo.

Outside, Jake, Bugsy and Heather, together with Boris, were already by the course, and I let out a little whine of delight at the sight of them. Thankfully, Gail understood what I was trying to tell her and we walked straight over to them.

'Hello, loves,' Heather said, as Gail placed me on the floor besides my larger doggy companions. 'This is all so exciting, isn't it?'

'It certainly is, old thing,' Jake said softly. 'You've done wonders here, boy.'

I felt the flesh beneath my fur flame with colour. 'I didn't do anything, you've all done as much as me, and besides, this agility course is all down to Boris here. I can't believe you got Matt to do so much.'

'It was nothing,' Boris whined. 'I only had to mention this to him, and he had it all sorted in about five minutes.'

'Well, we're all very grateful, Boris,' Peg barked.

'Yes, I think this assault course looks amazing, Percy!' Bugsy put in. 'I think I'm going to have a go.'

I turned to look at him in awe. The thing looked terrifying to a little dog like me. 'Are you?'

'Yes, you never said, lovey?' Heather barked in surprise.

Bugsy wagged his tail and jumped up and down. 'It all looks so brilliant, I can't wait to run and jump through the hoops.'

'But aren't you worried about the tunnel?' Peg quizzed anxiously. 'You hate tunnels!'

'And don't you think you might drown in the mud, Uncle Bugsy?' Hugo whined.

'No! I really, really, really think I'll be good at this,' he barked determinedly. 'And Bella says she'll go round with me if I want to do it and I do want to do it, and I am allowed to do it, aren't I, Percy? Even though the contest says no relatives, I'm allowed?'

I barked doubtfully. 'I think so, Bugsy, I can't see anyone stopping you.'

With that, he let out a howl of delight. 'Yippee! I'm on next, so I'm going to find Bella. Wish me luck. I want to win all the treats and then I can share them with you. But I'm going to keep the medal for myself, if you don't mind.'

Without waiting for a response, he turned around and pushed his snout through the crowds to find his owner. I shook my head as I lost sight of his rear end. There were times Bugsy really amazed me, and not always because he was chasing shadow monsters.

All too soon, the dog agility course began with a tiny black Cavapoo named Max, ably led around by his owners, Emily, Lucy and Daniel. As the four of them entered the arena, the audience cheered at the sight of the three children and the cuddly dog. When the bell sounded for them to begin, I saw to my delight the children had really mastered the competition. Between them, they had worked out a series of calls and whistles that encouraged young Max up the rope ladder, through the tunnel and even down the slide.

Bounding towards the finish line, Emily, Lucy and Daniel calling his name, Max finished in high spirits, no doubt delighted with his faultless performance. Eagerly, he rewarded them all with a lick to the face, knocking over each of them in the process.

As the kids got up from the mud and brushed themselves down, I barked up and down with excitement. For a dog so small Max had done surprisingly well, clearly having spent some time practising the course.

As Max and the children received another round of applause for a job well done, the bell rang again, and in walked Bugsy flanked by Bella, looking every inch the perfect dog owner in a wax jacket and pair of wellies.

'Go on, Bugsy,' I found myself barking.

'Yeah, go on, mate. You've got this,' Boris added.

Just as Bugsy hurried to the start, I turned to look at Gail to see if she was enjoying the show. Together with Sal, Simon and her parents, Gail seemed as though she was having a whale of a time and I was pleased for her. The last few weeks had been so stressful, if this event could bring a bit of joy as well as raise the funds we so vitally needed to send Hugo to school then it was all worth it.

Turning my gaze back to the assault course, I was delighted to see Bugsy had cleared the first hurdle and was now gearing up to walk up and down the ramp. Within seconds, he had cleared it, with much encouragement from Bella, and was now aiming for the dreaded tunnel.

Anxiously I held my breath as Bugsy bounded towards

it. Only, as he approached, he appeared to have put his own emergency brakes on and came to a skidding halt just outside the entrance.

'Come on, Bugsy,' I barked.

'You can do this,' Heather yapped.

'Yeah, come on, Bugsy, show that tunnel who's boss,' Peg tried.

But no amount of encouragement from us, or Bella, would get Bugsy to go through as he sank to the floor and covered his paws with his eyes.

'I don't want to go inside,' he whined. 'There are monsters in there.'

'No there aren't, old thing,' Jake barked loudly. 'It's all in your mind.'

'No it's not,' Bugsy replied. 'If I go in there, I'll be killed.'

'If he doesn't, the audience will kill him. Look at them all jeering and taking pictures on their stupid phones,' Peg barked.

I glanced at the crowd and saw to my dismay that Peg was right. Rather than encouraging Bugsy, they were pointing and laughing, enjoying the spectacle of my poor friend's misery. I tried to think on my paws, something had to be done, but what?

Just then, I noticed a movement in the arena. Peering through the mesh fence, I saw to my surprise that Hugo had pushed his way through the crowd and was making his way to the tunnel. Rather than approach Bugsy he walked to the opposite side and peered through the end.

'Uncle Bugsy, it's me Hugo,' he barked loudly.

Immediately, Bugsy removed his paws from his eyes and craned his neck forward to look through the tunnel.

'Hugo, what are you doing here?' he yelped in surprise.

'I want to see you race through the tunnel. Come on, it's just like the chase we play in the park.'

'What do you mean?' Bugsy asked doubtfully.

'I'll show you,' Hugo replied.

And just like that, my lovely son rushed through the tunnel and met Bugsy. Giving him a quick lick to his ear, Hugo then turned around and dashed through the tunnel again.

'Come on, Bugsy, come and chase me,' Hugo called, jumping up and down. 'No monsters, promise.'

It was all the encouragement Bugsy needed and, as he dashed through the tunnel to greet my son, the two of them finished the rest of the agility course together. As they crossed the finish line, the audience erupted into a huge round of applause and I felt a surge of pride.

Looking across at my friends, family and Peg, I saw their eyes were all shining with tears at Hugo's kindness. In just one short afternoon, Hugo had become a wonder dog.

Chapter Twenty-Three

There was no getting away from it, even a pug like me could see the whole event was turning out to be a huge success. After the incredibly popular agility course, which had seen dogs of all shapes and sizes take on the dreaded tunnel that had foxed Bugsy, the show moved inside for the rest of the acts who had been queuing up to take part.

In the days and weeks leading up to the show, I have to admit I had been worried that nobody would turn up, and the whole thing would be a disaster. Yet incredibly we had acts desperate to hand over their cash and be judged by Rik and Lee.

As I sat with Doreen, helping her take the money on the door, it took all my energy to stop her rubbing her hands in glee at the amount exchanging paws and hands.

'Look at all this, Perce.' She grinned, pointing to all the notes in the little petty cash box on the desk in front of her. 'We'll have enough to send all of you to doggy training school at this rate and plenty left over too.'

I fixed her with what I hoped was my sternest glare. 'No thank you, Doreen. I am a living, breathing example of a dog too old to teach new tricks.'

Doreen looked at me and chuckled. 'I might not understand many of your barks, but I got that one, love. I make you right 'n' all. I'd be too old to learn anything new as well. Oh look, there's Eric over there.'

Glancing across to where Doreen was pointing, I saw Eric standing in the doorway, looking wildly around him, as though he had lost something. Patting his grey trousers and scratching his balding head, I saw his eyes were filled with worry and I wondered how we could help.

'Cooeee, Eric, love, over here,' Doreen called at such a loud volume I had to cover my ears with my paws.

Thankfully, Eric quickly turned around and, seeing Doreen waving at him, made his way over.

'You all right, love?' Doreen asked.

'Fine,' Eric replied absent-mindedly. 'Listen, you've not seen my dog have you?'

Doreen looked at her husband in surprise. 'Hugo?'

'Yes, that's him.' Eric smiled. 'I'm sure he was with me a minute ago.'

'Well, yes, love, Gail's taken him inside with the others. Look, he's sat with Peg over at the front of the hall.'

As Eric followed Doreen's gesture, his face flooded with relief when he saw Hugo was just where his wife said.

'Oh thank God! I thought he'd wandered off.' He sighed.

Doreen shook her head and smiled. 'No, he's in there safe and sound all right.'

Nodding, he gave Doreen a little smile. 'Well, I'd better

go and get him then, make sure the little so-and-so isn't getting up to mischief. He has a tendency to do that, you know.'

'I know only too well.' Doreen grinned in reply.

Eric raised an eyebrow before beaming down at me. 'Spoken like someone who knows. This your dog?'

A flicker of concern flashed across Doreen's features and she smiled sympathetically at Eric.

'No, love, this is Percy, Gail's dog,' she said kindly.

Scratching his head, as though more confused than ever, Eric nodded. 'Yes, 'course, silly of me. Well, I think I'll join the others.'

'All right, love,' Doreen replied, a look of bewilderment flickering across her features.

As Eric wandered inside, I tried to ignore the waves of panic coursing through my fur. There was something very wrong with that exchange between Doreen and her husband, but for the life of me I couldn't put my paw on what it was. I looked back inside the hall and watched as Eric picked up Hugo and cradled him like a baby. Ordinarily, I would have been touched at such affection, especially as it would have been further evidence of the two of them bonding. Yet the way Eric clung to Hugo, almost as if he was scared of something, left me feeling very worried indeed.

*

Later all my concerns about Eric were temporarily forgotten as I sat in between Gail and Peg, enjoying the show.

So far I had witnessed a pair of black-and-white cats called Pico and Lola who could do magic tricks, a parrot named Polly that could mimic every word her owner said, and a poodle called Patricia who could mew like a cat much to the delight of the audience. Next was a Shetland pony named John, ably brought on stage by his owner Pam, a short older lady with blonde, curly hair, wearing jeans and a leather waistcoat.

As the applause died down, Pam beamed and called out to the audience. 'I need a volunteer. An animal one preferably not a human one, please.'

Immediately, I saw Hugo was up on his paws. 'Me, me, me,' he barked at the top of his lungs.

Pam smiled at Hugo. 'Let's hear it for this little pug. Could his human please bring him onto the stage.'

Once again, Jenny brought a clearly excitable Hugo onto the stage and I felt a sense of unease creep up on me. Hugo had been so good with Bugsy earlier but I also got the feeling that he was keen to show off and in front of such a large crowd I knew that this was the perfect opportunity for him. Anxiously, I looked at Gail to see if she was as worried as I was, but she was too busy smiling up at the stage, enjoying the spectacle playing out in front of her.

As Jenny placed Hugo on the stage, she took a little bow and stood to the side ready to help when needed. Meanwhile, Hugo barked a quick woof at John and Pam, then ran up and down the stage, all the while the audience cheering for more.

My sense of unease began to grow as I caught the look

of delight along with a hint of mischievousness in Hugo's eyes. As Pam stood to the front, she called Hugo to her side and incredibly he complied.

'Now, Hugo.' Pam smiled. 'I want you to help me out here. Do you think you could just give me one bark?'

'Of course,' Hugo replied with one very loud and clear bark.

As Pam grinned, John stood up on his hind legs, much to the delight of the audience who rewarded him with a thunderous round of applause.

Once the audience's appreciation died down, John stood back on all four of his hooves and waited for his next instruction.

'Can I help again?' Hugo barked cheekily up at Pam, but I already knew the answer.

'So, Hugo, can you give me two barks this time?' Pam asked hopefully.

I gazed around at the audience before Hugo answered. Their eyes were alight with amusement as they waited for Hugo's reply, while John looked good-naturedly down at my pug.

'No problem,' Hugo replied, giving Pam two sharp barks.

Immediately, John gave an excitable whinny then started to trot two steps to the right, then two steps to the left, much to the delight of the crowd.

Coming to a standstill in the centre, John almost knocked Hugo off the stage, which he took with good grace, righting himself and shooting John a sideways dirty look that had the crowd in stitches.

John of course took it in his stride, and batted his eyelashes at Hugo. Then to the further delight of the audience, John immediately fell to the stage with a slight thud, somehow covering his eyes with his hooves as a gesture of apology to Hugo. The audience erupted into roars of laughter at the pony's antics, but John's gesture clearly surprised my boy as he jumped in shock before quickly composing himself. His dark eyes brimmed with trouble, and I saw Hugo look out across the giggling audience. I recognised the signs all too clearly – Hugo had an idea. It didn't take long for me to find out what it was as Hugo glanced at John who was still lying on the floor, then he took a running jump at the Shetland pony, landing on his back.

'What is he doing?' Peg barked, in astonishment. 'He's going to steal the show at this rate.'

I shook my head. 'Say what you like about our boy but he's definitely a crowd pleaser.'

Behind me the roars and cheers from the crowd were deafening, as they got to their feet and applauded the two animals. I sneaked a look at Jenny who was now standing next to Pam, the two women clearly in a fit of giggles as they whispered at what the two would get up to next.

With the audience still clapping, Hugo bent down and barked something gently in John's ears. Whatever it was, the pony clearly agreed as all too soon he was back up on his hooves and, with my son still on his back, the two paraded around the stage in a circle while the audience got to their feet and cheered.

Recognising that both John and Hugo had reached

the peak of their performance, Tanya walked on stage with a beaming smile. 'Wasn't that fantastic, ladies and gentlemen?' she called, without once looking down at her script. 'We weren't expecting Hugo to become such a little star tonight, but I think it's clear we've seen the start of a beautiful double act! Now, please give a big hand for John, Hugo and of course Pam!'

With that, Pam took her cue to lead John off stage, while Jenny quickly scooped Hugo from John's back and gave him a kiss. As she brought him back down to sit with me, both Peg and I gave him a lick of appreciation.

'You're quite the showman, aren't you, Hugo?' I barked.

'I didn't mean to, Daddy,' Hugo replied excitedly. 'I just got carried away.'

Peg gave her son another lick. 'And you were brilliant. Just don't go forgetting about what's important here today though, OK?'

With that, we turned back to the stage and watched Tanya introduce the next competitor. After Hugo and John, I thought the rest of the acts would have a tough time measuring up, but it seemed Perivale was home to a lot of talented pets as the rest of the acts were eye-wateringly good. I met Boris's eye across the room and barked a silent thank you. If he hadn't got Matt involved I was sure that we wouldn't have had anywhere near as many acts turn up. But Boris had not only got Matt to ensure we had a prize of a year's worth of free vet services for any animal, along with a lifetime's supply of toys and treats, but he had also managed to organise a week's holiday for the owner in the Bahamas.

All in all, the prizes weren't to be sniffed at and, as our next act, an English sheepdog named Dave, who could dance the tango with his owner, took to the stage I couldn't help marvelling at his performance.

English sheepdogs weren't meant to be light on their paws, but Dave was proving to be the exception to the rule. Not only was he gliding across the stage with all the grace of a whippet at a dog track, he was making it look effortless as well. I glanced at Peg and saw she was caught up in the theatre of it all.

'Don't go getting any ideas,' I warned. 'I might want to lift you up and twizzle you about in the air, my love, but with my puggy breathing difficulties I think I might struggle.'

Peg chuckled under her breath. 'Well, that's it then, Perce. If you can't dance with me like that, I'm leaving you for that Dave. He's gorgeous.'

Heather looked alarmed. 'You're not serious, Peg? He's four times the size of you. He'd crush you to death if he tried to give you a lick.'

'He would really, really, really crush you, Peg,' Bugsy barked seriously. 'I would stick to Percy, he's very loving.'

'Yes, come, old girl,' Jake yelped quietly. 'I know Percy has his faults . . . '

'Thank you, Jake,' I yapped in protest.

'Sorry, Percy, slip of the tongue so to speak, old thing,' Jake continued. 'As I was saying, Percy really isn't such a bad catch you know. This Dave might be giving Pudsey a run for his money, but I do think there's more to a relationship than a few fancy moves.'

Peg stared at them all in shock before she let out a little desperate bark. 'I was only joking! I wouldn't trade my Percy for all the bones in the butcher's. And, Jake, Percy does not have any faults, he's perfect.'

With that she rubbed my snout affectionately, and I felt a warm glow move through my body. After giving Peg a lick on the cheek, I couldn't resist leaning towards her and barking softly in her ear. 'I wouldn't trade you for all the bones, in all the butchers, in all the world.'

'Oh, Percy,' Heather barked, her tone thick with emotion. 'You say such lovely things.'

Jake looked alarmed. 'Steady on, old girl. You know I feel the same way about you too, don't you?'

At this unexpected outpouring of emotion, Heather suddenly flew at Jake, and knocked him to the floor with an enthusiastic lick. 'Oh, Jakey, I love you too.'

As I helped Heather get Jake to his paws, I was aware of Peg nudging me in the ribs.

'Hurry up, look, they're just about to announce the winners.'

I turned to look up at the stage and saw Tanya was now in the spotlight, beaming at the crowd. As the audience whooped and cheered, she gave them all a clap and turned to Rik and Lee.

'Thank you, everyone. Wow! Who knew Perivale had such talented pets?' At that, the audience burst into applause again as Tanya beamed, waiting for them to settle down. 'Everyone's a winner here today in my opinion, but let's give a big round of applause to Hugo and making the decisions today, our fabulous judges, Rik and Lee.'

The audience got to their feet and joined in with their whoops and cheers as Rik and Lee joined Tanya on the stage. Each gave her a kiss on the cheek before they walked to the front and waved at the audience.

'Thank you, thank you,' one of them said.

'It's such a pleasure to be here amongst such incredible pets,' the other one replied. 'I don't know about you, Lee, but I want to take that English sheepdog to meet me hinny.'

'I flamin' don't,' the one I now knew to be Rik chimed. 'If I brought Dave home to meet my wife, I've a feelin' I know which one of us would end up in the doghouse.'

At that the audience burst into laughter. Glancing up at Gail, I saw she too was giggling away and I felt a wave of pleasure at seeing her smile. My lovely owner had the weight of the world on her shoulders at the moment. Seeing her enjoy herself felt like I had won the lottery, and I knew that even if I had entered and won an event today, I would trade in all the prizes for Gail's happiness.

'Now, I know you all want to know who's won, but before we get on to that I think we should all give the dog we're raising money for a very special round of applause,' Rik continued, as his eyes searched the crowd, before finally resting on us dogs at the front. 'Hugo, come up here and say hello to everyone.'

Proudly, Hugo got to his paws and padded towards the steps where Rik and Lee scooped him up and carried him onto the stage. Standing to the side, I suddenly saw a photographer appear. As he pointed his camera at the threesome, I saw my son blink in shock when the flash went off and I felt a surge of worry crawl through my fur. As the photographer continued to snap away, I looked at Hugo and noticed that rather than beam into the camera like Rik and Lee, he was tugging at the sleeve of Rik's jacket. I let out a little bark of warning, encouraging him to stop it, but he either didn't hear me or he ignored me as he carried on tugging.

Anger coursed through me. Being the star of the show had clearly gone to Hugo's head. Why couldn't he just behave? I was about to let out another, louder bark of warning when the presenters thankfully had the good sense to put Hugo down on the ground.

As Rik and Lee began to address the audience, thanking them for coming, I stared in horror as Hugo started to gnaw Lee's trousers, causing the hem to unravel.

'Hugo!' I barked furiously. 'Stop that now!'

But Hugo ignored me, looking everywhere but down at the audience.

'That little devil,' Peg hissed in my ear. 'I thought he'd turned over a new leaf.'

'Me too,' I whined desperately.

I glanced around to look at the audience and saw to my horror that they had seen my boy's bad behaviour. But rather than appear cross, they were all laughing hysterically, jostling and laughing so loudly that Tanya had to step forwards and call for quiet.

'Hey, everyone, settle down now,' she called good-naturedly, 'we're just about to announce the win—'

But she never got to finish her sentence as Tanya took another step forward and tripped over the hem of Lee's

225

trousers. I held my breath as she lost her footing and flew through the air to the other side of the stage. The audience gasped in shock as she landed in a heap of tangled arms and legs and lay stock-still.

Immediately, Rik and Lee rushed forwards to help her up and my jaw dropped as I suddenly saw Rik's sleeve fall from his jacket, thanks to Hugo and his chewing efforts. Anger pulsed through me, and as I bounded on the stage together with my friends to help Tanya, I looked frantically for Hugo. There he was, in the midst of the action, tending to Tanya with his own brand of doggy loving, by covering her poor bruised face with a series of very wet licks.

Chapter Twenty-Four

It had been twenty-four hours since the show and feelings had been running high since Tanya's epic fall. Thankfully, the only thing that had been bruised, aside from her eye, was the presenter's pride, but Jamie had told us that she would be sticking to the age-old entertainment mantra from now on – never work with children and animals.

As for Rik and Lee, they had taken the destruction of their suits in good humour, but they had avoided all animals once the prize-giving was over. The audience too had whispered and giggled as they left the community centre and I even heard one man joke with his wife that he wouldn't envy the school attempting to teach that pug as he clearly had a taste for attention.

Both Peg and I were mortified. We had such high hopes for Perivale Animals With Skill and to see it destroyed because of our boy's behaviour was something I couldn't get over. Afterwards, I'm slightly ashamed to say I didn't bark at Hugo. I just couldn't trust myself to woof something nice.

That night, Jenny had done her level best to console me, but the truth was I couldn't be cheered up and in a way I didn't want to be. I know Hugo hadn't misbehaved on purpose but I couldn't help feeling as though my son had let me down.

This morning, both Peg and I had agreed to bark to Hugo once more and find out if he could actually grow up enough to go to training school or not. Together with Jake, Heather, Bugsy and Boris too, Peg and I had talked long into the night about the best course of action.

'He's not a bad pup,' Bugsy barked earnestly. 'He means well.'

'If he means well, why did he chew the presenters' clothes and try to steal the show?' Peg growled.

'He's just young, lovey,' Heather reasoned. 'You're not honestly thinking about pulling Hugo out of the training school, are you? Now you've got the money and the place is secured it seems a waste. Besides, nobody noticed. I think most of the audience thought it was part of the show.'

Peg sighed. 'That's precisely my point. He shouldn't be thinking about things like being a star, he should be thinking about how to take care of his owner.'

'Exactly,' I agreed. 'If he won't behave and rise to the challenge isn't it more of a waste to send him? We could be depriving another really deserving dog of a chance to help their owner. I don't know, I so wanted Hugo to be the one to help Eric but I'm not sure he's capable. Perhaps we're better off sticking to the original plan of ensuring he's well behaved enough to find a normal forever home. Maybe he's not ready for this kind of responsibility.'

'But don't forget how he saved me,' Bugsy yapped sadly. 'If it wasn't for him, I never would have got through that tunnel. He helped me. He's ever so lovable really.'

'I know,' I replied, having thought just the same thing. 'And this is the problem. Hugo has a very good heart, he's a good dog really or certainly has the makings of becoming one. I don't know what to think.'

'Send him,' Jake put in wisely. 'You might very well find that this doggy training school is the making of him. I'm sure they've seen pups just like Hugo before. They'll knock the corners off him, soon get him into shape.'

'But what if they don't?' Peg barked, echoing my own concerns. 'What then?'

'Then we'll have to find another way to help Eric, and another family for Hugo,' I barked sadly.

*

Now, as the sun beat down and the grass tickled my nose, I found myself sitting next to the love of my life, staring at my son. For the first time in my life I was barkless. I had been grateful to all my friends' yaps of wisdom last night, and as I fell asleep I was sure I knew just what I was going to discuss with my boy. But now, as my eyes roamed across his face, it all disappeared out of the kennel door. Just how was I going to make this little boy see sense and recognise he had a duty to his family?

'I just want to bark that I'm truly sorry, Daddy,' Hugo yapped, getting in there first.

Peg wrinkled her snout. 'Are you? It didn't look that way to me.'

'I really am, Mummy. I didn't mean to chew the man's clothes and cause so much fuss. I was nervous,' Hugo barked, turning to his mother, his brown eyes filled with hope.

'Were you?' I asked in astonishment. 'You couldn't wait to get up those stairs and see the crowds.'

Hugo, to his credit, hung his head in shame, before he woofed again. 'I think I just got a bit caught up in the moment.'

'That poor Tanya's got a black eye because she was distracted by your antics,' Peg snapped.

'And what about Lee's trousers and Rik's jacket?' I put in. 'You didn't have to destroy those. They were ruined. Jamie told us last night they cost thousands. Replacing those means eating into almost all of our profits from the show.'

I fell silent, not mentioning how good Rik and Lee had been, insisting that they had seen the funny side and there would be no charge. No, for once I wanted Hugo to think about his actions.

'Does that mean I can't go to doggy training school then?' Hugo barked anxiously.

'I don't know, Hugo. I'm not sure you can be trusted to go to training school,' Peg replied, her bark even.

Hugo looked at us both, his eyes wide with fear. 'You can't not send me because of what happened at the show.'

I never would have behaved like that if I thought it would destroy my chances of helping Eric.'

'But, Hugo, you must see how difficult it is for us to believe this is what you actually want to do,' I barked seriously. 'You had the opportunity yesterday at the show to prove to everyone how worthwhile it would be to send a pug to training school and instead—'

'You acted like a clown,' Peg finished grimly.

'I'm sorry,' Hugo whined, pleadingly. 'Please don't punish me or Eric because I made a mistake. It will never happen again, Daddy, Mummy, please.'

I let out a shaky sigh. My child had left me barkless, and I just didn't think I knew the answers any more, never mind know what to do now. When our pups were first born I thought I would always know the perfect way to guide them through life. Now it seemed I didn't have the first idea.

Just then, Doreen and Eric walked out into the garden, closely followed by Gail clutching a tray teeming with tea and biscuits.

'Just set it on the little table over there, love,' Doreen said, gesturing to the metal side table under the cherry blossom. 'You're all right if we sit in the shade, aren't you, Eric?'

'Yes of course.' Eric nodded. 'As long as you've got some of those custard creams you know I like, I'll sit anywhere.'

Gail chuckled as she sat down and opened the packet of biscuits, spreading them out on a plate. 'Nothing changes, does it?'

Eric grinned as he reached for a handful. 'You can give

me all the fancy biscuits in the world, but there's nothing like a custard cream.'

Kissing her husband's cheek affectionately, Doreen gave him a cup of tea. 'Not too many you, you'll get too fat.'

Eric rolled his eyes. 'She says that all the time.'

'It's only because she worries about you.' Gail sighed, wrapping her hands around her mug.

Looking at them all so settled, I wandered over and sat with my head resting on my lovely owner's feet. For a minute I just needed a break from my son, and could think of no nicer way of calming down than by spending a few minutes with Gail.

As the sun beat down, I looked up and met her sparkling emerald eyes. Despite the drama of yesterday she seemed as though she didn't have a care in the world as she smiled down at me and fed me a custard cream.

'I wonder how that Tanya's getting on today,' said Doreen, reading my mind. 'Cor, didn't she have a shiner when we left?'

Gail bit her lip at the memory. 'It was such a shame. Honestly, I know Percy wanted to read Hugo the Riot Act for his behaviour.'

'It was funny though.' Doreen chuckled, meeting my eyes. 'I'm sorry, Percy,' she said, catching my frosty glare, 'I know it wasn't right and I'd be just as cross as you if my kids behaved like that, but you have to see the funny side.'

Eric nodded. 'That's the beauty of having children. You've always got to see the funny side.'

Doreen snorted. 'I don't remember you feeling that

way when our Gail stuck a poster to the wall after you'd just painted it. You chased her halfway around the house screaming blue murder.'

Gail blushed as Eric opened his mouth to protest. 'I did no such thing. And even if I was cross at the time I'm sure I apologised afterwards,' he said evenly, looking to Gail for support. 'Now, did someone say something about a biscuit and a cup of tea? Shall I put the kettle on?'

I held my breath as Doreen and Gail exchanged worried looks.

'Your tea's just to the right of you, love, and the biscuits are on the table,' Doreen explained patiently.

Eric rubbed his hands together with glee. ''Course they are. I tell you, you can give me all the fancy biscuits in the world, but there's nothing like a custard cream.'

As Eric reached for his second biscuit, I felt a pang of fear. Glancing up at Doreen and Gail, it was clear they felt the same as they both stared at Eric tucking into his snack with gusto, clearly unaware of the forgetful error he had just made. My heart went out to both of them. From what I could tell, memory losses such as this one were a sign of Alzheimer's and its progression. For the life of me all I wanted to do was help Gail and her family but this illness was devastatingly cruel and I didn't want to stick my paw in and make things any worse.

Just then I felt a snout at my side. I looked around and saw Hugo. He was sitting on the ground and looking at me dolefully.

'What is it?' I barked wearily, in no mood for any more of Hugo's cheek.

'I just wanted to say again how much I love Eric, Dad. I'm so sorry I messed up yesterday, but I can promise you that nothing means more to me than being there for him and helping him through this illness.' Hugo barked with a passion and intensity I had never seen before.

'I don't know, Hugo,' I barked sadly. 'Believe me, I want nothing more than to send you to school and see you do well and help your family, I'm just not sure the time is right. I think it's our fault. We asked too much of you before you were ready.'

Hugo paused for a moment, before looking at me, his eyes filled with openness and trust. 'I can't guarantee you that I'm ready either, Daddy. What I can tell you is that going to school and being with Eric feels like the right thing to do. No, it's more than that,' he corrected, his little face brimming with urgency. 'I feel like I have to do this, as though it's what I was born to do.'

As he finished, I watched Eric ruffle Hugo's fur and bend down in his garden chair to kiss my son's ears.

'Fancy a bit of biscuit, Hugo?' Eric crooned lovingly. 'I know they're bad for you, but a crumb or two won't hurt.'

As Hugo barked his grateful thanks and took the sweet treat from Eric's outstretched hand, I saw the look of love flicker between man and dog. In that instant I understood just how perceptive Hugo had been. He was right, he may not be ready for school and he may make mistakes, but Eric and Hugo belonged together and I understood that when a dog loved an owner with that much passion, then any number of miracles could happen. It was time to set Hugo free.

Chapter Twenty-Five

As Gail and I walked home along the tree-lined Perivale streets in silence I kept a cautious eye on my gorgeous owner. Before we left, she had insisted to her mother that she was fine, that the fact she had seen Eric lose his memory hadn't upset her. But now, as Gail looked forlornly at the cracks in the pavement, lost in her own world, I wasn't sure that was how she really felt. Turning the corner into Barksdale Way, Gail wordlessly let herself into the house.

'Hello,' she called, flinging her keys into the pot on the hallway table. 'Anyone home?'

Greeted by silence, Gail wandered through to the kitchen with me at her heels. As she flicked on the kettle, she flung herself into the nearest chair and leant her head on the table.

'Are you all right?' I barked anxiously, sitting by her feet.

But Gail said nothing, instead she started sobbing so hard her shoulders shook like jelly. Immediately, I climbed up onto her lap, and allowed her to gather me in her arms.

'Oh, Percy,' she sobbed into my fur. 'My lovely dad, I'm losing my lovely dad.'

'No, you're not,' I whined. 'Your dad is still your dad, he's not going anywhere, he's just got a bit confused that's all.'

But it was as if I hadn't spoken as Gail carried on crying. 'Forgetting whether he's had a cup of tea and a biscuit is just the beginning. It's only going to get worse. My dad is such a beautiful, strong and kind man. I can't stand to see him like this, it's not who he is.'

'He's still your dad,' I barked fiercely. 'No matter what happens, he's still your dad and he still loves you and adores you.'

Gail's shoulders continued to shake with her cries. 'It's just all so unbearably cruel. To watch the person you love lose their mind like this seems twisted and wrong. My dad wouldn't want me to see him like this.'

I nodded miserably and let Gail's tears soak straight into my fur. 'I know that, but sometimes being there for someone, helping them when they are at their very lowest ebb is really all we can do for those we love.'

Gail paused and looked up. I met her eye and gave a little start. Her eyes were red raw from crying so violently and she looked as if she had the weight of the world on her shoulders.

'I'm just not ready, Percy,' she said through tears. 'I'm not ready to lose my daddy, and that's what's happening,

I'm losing my daddy right before my very eyes and there's nothing I, Mum, or even you can do.'

I shook my head in disbelief. Gail was always such a positive person, and yet she had dealt with so much heartache. Not only had she had to watch, wait and wonder if her only child would live through a heart transplant, now she was coping with her sick father as well. Life really could be so unfair.

Unable to help myself, I let out a little growl. Alzheimer's was a devastatingly terrible illness. With no cure, sufferers were left to cope in the worst way, and I knew that it must be distressing for Eric when he forgot where, or who he was. I cast my mind back to the day before at the show where he had seemed lost and confused as he looked for Hugo. I couldn't shake the feeling that something was desperately wrong and in that moment I wondered if he had even known who anyone was apart from Hugo. For some reason my precious boy had stuck in Eric's mind, and I was grateful that we were sending Hugo to school now. It seemed like the most natural thing in the world.

If nothing else it was something to give hope to Gail. Thankfully neither she nor Doreen had considered Hugo's behaviour at the show bad enough to stop him from going to school, which was why I wanted to remind her of the strand of good fortune we still had to cling to.

'When Hugo comes back from training then things will be much calmer for everyone, you'll see,' I barked comfortingly.

Gail wiped her eyes with the back of her hand and gave me a watery smile.

'Look, this is hard for everyone, but where there's hope there's a dog,' I continued.

Laughing, Gail kissed the top of my head. 'I don't know what I would do without you in my life, Percy. No doubt Mum and Dad feel just the same about Hugo.'

*

The day before Hugo was due to leave for Cornwall, Jenny, Gail and Simon and I set off along the sunshine-filled streets and walked to the dog park one last time. There, by Hugo's favourite oak tree, stood Bugsy, Jake, Heather, Peg along with Lily, Ralph and Roscoe who had all come to the park to say goodbye to their brother. At the sight of them all I did a little jig of delight. It was so wonderful for the family to be together. There on the ground was a picnic filled with all Hugo's favourite treats. Bones, Boneos, cheese slices, bacon sandwiches and even doggy chocolates had been laid out by all my friends.

'Wow!' Hugo barked excitedly as he caught sight of the delicious treats ahead. 'Is that for me, Dad?'

I nodded cheerfully, caught up in my boy's enthusiasm. 'Looks like it, though I think you might have to share.'

It was more than good enough for Hugo who gave a yelp of delight as he rushed excitedly towards his brothers and sisters and of course the picnic, followed by Jenny.

Together with Gail, Simon and Peg, we walked at a slower pace towards the food.

'What a lovely thing for everyone to have done.' Gail

beamed. 'Looks just like the one we enjoyed when Jenny was in hospital, do you remember, Simon?'

Simon's face lit up at the memory and he wrapped an arm around his wife's shoulders. 'How could I forget? It was a wonderful end to a wonderful day.'

I barked nothing. Neither Gail nor Simon ever found out it was me and my pals who were behind the feast that had helped to save their marriage. Instead, we let each of them think the other had been behind it. I desperately wanted it to stay that way so purposefully kept the fact that Peg and my pals had been the ones to put this little lot together as well to myself.

'Do you mind driving Hugo down to Cornwall, Gail?' I barked quickly changing the subject.

'I'm looking forward to driving Hugo down.' She beamed. 'I'm going to stay overnight with an old friend in Barnstaple. It'll be a bit of a treat actually, a night away.'

'It certainly will, it'll do you the power of good after everything that's happened,' Simon said loyally, pulling his wife in close.

'And you don't mind having the kids and Percy for the night, do you?' she asked, kissing his cheek.

''Course not.' Simon shrugged. 'We'll slob on the sofa and eat pizza all night.'

Gail swatted her husband's arm playfully. 'You'd better not!'

'And do you think Doreen's all right about Hugo going?' I barked.

Gail sighed and looked down at me. 'I think she and

Dad will really miss him. He's given them both a whole new lease of life since Dad's diagnosis.'

I was about to bark something in reply when Peg came bounding up to me and rubbed my snout, causing Gail to smile.

'We'll leave you two lovebirds to it.' Simon grinned.

'Yes, Sal's over there and I want all the latest on her romance with that dishy bloke she's been seeing,' Gail added.

'That'll take all of about five minutes,' Peg barked good-naturedly. 'She's with him all the time, Gail. There's not a lot else to say,'

Gail roared with laughter. 'Oh, Peg, your barks always tell it how it is. You're a breath of fresh air, I'll give you that.'

With that, she and Simon walked off towards Sal, leaving me and the love of my life alone. Silently, I linked paws with Peg and together we turned our gaze towards our offspring. Lily was playing chase with Bugsy around the tree, while Roscoe chewed a tennis ball that Simon had just thrown for him. On the picnic blanket, just looking at the spread before him lay Ralph, while behind him, appearing thoughtful, Hugo was slumped to the floor.

'Do you think he's all right?' I asked, turning to Peg feeling concerned.

She shrugged her little shoulders. 'He's been quiet for the past few days, perhaps the seriousness of the situation is sinking in.'

'Let's hope so,' I barked. 'I'll go yap with him.'

'Good luck,' she replied as I padded across the park towards our son.

Gently, I greeted him by rubbing my snout against his, and licking his ear. 'Hello, boy,' I whined.

But Hugo barely glanced up at me. Instead, he slumped his head back down, chin resting on his paws.

'Hi, Dad,' he barked mournfully.

A wave of alarm coursed through my fur. 'You all right?'

'Fine,' he replied, his bark listless.

I slumped down next to him, mirroring his pose by slumping my own chin on my paws.

'You don't seem all right,' I barked. 'Are you worried about tomorrow?'

Hugo shook his head, his frown lines and wrinkles seeming to have become deeper overnight. 'No, I'm looking forward to it. It will be really good to finally feel as though I'm doing something to help Eric. He and Doreen have been so kind to me, all I want to do now is be there for both of them.'

I looked at him in surprise. Bark about turnaround. It was as though Hugo had become a different dog over the past few days.

'That's lovely of you,' I barked, giving him another lick to his cheek. 'I'm sure Eric and Doreen will be so grateful to you for all you're doing for them.'

Hugo barked nothing once more and kept his eyes fixed on the floor. I tried again. 'So, can you tell me what it is that's troubling you. I might be able to help.'

241

'You can't help, Dad,' Hugo replied sadly. 'It's just one of those things.'

I did my best to suppress a bark of laughter. Such seriousness in one so young was rare to find and funny when it happened.

'Why don't you try me,' I suggested gently. 'If nothing else, it might make you feel better.'

'OK.' Hugo sighed, as if he were a human teenager. 'I'm worried about Eric. I don't want to leave him for so long. I won't be there to care for him.'

My heart ached for Hugo. How sensitive and thoughtful my precious boy had become.

'Well, Doreen will be there,' I reasoned. 'They can take care of him while you're away.'

'I know,' Hugo replied mournfully. 'But they won't be there all the time like I am. What about when Doreen goes to yoga or line dancing, or even the shops? Eric will be on his own. I'll worry about him.'

'But it's just for a fortnight. Nothing will happen,' I soothed.

'You don't know that, Dad,' Hugo replied stubbornly. 'You saw how he forgot whether or not he'd eaten his custard cream the other day. What's to stop him getting even worse while I'm away and then something bad happens?'

I paused and looked at my sensitive little boy. 'Well, what about if I kept an eye on him?' I suggested casually.

Hugo's head snapped up and he looked at with eyes filled with hope. 'Would you really do that, Dad?'

'Of course,' I barked gently. 'You only had to ask. Me

and your mum will keep an eye out while you're not here. I promise, we'll take good care of him. I personally give you the dad guarantee that I will look after Eric just as if he were Gail.'

Suddenly all the heartache in Hugo's eyes fell away as he looked at me with something that resembled happiness. 'You would really do that for me?'

I gave him a lick. 'I would do anything for you, Hugo.'

Chapter Twenty-Six

It had been a whole seven days since Hugo's departure for doggy training school, and life just wasn't the same without him. Although I knew he would only be gone for two weeks, I found I missed him far more than I had when he had left me to go and live with Doreen and Eric. I woke up feeling alone, miserable and bereft. Even the weather echoed my mood, with dark clouds and an early evening chill signalling the end of the long hot summer as we approached autumn.

It felt as though everything around me was changing. Even Jenny, who had gone back to school last week, seemed different. She was more grown up and had her face buried in her phone even more if that were possible. Thank heavens for Gail. She recognised I wasn't feeling myself and worked wonders to cheer me up. She fed me my favourite bones from the butcher's and was always on the sofa ready with a cuddle and kind word.

Of course I knew it was all for the best and that when Hugo came back, trained and ready to help Doreen and

Eric, life would improve for everyone. Until then, I just had to keep my chin up and know I would be reunited with him soon. Only yesterday Gail had talked about us going down to pick him up with Eric when he completed his final training session, which would be a huge treat, not just for me, but Eric too who I knew missed my boy just as much as I did.

I had kept my word to my son, and visited Eric religiously. Not only had I ensured he was never left alone for a moment, I also helped Doreen around the house. Folding sheets, getting the washing in, cleaning the tiles around the mysterious island and reminding Eric to take his pills by fetching medicines if Doreen was out.

'Quite the little wonder dog, aren't you?' Eric said cheerfully one morning as I dropped his pills at his feet.

'I do my best,' I barked, as Eric bent down and picked up the tablets from the carpeted floor.

As he examined the orange glass bottle, he scratched his head thoughtfully. 'Now why have these got my name on them? I don't remember being given these? Are they antibiotics?'

'No, they're your dementia tablets,' I barked quickly. 'You take them every day. They make you feel better.'

Eric looked down at me and then back at the pills in his hands. Peering at the label, he looked quizzically at it once more.

'These say they were bought from a pharmacist in Perivale,' he said, a hint of wariness in his voice. 'But why are they from a pharmacist there? Why wouldn't I get my tablets from my local pharmacy in Barnstaple?'

A growing sense of unease crawled over me, and I was about to try to bark a reply when Doreen walked in, arms filled with ironing.

'There you two are,' she said, ruffling my ears, and bending down to give me a kiss. 'You're very lovely to come and take care of us while Hugo's away,' she said softly, 'but I worry about you getting here all on your own. However do you do it?'

'I creep out of the cat flap, and take extra care on the roads,' I told her seriously.

Doreen looked at me and wrinkled her nose in confusion. 'I don't know what you barked, lovey, but I do know it's a pleasure to see you.' She smiled at me before turning to her husband. 'What's the matter, love?'

'This house, love, who's is it?' Eric asked, taking me back by getting to the point so quickly.

Doreen fixed her husband with a concerned gaze. 'It's our house, sweetheart.'

'Is it?' he asked, looking around him in confusion. 'But why haven't we got any stairs any more?'

'Because we live in a bungalow in Perivale now, near our Gail's.' she said gently. 'We left the stairs in our house in Barnstaple.'

Eric looked at her blankly but didn't pursue the matter further. Instead, he looked down at the pills in his hand.

'These tablets, Dor. Why have I got them?'

'It's because you've got memory problems, my love. These are supposed to help you,' Doreen replied patiently.

'Well, I know that.' He sighed, clearly irritated. 'What

I don't know is why they came from a pharmacy in Perivale. We haven't been up there for months.'

Shock flickered across Doreen's features. 'We live in Perivale now, Eric. We have done for a few months.'

Eric's face flamed with colour as he took in his wife's statement. About to open his mouth to speak, he paused and smiled. 'Oh, yes of course, silly of me. I know we live here, of course I do, but I just thought that my old doctor had been in contact, got me some pills from down there.'

'Right OK,' Doreen said doubtfully. 'Well, we'll be back west in a few days. Gail has suggested we all go and pick Hugo up and I think the staff at the training school want to do a bit of work with you both.'

At the mention of my son, Eric's eyes lit up and he clapped his hands together in glee. 'Oh wonderful! I have missed Hugo. He hasn't met Big Tony from the bowling club yet, I'll take him down there next week. It's the club finals, I'm going to have to meet the lads for a powwow, make sure we beat those swines from Dawlish. Can't have them taking our trophy again.'

Doreen patted her husband's arm affectionately. 'Sweetheart, you don't play bowls with the lads any more. Not since we moved up here to London, but I'm sure we could pop in, say hello on the way there if you like?'

Eric looked at his wife in confusion once more, and narrowed his eyes. 'Yes, yes, of course,' he said quickly. 'I knew that. No matter, now, do you want a cup of tea love before you nip out to your yoga class?'

As Doreen nodded, Eric walked out of the kitchen, leaving his wife alone. Sinking into the chair nearest the window, she gazed outside and I noticed silent tears streamed down her cheeks.

Without waiting for an invitation I jumped up onto her lap, and let her hold me close.

'In sickness and in health,' she whispered into my fur. 'That's what we promised each other all those years ago when we stood in church and made our vows. But, Percy, God forgive me for saying this, I never knew Alzheimer's was part of that promise. The man I love is disappearing before my very eyes.'

With that, Doreen clung on to me tightly and I allowed my fur to be soaked through the skin by tears for the second time in almost as many days. I felt her body wrack with sobs against me and my heart went out to her as I realised the only thing Eric said that made any sense was when he was talking about Hugo. The sooner we could get him together with my boy the better, and I made a mental note to have a bark with Gail when I got home.

*

Thankfully, Gail couldn't wait to drive back down to Cornwall again and, as we pulled up outside the training school on a grey and windy September morning, it was all I could do not to leap from the car in excitement. There hadn't been enough room for everyone in the car, so Simon and Ben along with Peg stayed at home.

Now we had pulled into the car park I did a little jig with my paws on the back seat. I was going to see my boy in just a couple of minutes and I had never felt so excited about anything in my life.

Sitting between Jenny and Doreen, I looked up at my favourite little girl pleadingly. Meeting my gaze, she gave me a bright smile, and kissed the top of my head.

'Mum, come on, Percy wants to get out,' Jenny groaned.

'Me too, love,' Gail said pointedly, 'but I need to secure the car first, so you'll have to hold your horses.'

'I think we might have got here a bit quicker on horseback,' Doreen muttered under her breath.

Gail fixed her mother with a cold stare in the rear-view mirror. 'Something to say about my driving, Mother?'

'No, dear.' Doreen sniffed. 'I just wondered if I'd draw my last breath stuck in this car at the speed you've been going.'

'I've just been concentrating on driving safely,' Gail protested. 'I thought you would be grateful.'

'I'm very grateful, dear. I'd also be very grateful not to waste what I have left of my remaining years in the back of a car because you've suddenly become Driving Miss Daisy,' Doreen said, with a raised eyebrow.

I held my breath as I looked at my owner in the mirror and saw her jaw was clenched. It was certainly true that since the accident Gail had become a much more cautious driver. As well as driving at the slowest speed possible, she also went to great lengths to ensure the car was in perfect working order too by checking the lights, fuel, oil and even seat belts. I was sure it was something that would pass in time, but Doreen was a devil for finding humour in almost every situation she didn't deem serious, so no doubt she was hoping to offer Gail a bit of encouragement by taking the mickey. Sadly, this time it didn't appear to be working. As Gail opened her mouth to reply, looking for all the world as if she were about to bite her mother's head off, Eric sighed with exasperation. 'Can we get on, you two are – how do you kids say it, Jenny? – doing my head in.'

Jenny let out a peal of laughter. 'That's it, Granddad.'

With that, Jenny opened the door and I leapt to the ground.

I had hardly had time to put one paw on the ground before I saw a pug come flying out of the entrance. At first it was impossible to register who it was, so fast and furious was the bundle of blond and black fur that bounded towards me.

'Daddy!' A bark I immediately recognised as Hugo's sounded as he simultaneously knocked me to the floor as though I was no more than a feather.

A pang of joy flooded through me as I felt my boy's fur against mine.

'Hello, son,' I yapped, flinging my paws around his neck as we held each other, rolling around the rain-soaked floor.

'Have you missed me, Daddy?' he asked, his bark a mix of sorrow and excitement.

'Missed you doesn't cover it,' I barked, stepping away from him for a second. 'Here, let me look at you.'

As Hugo stood obediently in the car park for me to examine him, I couldn't help feeling a sense of sorrow. He had been away just fourteen days and yet already it seemed as though he had grown to be twice the size with three times as much energy. Whatever had they been feeding him at this doggy training school?

'Are you all right?' I barked desperately. 'Is everyone being nice to you?'

'Very nice,' Hugo replied solemnly. 'I've learnt how to assist people to the toilet, take washing from the machine, fetch pills at certain times and I've also learnt how to just be.'

'"Just be"? What does that mean?' I quizzed.

'It means that I have to allow myself time to relax,' Hugo told me seriously. 'As I'm a working service dog now, it means that time off is very important as well, so when I get the opportunity to relax I have to take it.'

'Are you two dogs going to bark at each other all day or are you going to give us humans some attention as well?' Doreen chuckled, stepping forwards to ruffle Hugo's ears.

Watching them together, I felt a swell of pride that Peg and I had produced four wonderful children everyone adored. My attentions turned to Eric and, as I glanced at him, I saw he was peering down at Hugo, silent tears streaming down his face.

I was about to open my mouth to let out a bark to attract Hugo's attention, but there was no need. My son was well aware of his best friend's plight and was already rushing towards his owner with all the enthusiasm of a dog that had been let loose in a butcher's. As my boy threw himself at Eric's legs, he let out whines of delight. He rubbed Eric's legs enthusiastically with his snout only for Eric to bend down and scoop him up into his arms.

Watching him squeeze Hugo tight, I felt a lump form. Eric peppered my boy's wrinkled snout with kisses. Looking across at Gail, I saw her eyes too were shining with tears at the sight of her dad and my boy wrapped in each other's company. There had never been a sweeter reunion.

Chapter Twenty-Seven

Inside the doggy training centre I was surprised to see how much it reminded me of the tails of the forgotten. Although it was obviously a lot smaller than the centre I had resided in before I was rehomed with Gail, there were a lot of similarities. It smelled just the same for a start with that undertone of bleach combined with human. Then there were the cubicles where the dogs slept, which were just the same, along with all the green uniforms the humans that worked there wore.

In a funny way it gave me a sense of comfort, as I knew how well I had been looked after at the tails of the forgotten, and I had a feeling that my son had been too. I looked at Hugo who, together with his trainer, Mike, an Australian with sun-bleached hair, was giving us a guided tour. With his ears primed forwards and nose in the air, not to mention the definite trot in his walk, he seemed so proud of the centre and for being a dementia dog that I found his pride rubbed off on me.

I noticed that the building itself was quite small, a

glass concrete affair over two storeys set in huge amounts of parkland. It was here the dogs could roam free, play amongst the trees and enjoy great big lungfuls of fresh sea air while they trained.

'So do you train many dogs here then, Mike?' Doreen asked, as he led us outside.

'A select few.' Mike grinned. 'Hugo here has picked up the training in no time, but then pugs are so intelligent, it's not a surprise.'

Sitting on a nearby bench with the sunshine peeping through the clouds, I shivered with delight. I had a feeling Mike and I were going to get on.

'And does everyone have a success story?' Gail asked. 'I mean do you have any dogs where the training doesn't work?'

Mike grimaced. 'It's only happened once in the five years I've been here. The dog, a red setter, just couldn't cope with all the to-ing and fro-ing. Although we're quite relaxed here, it's difficult for some dogs to cope with the rules.'

I let out a bark of amazement. 'But you're coping, aren't you, Hugo? There's a first!'

Gail chuckled as she sat on a bench and scooped me onto her lap. 'Don't be rude, Percy!'

Mike looked at my lovely owner with interest as Eric sat beside us still holding Hugo, while Doreen sat next to him. 'You understand your dog's barks?'

Gail nodded and beamed at Mike. 'Of course. I mean not every single one obviously, but I usually get the gist.'

'That's quite rare you know,' Mike replied with wonder. 'Even with dogs and owners who adore each other.'

I glanced at him. With his perma-tanned skin, he gave off the air of a confident youth, but I detected that actually he adored dogs and would lay his life on the line for any one of us.

'I think Percy is just very good at making himself heard.' Jenny smiled as she threw a tennis ball for Hugo.

Jumping up and down as she watched Hugo chew the ball, I let out a bark of affection. Jenny always knew just what to say to make me feel good about myself.

'So, how is Hugo doing? He's not failed, has he?' Doreen asked bluntly.

Mike laughed and shook his head. 'Far from it. He's doing brilliantly, and with just one test to go, I've been impressed.'

I couldn't help myself and let out another bark of astonishment.

'Percy, surely you can't be that surprised your son is doing so well?' Mike smiled.

I gave a little start. I wasn't used to other people understanding my barks apart from Gail, Jenny and, to a lesser extent, Simon. Knowing that I'd have to watch what I was barking would give the day an entirely different focus.

'Well, Hugo wasn't always known for doing as he was told back at home,' I barked delicately. 'Perhaps school has had a positive effect on him.'

'I think it's having more than a positive effect on him.' Mike beamed. 'I'd say Hugo is thriving. He's done really well, and it's brilliant you've been able to come down today to pick him up.'

Doreen looked at him perplexed. 'But I thought it was about more than picking him up? I thought you wanted us to come down so Eric here could have some training with Hugo.'

Mike nodded. 'That's true. We also have a support group that's meeting here now in the conference room. A few people here have partners working with an assistance dog. From our research we've discovered human carers need support just as much as those with dementia.'

Doreen put a hand up to silence him. I looked at her and saw her mouth was set in a firm line. 'No thank you. I don't need to discuss my private business with complete strangers.'

Gail gasped in shock. 'Mum! Don't be like that. Sometimes it can really help to talk things through with someone else. I know when Jenny was sick I got a lot out of talking to other parents who were going through something similar.'

Doreen sighed and fixed her daughter with an expression of sympathy. 'Well, you're not like me, love. You've always been quick to share your emotions; me, I like to keep things to myself.'

'Gran! Nobody thinks like that any more,' Jenny protested, throwing another ball for Hugo. 'You might get something out of it. Surely it's worth a try?'

Gail gave her mother a nudge. 'Exactly. You don't have to tell people your deepest darkest secrets, you could just listen. Sometimes you can get a lot out of that, you know.'

'Maybe,' Doreen said non-committally. 'Now why don't you do this training with Eric, love, and the rest of us will go and get a cup of tea?'

Mike laughed once more at Doreen's forthrightness as Hugo returned with the tennis ball. 'OK. Eric, Hugo, are you ready?'

Eric stood up and looked at Hugo, who was now loyally standing by his side. 'I'd say we're ready, aren't we, boy?'

'Born ready,' he replied.

With that, the two of them followed Mike into a room just off the main entrance leaving the rest of us in peace.

'Well, shall we get that tea then?' Doreen quizzed, getting to her feet and smoothing the creases out of her navy trousers.

Gail nodded. 'OK, but let's call in on the support group, find out more about it?'

'You won't leave this alone, will you?' Doreen sighed, arms folded.

Gail smiled. 'No, I won't. I'm only pressing this on you because I think it will help, not because I think it will hurt you.'

'All right,' Doreen grumbled, sensing her daughter wasn't going to give up.

As they all trooped inside, I stayed rooted to the spot.

'Aren't you coming, Percy?' Gail asked, swinging around to look for me.

I shook my head. 'I want to watch how Hugo gets on.'

'I want to watch Hugo as well,' Jenny said.

Gail looked at us doubtfully. 'All right. If it's OK with

259

Mike. But you'd better be quiet because you don't want to put him off what he and Dad have to do.'

'OK, Mum.' Jenny smiled.

'All right, we'll come and find you in a little bit,' Gail said, smiling too.

As they turned away, Jenny and I walked over to the other side of the courtyard and slipped inside the entrance Mike, Eric and Hugo had entered.

'So what do you think then? As good as the website made it out to be?' I asked.

Jenny nodded happily, slowing her pace to match mine. 'It's brilliant, everyone's so kind, and guess what, Percy?'

'What?' I barked, feeling buoyed up by my son's enthusiasm.

'I heard Mike say to Mum that Hugo is the best dog he's ever taught!'

Reaching the glass panelled room where Mike was training Eric and Hugo, I let out a little whine of pride. My son! The best the school had ever taught? Who would have thought it?

Mike put his finger to his lips and ushered us both to take a seat at the very back so we hopped onto the wooden bench. I looked at what the three of them were doing with interest. Mike had laid out a series of cones and appeared to be showing Hugo how to help Eric find his way from one corner of the room to the other with a blindfold.

'What's this about?' I barked quietly.

'It's so Hugo can help Eric find his way home if he needs to. This is just a training exercise to see if they listen to each other properly,' Jenny told me knowledgeably. 'If they don't then Mike will say they're not a good fit for each other and that all this isn't a good idea.'

A bolt of alarm surged through me. Even though Hugo was the best dog he had ever taught, it was possible all this could be for nothing. I bristled with annoyance. Of course Eric and Hugo were well suited, one glimpse at their reunion in the car park told anyone that.

I looked across at Eric slipping Hugo's lead onto his collar and found myself holding my breath. I didn't want to think about what would happen if Hugo and Eric failed this task and Mike deemed them an unsuitable pairing.

As Hugo started his journey guiding Eric through the cones towards safety, I relaxed just a little. Hugo looked as though he had done this a million times before, and Eric appeared to be finding the whole thing highly amusing as he smiled all the way through the exercise.

'My goodness!' I barked, as Eric took off his blindfold and found Hugo had taken him where he needed to go.

Once again, Hugo led Eric through the maze of cones and I shook my head in wonder. If only Peg could see this, I thought. Looking at Hugo now, rewarded with treats and gold stars for a job well done, I knew she would burst with pride.

'OK, you two sit back down,' Mike instructed. 'So, Eric, how did you find it having Hugo lead you everywhere?'

Pausing for a moment, Eric looked thoughtful. 'It was fine, I suppose. I mean, I would have rather taken myself where I needed to go, but I knew Hugo was going to get me safely to the other side of the room without incident.'

'And why did you know that?' Mike pressed. 'I'm guessing you've never done that exercise before together.'

'Because I trust him.' Eric shrugged. 'I've always trusted Hugo, and I think he trusts me.'

At that my son let out a little bark of agreement and shuffled closer to Eric.

Mike looked at them both before he spoke. 'That's the thing about this disease, Eric. It robs you of your ability to trust. There will be days when you won't know who you are or who your wife is.'

Eric nodded miserably and rubbed his temples. 'Today's a good day, but more often than not I forget where I live or when my last meal was. It's heart-breaking, for them and for me. I wish I could do something about it, I hate hurting my family like this.'

My heart went out to Eric. More than anything I wanted to run down and cover him with licks and let him know it was all OK, but I knew that wasn't appropriate. Reluctantly, I let Mike offer comfort instead.

'Alzheimer's is one of the most sadistic illnesses there is out there,' he said with a sigh. 'It's amazing there's no cure for it, but until there is we work hard here to ensure sufferers get to live lives that are as normal as possible. But that only works if there's trust. On the days when you don't know who anyone is and you don't know where you live it will be down to Hugo here to guide you, and that's where trust comes in. You may not know who Hugo is, but deep down you will know that you can trust him.'

'I'd trust this boy with my life,' Eric said affectionately, giving my boy a pat on his head.

'And that's good.' Mike beamed as Hugo gave Eric another lick to his ear.

Eric smiled at Hugo's affection, as he turned to Mike a little nervously. 'So do we pass the test then?'

'With flying colours.' Mike beamed. 'The two of you have one of the best relationships I have seen in the ten years I've been working here. You and Hugo here are going to be one of the school's biggest success stories. Congratulations.'

As Mike delivered the news, neither Jenny nor I could help ourselves. Together we let out delighted squeals and whines of joy, jumping excitedly up and down in our seats. At the commotion, Hugo looked across and let out another bark.

'I did it, I did it.'

'Yes you did, son,' I barked joyously.

And, looking at him now, as he gave Eric another lick, it was hard to believe I had ever doubted Hugo for even a second.

Chapter Twenty-Eight

Once Hugo had been released as a fully certified doggy dementia dog it was time to make the long drive back to London. With the night beginning to draw in, it was no wonder Jenny, Eric and Hugo all fell fast asleep the moment we got onto the motorway. I looked across at them, mouths open, snoring lightly, and gave each one a lick of jealous affection.

How I wished I could fall asleep too, but even though I was exhausted my mind was too busy going over the day's events. The whole thing had been an eye-opener and, although I hated eavesdropping, it sounded as though Gail and Doreen thought the same.

'It was a beautiful place though, wasn't it, love?' Doreen sighed from the front seat.

Gail nodded, her eyes twinkling as she glanced in the rear-view mirror. 'It was wonderful. All the staff there really cared for the dogs, didn't they?'

'Oh they did,' Doreen agreed. 'Nothing was too much trouble, and all the love they gave the animals.'

I gave a bark of agreement. After my time at the tails of the forgotten I had discovered how much love the staff were able to give the dogs they were looking after and had been delighted to find that it was just the same, if not better, at the school. Every dog was cuddled, played with and rewarded for a job well done. I had to confess it was something of a relief as I hadn't known what to expect but I knew now that Hugo had received the best possible care.

'And wasn't that Mike wonderful?' Doreen chuckled. 'Oh, the bond he had with Hugo.'

Gail nodded again. 'He has really got the best out of that boy. I can't wait to see how Hugo and Dad get on now.'

I barked again. 'It's going to be brilliant. You should have seen the rapport he and Eric had when Mike was leading the assessment.'

'You must be very proud, Percy,' Gail said, meeting my eyes as she glanced into the rear-view mirror.

'I am,' I yelped quietly. 'Hugo really has come a very long way in the last couple of months.'

Gail beamed at me. 'But then with you for a daddy, he was always going to do something to make us proud!'

I felt my fur-covered cheeks flame with embarrassment and kept my barks to myself as Gail turned to Doreen.

'And how did you find that support group in the end then, Mum?' she asked gently. 'I thought it best for you to go in on your own in the end. Thought you might feel as though you could talk more freely without me around.'

Doreen grinned. 'You know what, love, despite all I said before I went in, it was actually very helpful.'

'Get away!' Gail gasped with shock and took her eyes off the road as she looked at her mother.

'Gail, watch what you're doing!' Doreen thundered.

'Whoops, sorry,' she replied quickly turning her focus back to the road. 'Well, go on then, tell me more.'

Doreen shuffled her handbag on her lap, clearly uncomfortable about having to discuss her feelings. 'I don't know where to start really. But let's just say that Mike was right. It was actually very helpful to meet other people in my position.'

'And what did you discover?' Gail pressed gently.

'That I'm not alone really,' Doreen said quietly. 'Since your father's diagnosis, Gail, I've been feeling just that, on my own. Now don't get me wrong, I know you and the family all love me and you've been wonderful. But living with someone who's got Alzheimer's, well, it's very isolating and very frightening at times.'

Gail nodded quietly. 'I can understand that.'

'Anyway, I didn't say anything at the meeting itself,' Doreen continued, 'but I did get talking to a lovely lady afterwards, from Barnstaple would you believe!'

'Did you know her when you lived there?' Gail asked.

Doreen shook her head. 'No! And she only lives two streets from our old house. Isn't that funny?'

'Very,' Gail agreed. 'So I take it she's got someone close suffering from dementia too then?'

'Husband,' Doreen explained. 'We had a good chat over a cuppa in the canteen afterwards. It was so wonderful having someone else to talk to who really understood. I think her husband's at a similar stage as Eric.'

'So is their dog training at the centre too?' Gail asked.

Doreen shook her head. 'No, she was just there for the meeting. She goes every month, since she took her dog, Rocket, a Hungarian vizsla, to be trained last year. She was telling me the world of difference Rocket has made to their lives. Whenever her husband gets confused or agitated, Rocket calms him right down just by being near him.'

'Oh that's wonderful.' Gail smiled. 'It's nice she still goes back as well and mixes with all the people in the support group.'

Doreen nodded. 'Well, as she said to me, it's not far and she really appreciates spending time with other people who know just how she feels. She doesn't have to keep explaining herself, her situation or worry about other people's feelings. She can just speak honestly.'

'I remember that feeling,' Gail said, a hint of wistfulness creeping into her voice. 'It was those support groups that kept me going some days. Don't get me wrong, friends, family and so on are all so kind, but there's something very freeing about being around people who understand immediately what you're going through. I'm glad you were able to experience that today.'

'I'm glad you made me,' Doreen replied. 'I feel very lucky to have Hugo and Percy as well as all of my wonderful family to help us through this.'

'Well, we're all lucky to have such clever dogs.' Gail chuckled, meeting my eyes again in the rear-view mirror.

'We certainly are,' Doreen agreed. 'I'm beyond grateful to you, to you all.'

'You're welcome,' I barked.

But I had no sooner finished barking than I saw Doreen had tears pooling in her eyes.

'I mean it,' she wept. 'Having Hugo as a service dog will make all the difference. Today has shown me that in a way I never really understood before.'

I leant between the two front seats and pressed my paw into Doreen's hand. As she clasped her warm fingers around my fur, I felt a surge of affection for Gail's mum. We had all been through so much in this family, and it was a wonderful feeling when we could help each other.

I'm not sure how long we stayed like that, but by the time we arrived home over four hours later, I could hardly keep my eyes open. In fact I was so tired I didn't even bother to have a wee outside. Instead I simply licked each of my family good night and crawled straight into my basket. The moment my head hit the soft blanket, I fell straight to sleep and slept solidly until the morning.

*

Waking up, I saw Jenny smiling down at me she sat on her haunches next to my basket and stroked my head.

'Morning, Perce. Your breakfast is all ready for you.'

Wearily, I barked my thanks, got up and immediately became aware of how much I needed to use the loo. Bolting outside into the nippy autumn air, I didn't hang around and quickly made my way inside to wolf down the breakfast Jenny had lovingly laid out for me.

As Gail followed Simon down the stairs, yawning heavily and clutching a sleepy baby Ben, I saw she hadn't enjoyed anywhere near as much sleep as I had.

After giving Simon's leg a gentle nudge with my snout, I did the same to Gail and yapped a gentle hello as she sat down.

'Cuppa, Mum?' Jenny asked, shooting her mum a concerned gaze. 'You look done in.'

'You're all right.' Simon smiled, reaching for a pair of mugs from the cupboard. 'I'll sort your mum out. You get ready for school.'

'Are you sure?' Jenny asked doubtfully.

''Course.' Simon chuckled, ruffling his daughter's hair. 'I have made tea before you know.'

As Jenny bent down to kiss me on the head, she embraced her mother and brother then swept out of the kitchen. While the kettle boiled, I retreated to my basket and kept a watchful eye on Gail.

'Up all night were you?' Simon asked gently placing a steaming mug in front of her.

Gail nodded, bleary eyed. 'Yes, this one just wouldn't stop crying. I think he's teething again.'

'I thought all that had stopped.' Simon frowned.

Gail laughed at her husband. 'Sadly, no. Ben here might be fourteen months now but his teeth are still coming through and letting him know who's boss.'

'Sorry, love, I'll take a turn with him tonight,' Simon offered.

'That's sweet of you, Si, but you're working so hard at the minute. You need your rest.'

'So do you,' Simon replied, reaching for his son so Gail could drink her tea properly.

'I'll try and grab a nap in a bit.' She sighed. 'No doubt this one's as desperate for a bit of sleep as his mum.'

At that, Ben let out a shriek, and Simon immediately handed his son back into Gail's arms. 'Don't think it's me he's after.' He chuckled. 'Listen, why don't you take it easy this morning? I'll look in on your mum and dad later this afternoon, see how they're getting on now Hugo's back.'

At the offer, Gail's eyes lit up. 'Would you? That would be a huge help. I thought we'd organise a little celebration later to welcome Hugo back, and I also said I'd take some leaflets I printed off the internet for Mum about local support groups.'

Simon shrugged. 'No problem, I can pick up some party stuff after lunch and drop the leaflets off at the same time.'

'That's really good of you, thanks, love.' She smiled, relief flickering across her features.

'So our Hugo's done well then?' Simon said, through a mouthful of toast.

Gail nodded. 'Marvellously, according to Mike his trainer. He said Hugo was very talented and a natural service dog.'

Simon let out a peal of laughter. 'If you'd have told me that after he ate candles and potpourri a few months back, I would never have believed you.'

'I know.' Gail laughed. She turned to me and shot me a smile. 'But I think he takes after his dad, a born helper.'

I got to my paws and pushed my snout into her outstretched hand. As she stroked my head, I felt a surge of affection for my owner. Perhaps once Simon had gone to work we could all enjoy a cheeky nap on the sofa together.

At the thought of curling up together and shutting out the miserable autumn weather I let out my own sigh of relief. But on glancing up at the clock and seeing it was almost time for Simon to leave, a jolt of fear coursed through my fur. This morning was Monday and Doreen was taking Hugo to the vet's this morning for a quick check-up, meaning Eric would be on his own. Simon might well be going over to his in-laws' later but that was no good now. I had promised my son I would ensure his owner was well looked after and even though he was back now I intended to do just that.

Shaking my whole body to wake myself up, I peered out of the window. The sight of the grey clouds and trees rustling violently in the wind did nothing to encourage my desire to leave my warm comfy bed. But a promise was a promise and I wasn't going to let anyone down.

I padded across the floor to the cat flap, pushed my head through the door and set my paws onto the cold tarmac. I'd nap later this afternoon, but in the meantime I had a job to do.

Chapter Twenty-Nine

Despite the wind and rain, it didn't take me long to run through the streets of Perivale and reach Eric and Doreen's home. As I pushed my snout against the conservatory door, I opened it enough for me to squeeze my head and shoulders through the gap I had created. Once I had got the rest of my body inside, I padded across the striped rug Doreen had only recently bought from Ikea, and made my way into the kitchen.

I looked around in surprise. Everywhere was a complete mess with dirty bowls and plates piled high next to the butler sink with upended packets of cereal littering the surfaces.

I shook my head in astonishment. Doreen always kept such a tidy home. It was a running joke in the family that she would wash their mugs up before they had even finished a cup of tea. As for my water bowls, I had learnt that whenever Doreen was around it was best to ensure I didn't drain it dry as she would whisk it from me and start to give it a good scrub.

Just then, Eric bustled into the kitchen, his sparkling blue eyes alive with merriment as he hummed a tune I didn't recognise. Seeing me in the kitchen, he stopped suddenly and raised an eyebrow in surprise.

'Hello, whatever are you doing here?' he asked.

I regarded him warily. Although Eric wasn't usually a grumpy man, I had never seen him in such a good mood.

'Just popped in to say hello,' I barked, knowing full well he wouldn't understand me.

'Right you are,' he replied, turning his back on me and rifling through the cupboards, pulling out more food.

I looked at him aghast as he pulled out a loaf of bread, jam, porridge oats, and packets of bacon and eggs from the fridge.

'I'm making breakfast.' He grinned, setting a packet of sugar on the counter. 'Hugo's home and I want to celebrate.'

Glancing around nervously, I hoped against hope that Doreen was somewhere to be found. But one look at the filthy work surfaces told me there was no way Gail's mum was anywhere near her home. If she saw this mess, not to mention Eric's mental state, she would have kittens.

Watching Eric anxiously beat two eggs in a bowl and pour the mix into a saucepan, I tried to recall everything I had learnt at the doggy training school yesterday. After I'd witnessed Hugo's session with Mike, he had been kind enough to offer me a few pointers on how to cope with dementia sufferers.

One of the first things he had told me was that it was vital to try and keep Alzheimer's patients calm. Mike had explained that it was actually animals that had the best chance of soothing an Alzheimer's sufferer through the restful strokes and cuddles rather than a human they may not recognise. Noticing Eric now, busy making porridge on the stove, I padded quickly across the floor towards him and rubbed my head and body against his legs, almost as if I was a cat.

Immediately, Eric stopped what he was doing, looked down and grinned. 'What are you up to, eh, boy? You want a cuddle, is that it?'

Bending down, he ran his hand across my back, and I did my best to show him how much I was enjoying it by leaning into his touch. I wanted to encourage him to keep stroking me so he would continue to relax.

With every rhythmic stroke I sensed Eric's touch becoming less frantic and relief flooded through me. Eric was clearly not himself and I did the only thing I could think of and encouraged him to take it easy.

Once I felt Eric was more in control, I jumped out of his arms and walked across the kitchen towards the living room. I thought that if I could just get him to sit down and rest there was every chance he might feel better by the time Doreen and Hugo got home.

I had only made it as far as the door, when Eric started to get suspicious. 'Where are we going, boy? I'm sorry, I haven't got time to play with you now I've got to get breakfast ready. Hugo will be back soon, and I want to have everything just right for him.'

I looked at Eric aghast as he stood up and walked back to the stove, to stir the porridge.

'Bit more milk, I think' —he grinned— 'and as lovely as it is to talk to you, I must get the bacon on. Hugo needs feeding up after being away so long and deserves a treat. Now, what was I doing?'

As he scratched his head, looking in the fridge for the bacon, I saw it had already been placed by the side of the pan, and barked at him to tell him so. I must have done something right as he understood immediately and ripped it straight open. Then he reached below him for a frying pan from the drawer under the hob and lit the gas. He threw the whole packet into the pan and the smell of sizzling, salty bacon filled the air. Eric rubbed his hands together in glee.

'Look at that, eh? A breakfast fit for a king. Well, Hugo at least.' He chuckled, checking his wrist and examining what appeared to be a non-existent wristwatch. 'Would you look at that, boy? It's getting late, I'd better get upstairs and get myself showered and dressed so I'm all ready to take him for his walk.'

As Eric walked determinedly out of the kitchen, I ran at his heels, barking frantically. 'Eric you're already dressed and showered. Let's go and sit down in the living room. I'll sit on your lap and we can do a Sudoku puzzle together.'

But Eric wasn't listening as he paced up and down the corridor looking for all the world as though he had lost something.

'Where are they? Where've they gone?' Eric asked, his face full of confusion as he continued to walk up and down the corridor.

'Where's what gone? What are you looking for?' I barked, trying to keep pace.

But Eric paid me no attention as he continued to pound the floor, one long stride after the other, running his hands through what was left of his greying hair. 'They were here yesterday, I'm sure of it. Where have they gone? I can't get in the shower or get dressed if I can't find them, they've got to be here.'

I continued running up and down the corridor at Eric's side, desperately trying to make sense of what he was telling me.

'It's impossible to move stairs, isn't it?' Eric continued, his tone thick with confusion. 'If that's what had happened I would have known about it, wouldn't I? People don't just move stairs for no good reason, it's just not possible, is it? But why aren't they here? Where do you think the stairs could have gone? Could a burglar have come in and taken them do you think?'

'Eric, the stairs were in your last house I think,' I barked frantically. 'You live in a bungalow now, you remember that don't you?'

Suddenly, Eric sank to his knees and buried his face in his hands. I glanced at him in alarm as he let out a huge tortured wail, and he started to sob great gut-wrenching cries that were so violent they caused his whole body to shake with distress.

'I don't know anything any more. Where am I? This isn't my house, is it? I don't recognise it. Why will nobody help me? Please, someone help me.'

At the sight of Eric sobbing as if he were no more than

Ben's age, I felt a tug of emotion. I understood perfectly now just what Gail and Doreen had meant when they said Alzheimer's was a cruel disease that robbed you of your loved ones. The sight of Eric in so much distress was heart-breaking. He had always been a strong, stoic shoulder for Gail to lean on and seeing him reduced to this was one of the hardest things I had ever witnessed. But there was no time for my feelings, I had to do something. Mike's words echoed in my brain once more and I knew the best thing to do was to calm Eric down as quickly as possible.

Barklessly, I rubbed my snout against his side and then burrowed my way under his armpit. As if sensing my presence for the first time, he removed his face from his hands and looked at me, his eyes still brimming with tears.

'What's happening to me? I'm frightened,' he whispered, cradling my face with his hands. 'Percy, help me.'

A tennis ball-sized lump formed in my throat as I took in the very real fear in Eric's eyes. In that moment I would have gladly traded places with him if it would have helped ease his heartache for just a second. But I was just a pug, there was only so much I could do. Yet no matter how limited my skills, I was determined to do what I could.

'Don't be afraid, Eric' I whined, holding his gaze. 'I'm here for you. Come on, rub your hands across my fur, it will help.'

Eric had never understood a bark I had uttered before, but, in that moment, it was as though the penny had dropped. He looked at me for a split second and then began to run his hand along my back.

The action seemed to soothe him and, as I whined gently again, encouraging him to keep going, I made sure my eyes never left his.

'I'm here for you,' I whined gently, 'I'm not going anywhere. I won't leave you. You can trust me, I promise you, I'll keep you safe.'

As Eric continued to stroke my fur, his body seemed to relax with every touch. I made sure I stayed rooted to the spot, my mind continuing to whir. Although I had always known that Hugo wasn't exaggerating how worried he was about Eric's condition, I could now see why he was so concerned. He had never told me just how bad Eric could get, and as well as feeling sorrow for the elderly man kneeling before me, I also felt sorry for my son. He had been exposed to such cruelty and sadness at such a young age and guilt gnawed away at me. He wasn't ready to cope with something like this, he was far too young.

Looking at Eric, I saw that he had now stopped crying and his breathing had steadied. Sensing that he was now calm enough to walk, I pulled away and began to walk to the living-room door. Incredibly, Eric sensed I wanted him to follow me.

As I led him towards his favourite chair, I hopped onto his lap, and arranged blankets and cushions around the place with my teeth, ensuring he was comfortable.

'There,' I barked, when I was sure he was settled. 'Why don't you just shut your eyes now and have a little nap. You'll feel ever so much better when you wake up.'

Obeying my every bark, Eric took off his glasses, and let them rest on the little side table. Then he shut his eyes with his hands still resting on my back. As I nestled myself into his lap, I resolved not to fall asleep but to go and tidy the kitchen so it wasn't a mess for Doreen when she got back with Hugo.

But after such a traumatic morning, I was beginning to feel very tired and Eric's gentle strokes were very soothing. Settling myself into an even more comfortable position on Eric's warm lap, I found my eyelids beginning to close, and the sleepy sensation I was trying so desperately to fight off began to flood through my body, rendering me powerless.

Just a couple of minutes I told myself as I drifted off to the land of nod. I'll get up in two shakes of a pug's tail I promised, my eyelashes touching my wrinkles, then I'll clean the kitchen and nobody will be any the wiser as to what's happened here today.

Chapter Thirty

It was the thick black smoke that woke me as I felt the smog whirling around my head. With a sudden jolt, I knew something wasn't right and, as I opened one eye, I saw with growing horror great big plumes of evil spiralling around me like leaves at the dog park on a windy day.

Startled, I opened my other eye and realised the smoke was so dense I could scarcely see a paw in front of my face. Swiftly coming to, I realised the bungalow was on fire and I glanced around to try to see where it was coming from. Getting to all four of my paws, I was determined to investigate, until a charred acrid smell filled my nostrils. It was vile and smelled as though there was burning, rotting flesh flooding the room. As the smell overpowered my senses, I struggled to breathe and felt the smoke making me drowsy once more.

I turned around and looked at Eric. I had no idea how long we had been asleep for, but he was still slumbering in the chair. His breathing was laboured thanks to the smoke, but he was blissfully unaware of the devil and his work surrounding him.

'Eric,' I barked, sharply. 'Wake up.'

But there was nothing. 'Eric,' I tried again, louder this time. 'Eric, wake up, we've to get out of here.'

Yet still Eric remained fast asleep. I blinked away the tears that continued to form, but my eyelids were so heavy, I couldn't seem to keep them open never mind find the strength to wake Gail's dad. I tried again but it was as though my body had been taken over and I was no longer in control. Helplessly, I shut my eyes again, maybe if I just closed them for a second I would find the strength to help Eric.

The next thing I knew was the feel of something wet and slimy pushing against my wrinkled cheeks. I blinked my eyes open with a start and saw Hugo gazing at me, concern all over his face.

'Dad, there's a fire. We've got to get out of here,' he barked urgently.

'What are you doing here?' I barked sleepily.

'I smelled the smoke from the car park in the vet's and ran all the way back,' he explained. 'I didn't even go into see Gemma. I knew Eric was in trouble and came back straightaway. I didn't know you were here too.'

'I promised to keep an eye on Eric for you,' I barked, still feeling dazed. 'I didn't want to break that promise.'

'Oh, Dad, you daft thing,' my son replied mournfully.

As Hugo tried to rouse me fully awake, I felt touched my son had thought only of Eric and was intent on saving him. But this was a downright dangerous situation and the last place my little boy should be.

Giving him a lick, I glanced around the room and tried not to panic. Now, the smoke was even thicker than before, wrapping us in its fugue as though it were a suffocatingly hot winter blanket. As the darkness carried on swirling around us, I felt as if I was drowning. No matter how hard I tried, I couldn't catch a breath without choking and the smoke was now stinging my eyes so badly great rivers of tears were running down my wrinkled furry cheeks.

Hugo barked sharply, cutting straight through my thoughts. 'We need to wake Eric, now.'

I nodded, knowing he was right. Quickly, Hugo jumped onto Eric's lap and together we leapt up and down on his chest, our little paws scampering away like hammers.

'Eric,' Hugo barked at the top of my lungs, 'wake up, the house is on fire.'

'We've got to go now,' I barked.

As we finished barking, I felt a surge of hope as I saw Gail's dad shuffle in his chair. But rather than open his eyes Eric merely turned over as if he were enjoying a delicious dream.

I howled with frustration. Danger surrounded us and I knew I had to get us out immediately.

It was then Hugo caught my eye. 'Dad, I'm going to stay here and try to wake Eric, you go and see if you can find out where the smoke is coming from so we can find our best route to escape. I came in through the bathroom window but didn't see anything through there.'

'OK,' I agreed, following Hugo's orders.

Reluctantly, I jumped to the floor, anxious about leaving my son with Eric. Yet I knew that if we stood any chance of getting out of here we needed to investigate the source of the blaze. With the smoke still billowing all around me, I padded quickly across the living-room floor towards the kitchen. I had never been in a fire before, but a dollop of doggy common sense told me that's where hot things started and often finished so it was the most likely place.

As I neared the kitchen door, I felt the heat coming through the gap. Peering underneath, I saw the orange flames crackling under the door and felt a jolt of fear. This was worse than I thought.

I took a step back from the burning hot door and crouched low to the ground, instinctively covering my mouth with my paw. I found that this enabled me to take a deep breath and, as I enjoyed the feel of oxygen filling my lungs, I tried to think what to do for the best. I thought back to what I knew about fires, which for a pug like me wasn't much. I had picked up snippets watching *Casualty* with Gail on Saturday nights and knew that if I didn't want me, Hugo or Eric to burn to a crisp then we had to get out of here as quickly as possible.

A million and one thoughts blazed through my mind. If Hugo and I could wake Eric, then we could get him to open the front door as long as he remained calm and understood what was happening. But if we still couldn't get Eric to wake up then there was every chance we could creep through the bathroom and out through the window, and then we could send an alert through the dog telegraph.

Thinking of Eric's slumbering frame, I decided to try to see how bad the fire was in the kitchen, and crept closer to the door. I was only a paw strike away when I jumped back from the heat. Whatever was behind that kitchen door was so hot it made my fur feel as though it was on fire. I gulped with alarm as I thought of Doreen's beloved kitchen island. If only she had managed to fill it with water by now then perhaps the fire would never have started. Fires disliked water, that much I knew. I noticed that by now the sound of the flames was roaring and I let out a howl of anguish. Just then another thick plume of smoke billowed from the gap in the kitchen doorway and almost knocked me over with its ferociousness.

It was no good, the flames were too strong and I backed away from the door and hurried into the living room to find Eric and Hugo. Just as I feared, Gail's dad was still fast asleep in his chair, with Hugo trying desperately to get him to wake while the smoke surrounding him was becoming thicker and faster. As I got nearer, I saw a look of frustration in Hugo's eyes, before he stood on his hind legs, and reached his right front paw behind Eric's head. Alarm coursed through me as I saw him push Doreen's favourite glass vase filled with flowers that sat proudly in the middle. This was not the time for games, I thought angrily, as memories of Hugo upending flowers everywhere when Doreen and Eric first moved in flooded through my mind.

'Stop that now!' I barked. 'That's Doreen's good vase.'

Hugo turned to look at me in surprise. 'It's the only way, Dad,' he barked impatiently. 'And I've a feeling she loves her husband more than she loves this vase.'

Without waiting for an answer from me, Hugo tipped the vase straight over Eric, sending flowers and water all over him, soaking his trousers right through.

Immediately, he blinked his eyes open in shock. 'Hugo? Percy?' he gasped, as he took in the thick smoke around him.

I saw the shock and horror on his face as he registered what was happening to his beloved home. As he began to choke, Hugo covered Eric's mouth with his own paw to help him breathe easier. He glanced at Hugo, a mix of love and gratitude filling his eyes.

'Eric,' Hugo barked again, 'the house is on fire and we all have to get out of here.'

Eric nodded and suddenly sprang into action. 'The house is on fire. Let's go, stay low mind, smoke rises, so we'll have to remain close to the ground.'

As Eric got to his feet, I felt a surge of hope that Gail's dad might suddenly be enjoying a moment of clarity after his sleep. Sure enough, the way he expertly crouched down on all fours and crawled out of the living room and along the corridor made me relax ever so slightly.

'Well done, Hugo,' I barked loudly over the roar of the flames.

'We're going to be all right,' Hugo replied.

Following Eric's lead, Hugo and I stayed close to his heels as we made it out into the corridor and crawled out towards the front door. Despite the great plumes of smoke,

I could picture the delicious moment of freedom as we made it outside and breathed in great lungfuls of fresh air. I would roll around in the gorgeous cool grass, lick my beloved Peg, rub my snout against Hugo and, most excitingly of all, enjoy a cuddle with my precious Gail.

'Stay with me, boys,' Eric instructed. 'We'll be out of here in a jiffy.'

'OK,' we howled in agreement.

I looked at Hugo, who was watching Eric closely, but I was sure that despite what had happened, Eric would lead us to safety. As we neared the front door, I felt another surge of optimism as Eric gingerly got to his feet and began to stand up. Through the whirls of smoke, I watched, heart in mouth, as he held out his arm to lift the door handle. Liberty was just seconds away, only, as Eric stepped forward to grasp the knob, he began to sway left and right, clearly losing his balance.

'Eric, Eric,' I barked. 'Are you all right?'

'You've got this, Eric, you can get us out of here,' Hugo whined encouragingly.

But Eric couldn't reply. Quick as a flash, he teetered backwards, hitting his head on the corner of the pine hall table on his way down. As he lay in a crumpled heap on the ground, Hugo pushed past me and tried to rouse Gail's dad by licking his nose and barking in his ear.

'Eric,' he whined urgently. 'Eric, wake up.'

Hurrying to join my son, together we did our best to rouse him by soaking his face with a series of licks. But no matter how hard we tried, Eric refused to stir.

A sick feeling of failure ate away at me, as I realised I

had not only let Eric down, but I had also let down my son who had returned here to save us all for nothing.

'Dad, stop that right now,' Hugo barked, somehow reading my mind.

'I'm sorry,' I barked wearily.

The tiredness I had felt earlier was eating away at me now and I could barely keep my eyes open. The smoke was making me drowsy and all I wanted to do was sleep for just a couple of minutes. Before I could stop myself I slumped to the floor, and rested my eyes, happy to give in to the land of nod.

Only Hugo had other ideas, as I felt a sharp bite to my ear.

'Oh no you don't, Dad. You're helping us get out of here,' he yapped angrily, hauling me to my paws by the scruff of my neck.

'OK, OK,' I yelped, reluctantly following Hugo's command.

Anxiously, I glanced upwards and saw the thick black smoke was only getting denser. If we didn't get help soon the entire bungalow would be ablaze and I would never see my family again.

'Good,' he barked sharply. 'We need to act quickly, Dad, and I think there's only one thing for it.'

'Go on,' I coaxed.

'We're going to have to go through the kitchen and get out through the conservatory door. It's risky, but it's the only escape as the fire's now spread out to the bathroom. If we stay low, we can manage it.'

'OK,' I agreed.

Fully awake now, we each gave Eric one final lick to the cheek, then reluctantly left his side and hurried back across the corridor. We were several paw strides away from the kitchen and I could already tell that whatever was behind that door was now a lot hotter than it was earlier. I felt my resolve fail, but, looking at Hugo who was striding confidently towards whatever lay on the other side of that door, I knew I had no choice but to follow my brave son.

As he threw himself at the door and hurtled his way into the kitchen, I followed hot on his paws. The scene took my breath away. Everywhere I looked were bright orange flames, eating their way across the kitchen, destroying Doreen's kitchen cupboards, fridge and even her precious island. It was terrifying, but it was the noise that startled me the most. All I could hear in my ears was this great roaring sound that left me feeling weak-kneed and lily-livered. But I knew this wasn't the time to back out. As well as the flames, there was even more black smoke to contend with, making it impossible to see a thing let alone breathe, even at my height. I tried to see through the fugue and find the entrance but the clouds of darkness made it impossible.

'Are you OK, Hugo?' I barked anxiously.

'Fine, Dad,' he barked at the top of his lungs, pushing on through the flames. 'Come on, the door's just here, we'll be out of here in no time.'

Following my son across the kitchen, I let out a howl of despair as the flames from what used to be the oven danced near my paws. How was I ever going to put even one more paw in front of the other in this orange hot room, never mind make it all the way across the floor to the conservatory? I would be eaten alive. Through the smoke I watched Hugo crawl across the floor, just as Eric had done moments ago, and did the same, keeping my belly as low as I could to the ground. But, dear dog, the fire in this part of the house was now so hot I could feel the flames singeing my fur. Holding my breath and squinting through the smoke, I crawled my way forwards, all the while hoping that the conservatory door hadn't somehow banged shut in the wind.

Then suddenly like a treat from an outstretched hand, after months of dieting, it was there, the door was there, still wedged open from my entrance earlier that morning.

Never in all my days had I been as glad as I was in that moment to see a door. Gingerly, I saw Hugo press his snout against it and together we slipped into the smoke-filled conservatory, then dashed through to the French doors and stepped outside.

I all but threw myself onto the grass, and inhaled great lungfuls of air. Never in all my years had oxygen tasted so sweet. But there was no time to relax. Inside there was a man depending on us to save him. No matter how tired I was or how burnt my lungs, I had to get help.

Opening my jaws wide, I was about to bark for all I was worth, when I suddenly saw Hugo turn back towards the house.

'Where are you going?' I yelped.

'Back inside to try and save Eric,' he replied. 'You're

tired, Dad, but try and get help through the telegraph, and I'll be out in a minute.'

A cold sense of fear coursed through my fur and I rushed back to the French doors to block my son's path. 'No you don't, Hugo, you're not going back in there, we'll get help together.'

Hugo looked at me determinedly. 'Imagine if it was Gail lying there. Would you just leave her?'

It was then I knew there was no stopping Hugo. He was right, I wouldn't leave Gail in a burning building any more than Bugsy would ignore a shadow. I had no choice but to let him go.

Watching him push past me and run back into the burning flames, I barked and barked for all I was worth, hoping against hope that the dog telegraph wouldn't fail me and that my pleas to save Eric and my son would be answered.

Chapter Thirty-One

Blinking my eyes open as I slowly came to, I wasn't sure where I was at first. Turning my head left and right, all I could see was white. White tiles, white ceiling, even a little white blanket for me to curl up into. The place was clinical and sterile and the smell of bleach and lemons overpowering.

I got up on all fours to try to get a better look but the only thing I could really make out was that I was in some sort of large puppy cage and it was then I realised I was in the special care section at the vet's. Alarm coursed through me as memories of the fire came flooding back. Where was Hugo? Where was Eric? Had they survived?

Anxiously, I started to bark at the top of my lungs even though it hurt to do so. I needed answers and I needed them now. Immediately, I heard the pitter-patter of footsteps and a familiar face came into view, beaming down at me.

'Gemma,' I whined. 'What's happened?'

'Your family has been so worried about you,' she told

me gently, opening the cage door and scooping me into her arms. 'Now you're awake I need to check you over.'

'Is Gail here?' I whimpered. 'Where's Hugo?'

But there was no time for Gemma to answer as she led me straight past a lot of other comfortable-looking cages containing all sorts of cats, dogs and even rabbits and into a consulting room. After she plopped me on the large black table, Gemma opened another door and beckoned someone through.

I craned my neck and let out a little bark of delight at the sight of Gail, Jenny and Simon. Their faces were a picture of worry as they rushed into the room and swept straight past Gemma towards me. Gail was the first one to reach me and, as she cradled my face in her soft hands, I saw she looked grey and tired, with tears running down her cheeks.

'I've been so worried about you,' she gasped, covering my face in kisses. 'Never, ever, ever go off without me again.'

'I'm sorry,' I whined gently.

'Don't be sorry,' she whispered. 'You're a hero.'

As she pulled away, I looked at her in confusion. What was she talking about?

'You don't know do you, Percy?' Jenny said, stepping forward past her mother and dropping a kiss onto the top of my head.

'Know what?' I croaked again, wishing someone would hurry up and tell me what was going on.

'You and Hugo saved Granddad,' she said simply.

As soon as she uttered the words, my thoughts flew to Eric and the reason I was here slotted into place.

'They're OK?' I barked desperately.

'Eric's more than OK, mate,' Simon said, grinning, in a rare moment of half understanding what I was barking. He bent down to tickle my ears. 'He's alive and very well all thanks to you.'

'And Hugo?' I barked desperately. 'Where's Hugo?'

But I didn't get my answer as Gemma bustled Simon out of the way. 'Come on, let me examine the hero here and then you can tell him all about what happened. He had very bad smoke damage to his lungs and I want to check that the medicine we gave him has helped.'

Eagerly, my family stood back to let Gemma do her checks. As she held a stethoscope to my chest, I tried to remember what had happened but the last thing I could recall was standing in Doreen and Eric's back garden hollering at the top of my lungs as Hugo dashed inside.

At the memory I winced in pain. How could I have let my son go inside like that? I should have stopped him, reasoned with him at least. But then I remembered the determined look in Hugo's eyes. It was a look I had recognised as my own, and I knew that nothing would come between Hugo and his precious owner.

'Where's my son?' I barked stubbornly.

'Hang on a minute, Perce,' Gemma said, taking my temperature. 'I'll get everyone to explain everything in a minute.'

I winced again and was grateful when Gemma had finished her checks.

'Right,' she said brightly. 'Percy is doing brilliantly. All his vitals are good and, as he's been with us a couple of days now, I'm happy for you to take him home, but I do want you to keep him inside for a couple more days. Keep him quiet and if anything changes please bring him straight back. Can't have our hero on the critical list again.'

'Thanks so much, Gemma.' Gail beamed, scooping me up into her arms.

I expected her to carry me straight out into the reception area, but instead she turned left and walked towards another consulting room.

By now I had reached breaking point. 'Will someone please tell me what is going on?' I barked in frustration.

But, as Gail pushed open the door to the little room, my heart skipped a beat and I leapt out of my gorgeous owner's arms, straight onto the table where another pug stood blinking up at the window in confusion.

'Hugo! You're alive!' I croaked, covering my beloved son with licks and wrapping my paws around his precious neck.

'Oh, Dad,' he whined like the puppy I still knew him to be. 'I've been so worried about you.'

I could have stayed like that for hours, simply holding my son in silence while the rest of the world kept turning. Sadly, Gemma had other ideas and gently unravelled my paws from around Hugo's neck.

'There will be plenty of time for celebration in a minute, you two. I just need to give Hugo his final check-up.'

'But he's OK, isn't he?' I barked as Gail picked me back up.

Gemma smiled at me and nodded. 'Hugo is fine. Like

you, Percy, he's got a bit of smoke damage to his lungs, nowhere near as bad as his dad, but other than that he's fighting fit.'

'So we can take him home?' Jenny asked eagerly.

'You can take them both home.' Gemma grinned. 'And if you ask me they both deserve a bit of pampering.'

'Come on then, you two,' Simon said, bending down to pick Hugo off the table. 'Let's go.'

'And with a bit of luck I don't want to see either one of you for quite some time.' Gemma laughed as she waved us goodbye.

Gail offered her thanks to Gemma and then carried me out of the consultation room, through reception and out into the car park.

'I'm glad you and Hugo are all right. You've missed ever such a lot of drama while you've been here,' she said, opening the car door.

'But that's what I don't understand,' I whined, as I glanced up at her. 'Will someone please tell me what's going on?'

'You and Hugo are heroes, Perce! That's what's been going on,' another familiar voice barked.

I whirled around and my heart leapt into my throat as I saw Peg sitting on the back seat beside me. With her tongue lolling out, she leant over as Simon settled me and Hugo in the car and licked my cheek.

'I had to come and see you were both all right,' she whimpered. 'I hope that was all right.'

'All right? It's wonderful to see you,' I barked tenderly.

'Mummy,' Hugo barked, rushing towards his mother,

despite the constraints of the puppy cage he was secured into.

'Easy, son,' she yapped tenderly. 'I'm right here, but we don't want any more accidents so you just settle down.'

'Sal said Peg was as worried as we were,' Jenny said, hopping into the seat next to me, and ruffling my neck.

I licked her hand with affection. It felt so good to see everyone again, but had I really been gone two days?

'Yes, you and Hugo have really been at the vet's for a couple of days,' Peg explained, reading my mind as always. 'You were both unconscious mostly, but Gail said you were in and out a little bit. She's been by your side as much as she can, along with Jenny and Simon, of course.'

'We were all so worried about you both,' Jenny said. 'When the fire brigade turned up and saw the house on fire, they didn't find you straightaway as you'd passed out in the garden.'

'What about Hugo?' I demanded.

'He was found trying to rouse Granddad,' Jenny said affectionately. 'Jumping up and down on his chest.'

My heart went out to my son, and I pushed my paw through his cage and stroked his fur with a surge of love. When did my little one become so brave?

'Where's Eric?' Hugo demanded. 'What's happened to him?'

'With Doreen,' Peg barked. 'Like the two of you he had smoke damage to his lungs. Doreen's under strict instruction to keep an eye on him.'

'I tried so hard to save him,' Hugo whimpered. 'I

thought we were going to make it out all right until he fell over and hit his head on the table. Then I thought my worst nightmare had come true. I had to go into that fiery room, and find us a way out.'

As the memory of all those flames flooded through my mind again, I suddenly felt very cold and cuddled up to Jenny for warmth.

'But you did it, Hugo. You did save Dad,' Gail said, turning round to smile at Hugo and me.

'I couldn't have done it without my own dad,' he barked, looking at me.

I shook my head. 'No, Hugo. You were the brave one. You came back to rescue me and Eric. If it hadn't been for you, well I don't know what would have happened. I'll never forget what you did that day.'

'None of us will,' Peg added with affection.

'You were a hero, Hugo,' Simon said with a smile. 'Accept the compliment, lad.'

'I wasn't a hero,' Hugo whined. 'I was so scared.'

'All heroes feel scared,' I told him.

'And anyway, you didn't give up, Hugo, no matter how scared you were. If you hadn't gone back inside and Percy hadn't barked as loudly as he did then who knows what might have happened,' Simon put in.

Gail shuddered as Simon finished speaking. 'Don't go there, love, it's not worth thinking about. It's bad enough knowing Percy slipped out without me knowing and found what he found.'

'Sorry,' Simon whispered, taking his hand from the steering wheel to comfort his wife. 'But everything's OK now. Percy's out of doggy hospital, your dad's going to be fine.'

'Did everyone on the dog telegraph pick up my message?' I barked. 'That's the last thing I remember.'

Peg nodded. 'Yes, Bertie the terrier lives on Yappersley Road so even though they were out at the park he was able to raise the alert and his owner was the one that called the fire brigade.'

I let out a sigh of relief before remembering the state of the house.

'Just how bad is the damage?' I asked.

Peg made a face. 'It's not as bad as you would think, mainly just cosmetic. Simon and a couple of his mates have been working non-stop so Doreen and Eric can move back in. They went home last night, and Simon thinks he'll have the work finished in the morning.'

'Do they know how the fire started yet?' I piped up again.

'Saucepan left on the stove was the cause,' Jenny explained. 'Gran's beside herself with guilt, says she never should have left him.'

'Which of course is complete nonsense,' Gail shouted from the front of the car, 'as if she could have possibly known that Dad would start making porridge at nearly lunchtime. She'd made him a sandwich and left it in the fridge with a Post-it on the door saying "eat me".'

I hung my head in shame. Doreen wasn't to blame but I was. I had made a promise to my son to take care of Eric and I had let him down. I had seen first-paw just how bad Eric was that morning. He was beyond confused,

300

making all sorts of breakfast dishes. I saw him put the porridge on the stove and I should have barked at him in warning to turn it off – that's what service dogs did, they served.

I let out a little whine of despair. It was a good job it hadn't been me that had been sent to doggy training school, I'd have been thrown out in the first five minutes and rightly so.

'Don't blame yourself,' Peg barked gently.

I lifted my head. 'How did you know?'

'You've got that look on your face where you're going through all the motions of what's happened and looking at what you could have done differently. This wasn't your fault, this was the fault of Alzheimer's, nothing more. You did all you could, and when the time came you saved Eric. You should be proud of yourself not chastising yourself,' Peg insisted.

'I'm not sure,' I whined. 'I could have stopped him.'

'Percy, Eric has Alzheimer's. It would have been very difficult to stop him. You did all you could. You need to stop being so hard on yourself. Doreen can't wait to see you and Hugo. What with you and Eric in the hospital she's been out of her mind with worry.'

At the thought of Gail's mum I gave a little smile. It would be so good to give her a cuddle.

'Eric thought he still lived in Barnstaple,' I barked forlornly. 'He was so upset that he couldn't find the stairs I was terrified he was going to hurt himself so I thought he would need a little nap and then feel right as rain but then I fell asleep too. It was the fumes, I think.'

Hugo pushed his paw through the puppy cage. 'You did all the right things, Dad. You were incredible.'

'The fire brigade think you're both pretty awesome too,' Jenny chimed.

As we turned into Yappersley Road and pulled up outside Eric and Doreen's home, I gave a little whimper, unable to believe my eyes.

Not only was the bungalow looking just as it had before, without a hint of the fire that had nearly gutted it just days earlier, but hanging from the front door stood a massive banner that Jenny told me read, *Welcome Home, Percy and Hugo*. Underneath it stood all of our friends and family. Sal, along with Doreen, was there, holding what looked like a special dog-friendly chocolate cake in the shape of a bone. And next to them was Bugsy, Boris, Jake, Heather along with Lily, Ralph and Roscoe who were all with their owners. And in the middle, sitting in a wheelchair, wearing a great big smile was Eric, shouting and waving at the sight of the car pulling into the driveway.

Too excited to wait for someone to carry us, Hugo bounded out of the car door as soon as Simon opened it and rushed forward to greet Gail's dad, his paws making little crunching sounds as he sped across the gravel.

'Eric! Eric!' he barked, ignoring Doreen's warnings to calm down as he somehow hopped straight onto Eric's lap and covered him with licks to his face. 'Are you all right? Does anything hurt? I've missed you so much.'

A tear rolled down Eric's cheek as he hugged my boy tightly to his chest and buried his head in his fur. 'And

I've missed you. Oh, Hugo, I can't believe I nearly killed you because of my stupidity. I'll never forgive myself.'

'No, Eric,' my son admonished firmly with a single bark. 'You did nothing wrong. Don't ever say anything like that.'

'But, Hugo, you mean the world to me,' Eric told him tearfully. 'These past few days without you have been terrible. I've realised just how much you mean to me, Hugo. You're my best friend, the boy I never had.'

Hugo didn't utter a single bark. Instead, he simply licked Eric's cheek and rested his head on his shoulder. That simple action told everyone all they needed to know – Hugo and Eric belonged together, it was so simple.

Just then, Doreen pushed her way through the pack of dogs. She scooped Hugo from Eric's lap and took him into her arms. I watched as she held my boy, tears streaming down her face like rivers.

'I'll never forget what you did for my Eric. What you both did,' she added, turning her gaze towards me and smiling with love in her eyes. 'You are the best pair of dogs in the world and I love you,' she whimpered.

'I love you,' Hugo whined, pushing his snout into her face and wiping away her salty tears. 'I'm so glad to be home with you and Eric.'

'And I'm glad you're here with us now forever,' Doreen whispered, finally understanding Hugo's barks.

A lump formed in my own throat as I watched Hugo, Doreen and Eric wrap their arms and paws around each other in a group hug filled with love.

Watching the scene play out in front of me, I thought

back to the fire, and the very real fear I had felt that the flames would destroy me and my loved ones. It was so good to see that the blaze hadn't destroyed anything, in fact it had ensured my precious son had truly secured his forever home. I ought to have felt on top of the world, so why did I feel so sad?

Chapter Thirty-Two

After Hugo and I had been hugged almost to death, we followed everyone else inside. While Hugo joined the rest of the party in the living room, I wandered into the kitchen and took in my surroundings. I was amazed to see that all trace of the fire had been eliminated, and incredibly Doreen's island was still standing, even without any water. Simon had clearly worked wonders over the last few days repairing and repainting. If you didn't know any better you would have been hard pushed to know there was ever a fire at all, aside from a scorch mark on one of the kitchen drawers Simon had obviously just missed.

With a start I saw that my basket had been placed next to Hugo's, and I wondered why it was there, along with my favourite blanket.

Suddenly I heard footsteps behind me and saw Gail, her eyes filled with concern as she peered down at me.

'You all right, Perce?' she asked, bending down to tickle my ears.

I gave her a grateful lick. 'I'm fine, just a bit over-whelmed I think and wondering why my basket is here.'

'Thought you and Hugo might like to spend the night together. Me, Simon, Jenny and Ben are all bunking down too. Want to make sure we're here just in case Dad needs anything,' she explained, pulling a large slice of cake from behind her back and setting it down on the kitchen floor. 'Wanted to make sure there was a slice for you, with all those gannets in there.'

I rubbed my head against her hands. 'Thank you,' I barked, taking a tentative first lick. 'This is delicious.'

She sank onto the floor next to me and watched me eat. 'It's no more than you deserve. After everything you've done for Dad, well, I can't tell you how grateful I am. You and Hugo saved his life!'

'It was Hugo really,' I barked dolefully. 'All I did was get in the way.'

'You've got to stop being so hard on yourself, Perce. You could have died in there trying to help my dad!' she said urgently.

At such a sombre statement I stopped chewing and gazed up at my owner. There was no getting away from it, she looked as awful as she had in those dark days when Jenny was in hospital fighting for her life. Bags as black as my fur hung heavily from her eyes, while the sparkle and joy she seemed to radiate as soon as she came into a room had long since disappeared. I could tell she was exhausted and my heart went out to her. So much for life getting easier for Gail once her parents moved up from Devon. If anything things seemed to have got worse.

'Are you all right?' I asked.

Gail nodded as she idly stroked my fur. 'I'm tired, Perce, but there's nothing new there.'

'You seem more tired than usual,' I barked.

She smiled weakly. 'It's called life, Percy.'

'But I should be helping you,' I protested. 'It's my job to be there for you. The whole reason you took me home all that time ago was so we would be friends. I've let you down.'

'You have not let me down! Don't you dare think such things!' Gail admonished. 'You, Percy my love, well I'm speechless at all you've done for my family. We all are. You have never, could never let me down.'

I rested my head on her lap. 'Thank you for organising such a lovely party. It's so nice to see everyone.'

Stroking my head, Gail whispered in my ear, 'You're more than welcome.'

'And it's lovely to be spending a couple of days with Hugo. It'll be like old times again.'

'Not quite I hope.' She chuckled. 'He seems different now,'

'More grown up,' I barked sorrowfully.

Gail said nothing, she just stroked my head with her hands. 'It's hard when your children grow up, Percy,' she said quietly, piercing the silence. 'You plough so much energy into raising them right, giving them the best of everything, and then they find their feet, or paws in your case. You're proud of them but sad they're leaving you.'

I nodded, that was how I felt exactly.

'But no matter what happens to your children or how old they get, they will always carry you in their hearts, Percy, and you will too,' she said earnestly.

I looked up at her then and blinked back the emotion welling in my eyes. My owner was such a wise, wonderful woman. I knew something had been wrong since the moment I saw Doreen with Hugo, but for the life of me couldn't work out what it was. Thanks to Gail I now realised it was fear. For so long I had nurtured, loved and cared for Hugo, all the while wanting him to find his forever home. Now he had found it, I felt deflated and empty. My son no longer needed me any more. Where did that leave me?

'You don't need to find the answers tonight, Percy,' she whispered, once again reading my mind. 'Just enjoy the moment. You're safe, sound and your son is here with us, as are all your pups. Everyone's healthy, happy and alive so just think about that for now.'

'OK,' I barked wearily, suddenly feeling really tired.

Just then the sound of paws across the kitchen floor caught my attention. Looking up, I saw Peg standing at the doorway her eyes filled with affection.

'Are you feeling maudlin?' she barked.

'A bit,' I replied sheepishly.

She trotted across to Gail and me, then softly licked my cheek. 'Come back and enjoy the party, we're here to celebrate you and Hugo.'

I looked at Peg. Her eyes were filled with love and not for the first time I felt so grateful to have found a soul mate like her.

'I told you already, I didn't do anything, it was all Hugo. He deserves the party, not me.'

'And I,' Gail began, looking at Peg and smiling, 'we, disagree! You're a hero, along with your son. Now stop being shy and let us cheer you on. Then we'll let you get an early night.'

Knowing I was beaten, I watched as my owner raised her arms overhead and yawned, then got to my paws.

'Cooee, Gail love,' Doreen called, walking into the kitchen and looking aghast at her daughter. 'What are you doing prancing about the kitchen? You've got guests out there and most of them want tea or wine, or both.'

'I was just chatting to Percy and Peg,' Gail said getting to her feet. 'I'll come now.'

'I should think so,' Doreen said, walking across to the fridge and pulling out a bottle of wine. 'Folks have got dry mouths waiting for you.'

'Including you it seems,' Gail said wryly, as she watched her mother pour herself a large glass from the bottle.

Doreen sniffed. 'I've been through a trauma, Gail. I've lost my home and my husband's in hospital. Is it any wonder I need a glass of wine to help see me through?'

Gail chuckled. 'You haven't lost your home. It's almost as good as new in case you hadn't noticed.'

Taking a large slug of wine, Doreen eyed her daughter. 'That reminds me, you know there's a woman from the hospital coming over tomorrow don't you, to talk about your father?'

'Yes, you mentioned it this morning. Why didn't they just talk to us at the hospital?' Gail said, puzzled.

Doreen shrugged as she took another gulp of wine. 'Who knows, love. The powers that be I'm sure know what they're doing. Anyway they'll be here first thing so the place had better be ready for a royal visit before she arrives.'

Gail nodded as she filled the kettle and set it to boil. She was just reaching for more mugs from the cupboard when the unmistakeable sound of Ben's wails echoed through the house.

'Gail love,' Simon shouted down the corridor. 'Ben's crying, can you do something?'

'And can you bring some soapy water too, Mum?' Jenny shouted. 'He's just been sick.'

Wearily, Gail wordlessly filled a bucket and walked out of the kitchen.

'No rest for the wicked,' Doreen called, helping herself to another glass of wine.

*

It wasn't long before I was ready to admit defeat and go to sleep. As I clambered into my basket and listened to the sounds of everyone leaving, I shut my eyes ready to enter the land of nod.

Just then I felt something warm, wet and sandpapery licking my fur. Opening my eyes in surprise, I came face to face with Hugo.

'Hello,' I barked tenderly as I returned his lick. 'Are you all right? Not too tired?'

Hugo shook his head. 'I'm fine. I just wanted to say thank you, Daddy.'

I looked at him blearily. 'Whatever for?'

'For helping me find my forever home. You always said you would and you did. I would never have done it without you, and who would ever have thought that Gail's dad would be my Gail,' he barked quietly. 'I just wanted to say thank you and goodbye while it's just the two of us, Dad.'

I felt a lump form in my throat. I had already said my goodbyes to Hugo earlier, but now in the darkness, all alone with my beautiful boy I felt a wave of emotion crash over me.

'It's been the best thing I've ever done, raising you,' I barked. 'I've enjoyed every moment and now, seeing you take care of Eric, be a service dog, Hugo, well there aren't enough barks in the world for me to express just how proud I am of you.'

Hugo licked the end of my nose. 'You're the best daddy in the world, did I ever tell you that before?'

I shook my head. 'No, but I haven't probably ever told you that you're one in a million, and I'm honoured to be your dad.'

Immediately, Hugo put first one paw into my basket and then another. The next thing I knew he had clambered in beside me and was nestling into my fur, just as he used to when he was tiny. He was so close I could feel his heartbeat pumping next to mine, and I held on to him, enjoying the feel of his fur next to mine.

'I was so scared when I smelled that smoke, Daddy,' Hugo began. 'I was terrified I was going to lose you and Eric. I rushed back so quickly Doreen didn't have a clue where I was. I think she thought I had dashed out to the shops again.'

I barked nothing, and just held Hugo tighter as he continued. 'All that mattered in that moment, all I could think about, was saving you and Eric. I would never have forgiven myself if you had died.'

I paused for a moment and reflected on what Hugo had barked before I added my own yelp. 'The thing is, Hugo, I never would have forgiven myself if you had been killed. You showed tremendous bravery that day. If it hadn't been for you waking me from the smoke not once but twice, I would have died. You saved my life, boy. I will never ever forget that and I want to shout it all across the dog telegraph that you're my son.'

'I would lay my life on the line for you, Daddy,' Hugo whined as he snuggled in closer.

I rubbed my snout against his. 'And I you, as your dad, Hugo, it's my job to take care of you, not the other way around, no matter how old you get.'

'But I want to take care of you all,' Hugo barked softly. 'I still need you, Dad.'

'You don't,' I replied with a soft bark. 'And that's the greatest compliment a parent can ever have from a child. You're kind, clever, brave and thoughtful, Hugo. You've got all the answers now and there's nothing more I can teach you.'

Hugo was silent for a moment. 'OK. I may not always need you, Dad, but I'll always want you. There's no other dog like you.'

I bent my head down to his and breathed in the scent of my son's fur. It smelled sweet, rich and just the tiniest bit smoky. 'And I, my boy, no matter whether you need me or not, will always love you. I will never stop loving you, Hugo, until the day I die.'

Nestling against him, I knew that was true. That although Hugo no longer needed me any more and I was unsure where that left me, the one thing I knew I could always count on was the unconditional love that would always ebb and flow between us.

Chapter Thirty-Three

Despite all the excitement of the day before, I woke early and found my first thought as I opened my eyes was how much I wanted to help my family get back to normality. Getting to my paws, I realised the house was silent, until I saw Hugo sat by Eric's feet as he read the newspaper in his chair.

'Where is everyone?' I barked sleepily, padding over to my son and rubbing his snout in greeting.

'All still in bed,' Hugo yelped, returning my grin. 'I know Eric always likes to get up early so I thought I would sit with him.'

'That was kind of you,' I barked. 'Can I help you with anything?'

Hugo shook his head. 'No thanks, Dad. I need to get Eric his pills in a minute and then I think I might try to encourage him to go for a walk. Exercise is just as good for him as it is for me.'

At all the noise, Eric put down his paper, looked at

us both and smiled. 'Well aren't you two a sight for sore eyes, eh?'

I felt concerned. 'Are your eyes sore, Eric?' I barked, turning to Hugo. 'Son, if Eric's eyes are sore we should perhaps get him to see the doctor. Could be a problem from the fire?'

'No, Dad,' Hugo barked gently. 'It's just an expression. Eric's fine, it doesn't mean he's got sore eyes.'

'Oh right,' I barked, feeling wrong-pawed. Already my boy knew more about life than I did.

With that, I watched Hugo pad towards a cupboard, nudge it open with his nose and reach inside for a little parcel of pills I knew to be Eric's.

As he dropped them at his owner's feet, Hugo pushed his head against Eric's legs. 'Come on, Eric, take these then we'll go for an early morning walk.'

'Good idea,' Eric replied, reaching for the pills and swallowing them whole with the little glass of water that stood to the right of him. 'Perhaps we can drive down to Instow, eh? Enjoy a little paddle in the water?'

I looked at Hugo warily. Eric still appeared to think he lived in Barnstaple. How would Hugo handle it? Yet my boy took it all in his stride and immediately rubbed his head against Eric's hand once more, before stepping back to look at his owner.

'That's a lovely idea, Eric, but how about we just go to the dog park this morning. It's bracing up there, and the café will probably be open too so you could get a quiet cup of tea,' Hugo barked softly.

Eric rubbed his chin thoughtfully. 'Yes, we could just nip up to the dog park. Good idea, I'll get my things.'

As Eric left the room, I turned to Hugo in astonishment. 'You knew just how to help him when he was confused,' I barked incredulously.

Hugo's flesh flushed red under his fur. 'It was all part of the training. Keep your owner calm. I knew that if Eric thought any more about Barnstaple he would get even more upset. It's better to try and stay in their world.'

I nodded, as Hugo went off to follow Eric, touched at the affection my boy had shown his owner. It was clear Hugo was devoted to Eric in just the same way I was devoted to Gail. As Eric and Hugo walked out of the door, a sudden realisation dawned. My purpose was the same as it always had been – to be there for my family.

Wandering back into the kitchen, my heart feeling lighter than it had in days, I caught sight of my lovely owner. With a navy towelling dressing gown wrapped tightly around her and wearing a look of stress across her features, she was feeding Ben his bottle with one hand and pulling Jenny's school uniform from the dryer with the other.

'Here let me help,' I barked, quickly tugging the skirt and blouse with my jaws.

'Be careful, Perce,' Gail cautioned, 'I don't want you going back into doggy hospital. You should be resting.'

I dumped the clothes into the laundry basket and whined. 'So should you. You're tired.'

Gail said nothing. Instead, she put Ben in his high chair

and went over to the kettle. She had only just flicked it on when Simon appeared, clearly raring to go.

'Oh nice one, love, you couldn't do us a coffee could you? I've got ever so much to get through here today.'

Gail raised an eyebrow as she took out another mug. 'And the rest of us haven't?'

'Oh God! Sorry, love, you've got that woman from the hospital coming first thing haven't you?' Simon smacked the palm of his hand against his forehead.

'Yes, there's a lot happening.' Gail sighed. 'Listen, I don't think I've said it yet, but thanks so much for sorting out Mum and Dad's house, I do appreciate it you know.'

'And I appreciate all you do here, just in case I don't say it enough. I love you, Gail,' Simon said. He gently kissed his wife on the cheek.

As the door shut behind him, Doreen suddenly appeared with Jenny just behind.

'Oh goody the kettle's on.' Doreen grinned. 'You couldn't make us one could you, love? I'm all over the place with this visitor this morning.'

'What time is she coming?' Jenny asked, before kissing me on the head and pulling her freshly laundered clothes from the table.

'In about half an hour,' Doreen replied checking her watch.

'What?' Gail gasped. 'You didn't say it was so soon. I'm not dressed.'

'Well, I don't know what you were thinking of sleeping

in till this hour.' Doreen sniffed, before taking a sip of tea from the mug Gail set in front of her.

'I've been up since four!' Gail blasted. 'I've been doing the laundry, dealing with a teething baby, sorting out lunch boxes and organising an event for Jenny's school fete.'

'Oh you didn't have to do that.' Jenny gasped. 'You've got so much on your plate as it is.'

Gail put an arm around her daughter and kissed the top of her head. 'You're a sweetheart, love, but I'm not going to let you down just because I'm busy.'

'But did you make that cake, love?' Doreen pressed. 'You know that one in Delia I showed you last night?'

Gail looked at her mother in surprise. 'A cake? No, of course I didn't make a cake! Why would I have made a cake?'

'For that hospital woman that's coming around any minute,' Doreen said in alarm. 'We want to impress her.'

'Well, why didn't you make the cake then?' Gail hissed.

'Because I was exhausted last night, love! Might I remind you I've nearly lost my house,' Doreen said, eyebrows raised.

Just as Gail was about to say something I had a sneaking suspicion she might regret, the doorbell went.

'Christ, that'll be her!' Gail gasped, clutching her dressing gown. 'Jenny, let her in while I nip into the spare room and put something on.'

'Make it quick,' Doreen called, 'we don't want to keep her waiting.'

By the time Jenny left for school ten minutes later, Gail was not only dressed but looking lovely in a pair of jeans and a soft white shirt. As she ran down the corridor I followed her into the living room while Hugo and Eric still slept the morning away. Inside the little room, I was delighted to see the fire had been lit to take the edge off the autumn chill.

'Gail love.' Doreen smiled, getting up from the sofa to make the introductions. 'This is Mrs Shah, she's a social worker.'

As Gail stepped forward to shake her hand, I took the opportunity to look our visitor up and down. Tall and slender with warm brown eyes, she radiated kindness. I took a seat next to Gail and waited to see what she had to say.

'Well, this is all a surprise getting a home visit,' Gail said nervously, exchanging smiles with Doreen. 'But I thought someone from the hospital was coming?'

Mrs Shah smiled as she sat back in the chair nearest the window. 'I do work with the hospital, that's perhaps where the confusion has come from. However, I was just saying to your mother that we sometimes do like to come and visit families at home when there are certain issues to discuss.'

At the mention of the word 'issues' my ears pricked up in alarm – this didn't sound good.

'What do you mean?' Doreen asked in alarm. 'Is something wrong?'

Shaking her head, Mrs Shah leant forwards in her chair. 'No, I'm sorry, your husband is fine. He is fine, isn't he?' she asked looking around the room. 'I don't see him here this morning.'

Doreen shrugged. 'He's just napping in the bedroom with Hugo after their walk. The two of them have been through ever such a lot, I thought it best to let them sleep while they recover.'

Mrs Shah looked confused. 'Who is Hugo?'

'Eric's service dog,' Doreen replied with a touch of defiance in her voice, as she gestured towards me. 'He's Percy's son. Hugo saved my husband's life don't you know.'

'I do know.' Mrs Shah smiled as she looked down at her notes. 'Now, I'm sure you're probably wondering why I'm here and, if I'm honest, it is perhaps a blessing Eric's not here just now.'

Gail narrowed her eyes. 'Why, what do you have to say?'

'Please don't worry, it's nothing bad,' Mrs Shah said gently. 'I just want to talk about Eric's future and whether or not alternative care might be a better option.'

'You think he needs a home help?' Doreen gasped. 'But I've been taking care of him.'

'I know you all have, and you've been doing a wonderful job.' Mrs Shah smiled. 'But it seems Eric's condition is deteriorating rather rapidly despite the medication he's on.'

'But I thought he was doing well,' Gail said. 'Just because he left the gas on, well, I mean we've all done that, haven't we?'

'Yes, but we don't all burn our houses down,' Mrs Shah replied evenly. 'We wonder if it isn't time to think about placing Eric in an assisted living facility.'

'A care home you mean!' Doreen's hands flew to her throat in horror. 'Over my dead body. Tell her, Gail, tell Mrs Shah we're not putting your dad in a care home.'

Gail glanced at her mum and then back down at me. That familiar feeling of unease that I had begun to experience more and more of late gnawed away at me as Gail opened her mouth to speak.

'What sort of care home have you got in mind?' she asked.

'Gail! No!' Doreen growled. 'We're not interested. We can manage.'

Gail swung around to her mother, her face pinched with anger. 'But maybe this is for the best. Nobody's saying he's got to go in one now, but we can't ignore what happened, Mum. If it hadn't been for Hugo and Percy then who knows what might have happened.'

Doreen looked at her daughter as though she had just slapped her. 'But, love, your dad wouldn't want this. You must see that.'

'I do. But not so long ago you were looking at care homes yourself. You must have done that because you thought this day might come? Perhaps this is the day, Mum. Dad's not himself just now. Like you, I only want to find out about the options, that's all.' Gail sighed. 'Where's the harm?'

Mrs Shah leant forwards in her chair again. 'There are some very good facilities in the area.' She produced a brochure from the black leather briefcase at her feet and handed it to Doreen and Gail, who looked at it with interest.

'The Laurels,' Gail mused. 'It is very nice. Isn't it, Mum? Look, the gardens are huge. Dad would love sitting out there.'

Doreen turned away. 'It's very nice, but your father's not going in a home, Gail, and that's the end of the matter. You remember how he got when I brought the subject up a little while back.'

'Your husband's condition has changed quite quickly and he does seem very confused,' Mrs Shah put in. 'He seems to think he still lives in Barnstaple. Have you lived in London very long?'

'Just a few months,' Doreen replied sadly. 'We'd not been here long before Eric started getting symptoms.'

'The move didn't bring it on, did it?' Gail asked in fear.

Mrs Shah smiled. 'No, of course not. I'm just trying to understand more about your dad's condition that's all.'

'Is there no other alternative?' Doreen asked, her face ridden with anxiety. 'What about a home help or something like that? I mean we've got Eric's dog Hugo back with us now. He's a fully trained service dog, that will help, won't it?'

'It will be a huge help,' Mrs Shah agreed. 'Service dogs are wonderful animals. My main concern is that it's easier to think about the future and your options before you're forced to. All I want you to do today is think about this. I'm not asking you to move Eric in there now. And let's hope that he may not ever need alternative care.'

'Do you honestly think putting Dad in a care home is the best thing?' Gail asked forlornly.

Mrs Shah paused as she looked from Gail to Doreen who was by now sobbing quietly into her handkerchief. I watched as she rubbed her hand across her chin, as if wondering how best to say what she knew she needed to say. I looked at her, willing Mrs Shah and her warm brown eyes to deliver whatever she had to say kindly.

'Yes, I do,' she said softly. 'I'm sorry, I do know how hard this is to hear, trust me. I shouldn't say this, as we're not supposed to talk about ourselves, but my own father has Alzheimer's and so I do know something of what you're going through.'

'Would you put him in a care home then?' Doreen asked sharply, blowing her nose.

Mrs Shah nodded sadly. 'I did it last year. It wasn't an easy decision. But it was better for him, and now he's with trained professionals all day, every day, who know how to take care of him.'

'So you think The Laurels is the best place around?' Gail asked quietly.

Again Mrs Shah nodded. 'As I say, there's every chance Eric might not need to go into a home, and I'm certainly not here to drag anyone kicking and screaming. All I'm suggesting is that you think about it for one day in the future.'

Once Mrs Shah finished, I saw Gail look at the floor in defeat. As she let out a long sigh, she glanced across at Doreen and squeezed her hand. 'We'll think about it, won't we, Mum?'

Wordlessly, Doreen nodded, as she dabbed her eyes with her handkerchief.

With that, Mrs Shah stood up to leave and, as she turned to go, I caught Hugo standing in the doorway. The expression on his face was hard to read, but my heart went out to him. If he had caught just a few words of that conversation he would no doubt be in turmoil.

As Gail and Doreen bade Mrs Shah goodbye, I rushed over to Hugo and was alarmed to see anger and determination in his eyes.

'I won't let them take Eric from me,' he barked quietly. 'I didn't go to doggy training school and save his life so he could be taken away from me. I'll do whatever it takes to see Eric safe from now on. Nothing will stop me, not a fire, not Alzheimer's and not Mrs Shah!'

Chapter Thirty-Four

As Gail threw me a tennis ball in the park, the wind blowing gustily through the trees, I chased after it hungrily, relishing the simple distraction playing gave me. In a funny way it felt as though my entire world, along with my family's, had been turned upside down, but now I was hopeful things would settle down and return to normal. And for me there was nothing more normal than playing with a tennis ball and giving it a good chew.

Licking the furry ball, I was suddenly aware of the sound of footsteps just behind me. Whirling around, I was delighted to see Eric, Doreen and Hugo trotting up the path towards the dog track.

Immediately, I dropped the ball and raced towards my son and his owners, delighted to find that feeling of knowing my son had a forever home still gave me comfort.

'Hello all,' I barked. 'How are you?'

'We're good, Dad,' Hugo replied, greeting me with a lick.

'Hello, Perce.' Eric grinned, bending down to give me a stroke. 'Still looking after everyone, I see.'

'No change there.' Doreen smiled, tickling my other ear, before looking me in the eye. 'Where's Gail?'

'Just behind that tree up there,' I barked with a jerk of my head.

But Doreen looked at me blankly. Instead, she turned to Eric who was busy tying one of his shoelaces that had come undone.

'Eric, love, do you fancy a cuppa?' she called. 'We can pop into the café, see if Gail fancies a cup.'

'All right,' Eric replied, standing up. 'But we can't be long, I need to pop down the bowls club later, see if Dougie's got everything in hand for the competition against Exeter next week.'

Doreen said nothing, she simply patted her husband's hand and linked her arm through his. 'All right, love. Let's get inside first and we'll think about it later,' she said, a hint of sadness to her voice. 'Boys, don't go far will you?'

''Course not, Doreen,' Hugo barked obediently.

With that, the older couple walked back across the grounds, the late autumn sunshine low in the clouds. As they reached the stone building with misted-up windows, I turned to Hugo, my eyes wide with concern.

'Eric still thinks he lives in Barnstaple then?' I barked softly.

Hugo nodded. 'It comes and goes, but yes. He lights up when he talks about Barnstaple. He doesn't seem to have any memories of being here, unless it's to do with Gail or Jenny.'

I barked nothing, just encouraged Hugo to keep talking. 'It's been an eye-opener looking after Eric properly now.'

'But you look like you've got it all in paw,' I yapped.

Hugo nodded once more. 'Yes. It's very different in some ways to what the training school told us to expect, but they also told us to think on our paws.'

'Well, that's no problem for a dog as clever as you,' I put in.

Hugo met my eyes and I saw at once he was conflicted. 'What's wrong?'

'I think it won't be enough, me looking after Eric, I mean,' he began nervously. 'I think something else needs to change. He gets so upset when he realises he lives in London.'

I wrapped a paw around my son's neck. Something told me that Hugo had already worked out the answer, he was just having trouble telling me what it was. 'And what do you think that change might be?' I asked gently.

Hugo gulped before he barked. 'I think Doreen and Eric should go and live back in Barnstaple. Eric seems to think that's where he lives now and they say familiarity is good for people with Alzheimer's and—'

'And that means of course that you'll go with them,' I finished.

A mixture of sadness and defiance flooded Hugo's features. 'How did you guess?'

'Because it's obviously the right thing to do,' I barked softly. 'Isn't it?'

Hugo nodded again. 'I think it is, Dad. I think being back in Barnstaple where Eric's spent the past seventy-odd years will be less confusing for him. I think it's best all round. I know Doreen wants to go back too.'

I let out a bark of surprise. 'Does she? I thought she wanted to be close to Gail and Jenny as well as baby Ben?'

'She does.' Hugo nodded. 'But I think she too misses her friends and their old way of life. I think Doreen would find living with Eric's Alzheimer's easier to cope with herself if she was surrounded by her own support network. I mean Barnstaple isn't far, they could visit all the time, just like you.'

I fell silent at the thought of Hugo so far away. Yes, of course I could visit and of course it was only a couple of hours or so by car. But the idea of my child living miles away frightened me. I felt blessed to have all my brood around the corner so I could see them at the park at least once a week. I had hoped that when we found Hugo's forever home it would be just the same. The idea of him leaving me for good left me feeling winded. But, at the same time, I also knew Hugo was right and like any good dog should, he was putting his owner first rather than himself. It was time for me to do the same.

'I'll bark with Gail,' I yapped, watching with astonishment as Hugo's eyes lit up.

'Would you?' he barked, a sense of relief flooding his face. 'I was going to try, but she doesn't understand me as well as she does you.'

I unravelled my paw from Hugo's neck and licked his ear. 'Leave it with me, son. What else do you think your old dad's for?'

I hoped to find a quiet moment to yap with Gail later that day but she was so busy taking care of Ben and making dinner for Simon and Jenny when they returned home from work and school that I didn't manage to pin her down for a bark until the following afternoon.

Once Simon had gone to work, Jenny had gone to school and Ben had been put down for his nap, I seized my moment as she finished making a coffee in the brand new fancy machine Simon had treated her to recently.

After she wiped the milk from the spout, Gail took her coffee to the living room and I took a deep breath. I didn't want to break Gail's heart, but for the greater good of our family, I was going to have to encourage her to let her own parents go.

'You all right, Perce?' she called, taking a seat on the sofa. 'You look worried.'

'I'm fine,' I barked, padding across the carpet towards her. Quickly, she set her coffee on the table next to her and scooped me up from the floor and settled me onto her lap.

'So what's on your mind?' she asked, running her fingers through my fur.

I braced myself to be brave, and took a deep breath before I barked. 'Thing is I've been doing some thinking about Doreen and Eric. I think I've come up with an alternative solution to Eric being in a care home.'

Gail said nothing. I glanced up at her tired face – she was giving nothing away so I decided to carry on.

'You won't like it, but I think it might be best if Doreen and Eric go back to Barnstaple and live there with Hugo.'

Gail gasped in shock. 'Percy, I don't think I understood your last bark. I'm sure you yapped something about Mum and Dad moving back to Barnstaple but you can't possibly have suggested that.'

'You know that's just what I did suggest,' I barked gently. 'I don't want them to leave either. It will break my heart to see Hugo go, but it's for the best, Gail. Doreen has a support network in place and Eric will feel more comfortable somewhere familiar.'

As Gail took a sip of her coffee, she remained tight-lipped. 'I don't want to talk about this any more, Percy,' she said with a sigh. 'Mum and Dad live here now. That's what's for the best. At a time like this they need their family around them.'

Just then the familiar sound of a key being turned in the lock rang through the living room, as not one set of footsteps but two descended inside.

'Mum? We're home,' Jenny shouted, the sound of her throwing her keys into the bowl by the door ricocheting through the hallway.

'Who's we?' Gail called warily, setting her cup down.

'Me, of course.' Doreen smiled, as she walked into the living room. 'I was near Jen's school at chucking out time so thought I'd see if she fancied a lift.'

'Thanks, Mum.' Gail brightened. I jumped from her lap allowing her to get to her feet. 'Coffee? I've just made one.'

'Yes please.' Doreen smiled, rubbing her hands together

to warm them through. 'It's getting nippy out there now. Christmas is just around the corner.'

'Tell me about it.' Jenny sighed. 'Miss James made us play hockey in the freezing cold today.'

Gail let out a laugh as her daughter huffed and puffed while putting her PE kit in the washing machine. 'You're not the only one. We all had to suffer at school, love. Be grateful you remembered your kit and they didn't make you borrow something from lost property.'

Slamming the machine door shut, Jenny let out a gasp of horror. 'That's gross! Is that what you had to do at school?'

'Afraid so,' Gail laughed. 'And no, it wasn't very nice.'

'Worse in my day.' Doreen sniffed. 'You were made to do it in your underwear if you forgot.'

Jenny shook her head. 'You're just making stuff up now, Gran!'

'I'm not.' Doreen giggled at her granddaughter's outrage. 'You youngsters today with your mobile phones and your apps for this, that and the other, you don't know you're born.'

'All right, Gran!' Jenny said, kissing her grandmother's cheek. 'I get it, I should be grateful for everything I get.'

'Too right you should,' Gail added, with a hint of a smile. 'Now do you still want a lift over to Jamie's later?'

'Yes please,' Jenny replied, her head now buried in the fridge.

Doreen wrapped her hands around her mug, now finally warm enough to have removed her navy parka. 'A lovely boy that Jamie,' she put in. 'How's his Aunt Tanya? She recovered from that black eye yet?'

'I think so,' Jenny replied, her voice muffled. 'Though she says she still won't work with kids or animals again.'

'Can't say I blame her,' Doreen muttered under her breath.

Gail shot her mother a stern look across the table. 'Come on, you haven't called in to wind Jenny up! What can I do for you?'

At that, Doreen looked nervous. 'What makes you think I want something?'

Gail shrugged, her chestnut hair spilling over her shoulders. 'Call it a lucky hunch. Or the fact I know you too well. Now, out with it.'

'All right,' Doreen replied, pausing as she took a deep breath. 'I want to talk to you.'

'Go on,' Gail coaxed before raising a hand to stop her mother. Turning to Jenny who was eating a sandwich at the sink, she raised her eyebrows at her daughter. 'Haven't you got homework?'

Jenny paused before taking another bite. 'Yes, but I'm just having a snack.'

'So put it on a plate and take it upstairs while doing your homework please,' Gail said firmly.

'Oh, Mum!' Jenny whined. 'I know you just want to get rid of me so you two can talk.'

'Well if you know it, then hop it,' Gail replied with a smile.

With an exasperated sigh, Jenny left her mother and grandmother alone at the table. With Jenny out of the room I felt the temperature drop as I sensed that somehow Gail wasn't about to like whatever it was Doreen had to say.

'OK, Mum,' Gail encouraged again. 'I'm listening.'

'Well, you know how your father's so confused just now. He's convinced he lives in Barnstaple,' Doreen explained.

'Yes, but I suppose that's the problem with Alzheimer's, isn't it? Sufferers have short-term rather than long-term memory issues,' Gail put in.

Doreen sighed. 'It breaks my heart to see him like that, love. He gets so distressed, and it's got me thinking.'

There was a pause as Doreen seemed to gather the confidence she needed to find the words. I looked up at Gail from where I was sitting next to her feet and caught the worry lines across her forehead.

'I think the best thing all round is to move back to our home in Devon,' Gail's mother finished.

'You're not serious. But you just got here. You need us to help you now more than ever,' Gail wailed.

'That's true, love, I do,' Doreen cried. 'And you've been a wonder, you all have. Especially you, Percy.' She beamed, bending down and tickling my ears. 'But we've friends at home, your dad knows where everything is, it'll be better for him, he's got a routine. And of course with Hugo by his side, well, that dog's done wonders already. Just having Hugo nearby has kept Eric calm all afternoon.'

Gail shook her head, tears pooling at her eyes. 'Have you been talking to Percy? He barked as much to me earlier on.'

Doreen looked down at me in surprise. 'You've always been an intuitive soul. What do you think about this?'

I looked helplessly from Gail to Doreen. I so wanted to side with Gail, she was my owner, I loved her. But in my heart I knew it wouldn't be right. This move to Barnstaple was in everyone's best interests.

'I'm sorry, Gail,' I yelped sorrowfully. 'You know what I think. I know how much this will hurt now, but it's the right thing for your dad. Deep down I think you know that.'

A wet tear fell from Gail's nose and landed onto my fur, before she turned to her mother pleadingly. 'This can't be right, Mum. You can't go now, I need you here. I know it's selfish. For so long I wanted you to be with us, for us to be a family, you can't go now, I need you both.'

Doreen leant across me and clasped her daughter's hand. 'Sweetheart, your wonderful family are all right here. And frankly with Percy the superstar to rely on you've no need for me or your dad.'

'I know,' Gail wept quietly. 'Deep down I think I've known for a long time, I just didn't want to face it. It's time for you to go.'

With that Gail and Doreen fell into an embrace with me caught firmly in the middle. As I leant into the two women, and felt their love surround me, a sudden realisation dawned. Although I was heartbroken to be saying goodbye to Hugo I felt a sense of peace descend across me. My purpose had always been to love my family. Just because each and every member of that family wasn't around the corner, that didn't mean we wouldn't still be in each other's hearts, which was surely the very best place to be.

Epilogue

As the darkness begins to fall and the cool December wind whips around my ears, I stand closer to Jenny's legs to guard against the chill. Surrounded by so many humans and dogs I don't imagine it will take long for me to thaw out, but there's something about the Devon air in this gorgeous park that's chillier than the weather in London and I'm struggling to stay warm.

Despite the chatter of the carol singers that surround me, I yawn noisily. Consequently, I earn myself a giggle from Jenny, who, sensing that I'm cold and a bit sleepy, picks me up and holds me tightly in her arms.

'Hope you've brought your appetite,' she whispers into my ear.

'Why?' I bark feeling confused.

'Because after we've all sung carols, we have to eat mince pies, and you know how much I hate them, so you'll have to eat mine too,' Jenny replies, still holding me tight.

Just then I hear another bark and peer down to see

Hugo looking at us both quizzically. 'Did Jenny just mention something about mince pies?' he yaps in delight. 'I love mince pies.'

Jenny chuckles. 'Like father, like son.'

'Who are you on about?' Doreen asks, as she takes a big gulp of something red and dark that smells like cloves.

'Percy and Hugo,' Jenny explains. 'Unsurprisingly, Hugo loves mince pies just as much as Percy here.'

Doreen chuckles as she takes another sip of her smelly drink. 'I know, I've had to keep them out of Hugo's reach. He snaffled one clean off the worktop last week.'

I look down at Hugo once more, ready to tell him off, when Eric appears at Doreen's side and catches my eye. 'All right, Percy?'

'I hear Hugo's been tucking into Doreen's mince pies,' I bark mock crossly, as Eric bends down to pick up my son.

'Oh we're both guilty of that aren't we, boy?' Eric chuckles. He leans over and kisses Doreen's cheek. 'It's this one's fault, she's too good a cook.'

Doreen returns her husband's kiss and then leans over to press her lips onto Hugo's head. 'You two know I don't mind. If all it takes to keep you both happy is a couple of mince pies then I'm happy.'

From my position nestled in Jenny's arms, I look around and feel a sudden thrill at the sight before me. The park in Barnstaple is beautiful. A large Christmas tree stands in the middle, decorated simply with fairy lights, and all the park-goers, ready for an evening of mince pies and carol singing, are gathered around it, drinking a glass of the same stuff as Doreen and chatting amongst themselves before the festivities begin.

Just in front of me is Simon. He has his arm draped around Gail and baby Ben, who seems less of a baby these days. As they turn towards us, I see Gail catch Doreen's eye, and her mum raises her glass as if to toast her daughter, which naturally makes my owner smile.

I chuckle to myself at the sight of my lovely family enjoying each other's company this Christmas Eve when it could all have been so different. From nowhere, the memory of the fire that nearly lost me my life, never mind Hugo's or Eric's, floods into my mind. It's not something I like to dwell on, but some good came out of it. Without the blaze, I don't believe that Gail's mum and dad would have moved back to Devon and it's been the making of Eric and Hugo. Being around familiar surroundings again, and with Hugo by his side, Eric has become a lot happier and less agitated overnight.

Doreen couldn't believe the difference in her husband and she admitted to Gail on the phone shortly after they moved back that it was almost like having the old Eric back. He seemed less forgetful she said and, while she knew it wouldn't necessarily always be that way, she was determined to enjoy it while she could.

I think returning to Barnstaple has also helped Doreen as she's reconnected with all her old friends and even started visiting the doggy training centre. There, she's taken part in the group sessions and even made new friends, developing a bit of a soft spot for Mike.

As for Hugo, well, my whole heart aches for him each

day when I wake and he's not there. However, we have developed an unshakeable bond and it's impossible to describe how proud I am of the pug he has become.

We often talk long into the night on the dog telegraph and I'm glad as it makes me feel he's not so far away. Sometimes even the kids and Peg join in, and together we exchange messages and news like the one big family we are.

Speaking of Peg, I notice her and Sal suddenly enter the park and at the sight of her feel another rush of adoration for my gorgeous love. When we all agreed to come down to Barnstaple, Peg was insistent that she came too as she was desperate to see Hugo and naturally, Sal, Gail and Simon all agreed.

'Merry Christmas, everyone,' Sal calls, waving a bottle of something.

'Merry Christmas, love.' Doreen smiles, kissing Sal on both cheeks and picking up Peg for a cuddle. 'What have you got there?' she asks, gesturing towards the bottles.

'Just a bit of Christmas spirit.' She laughs, undoing the lid and topping everyone's glass up.

'Funny, looks more like mulled wine to me.' Gail giggles, lifting her glass to say a silent thank you.

'Can I have a glass, Mum?' Jenny asks quietly.

I watch Simon frown. 'I'm not sure, love . . . '

''Course she can,' Gail gasps. 'It's Christmas. Half a glass won't hurt. But, Jen,' she says warningly, 'just half a glass.'

Jenny grins at the fact she's being treated like an adult, and I must bark I am delighted to see Gail's found her old sense of fun again.

'What about our treats?' Peg woofs, turning to me.

'I think we'll be getting some mince pies later,' I reply with a bark.

Peg's face lights up. 'Doreen's?' she asks quickly.

'Of course Doreen's,' Hugo barks authoritatively. 'You know she makes the best mince pies.'

'The very best,' Peg barks.

As I watch the humans clink their glasses together and take a sip, Eric suddenly holds up his hand. 'Stop,' he shouts.

Everyone raises their eyebrows in surprise at the sudden outburst, and Sal is so shocked she almost drops her glass, earning her an eye roll from Peg.

'What's the matter, Eric?' Doreen asks urgently.

Eric shakes his head and smiles. 'Nothing. But we can't drink without raising a toast.'

There's a collective gasp and smile at the mistake as we each realise we thought something terrible was wrong.

'So what shall we toast then?' Gail asks, linking her arm through Simon's.

'Christmas?' suggests Jenny.

'We'll be doing that tomorrow over dinner, won't we?' Simon puts in.

'True, love.' Doreen nods. 'And it's a bit early for New Year.'

'What about the season?' Sal suggests to guffaws of laughter.

'Season?' Simon mocks. 'Are you going all American on us, Sal? Next you'll be telling us you don't go on holiday, you take vacations.'

'Leave it, Si,' Gail says, playfully swatting her husband on the arm.

'Exactly, it's not like you've come up with anything better,' Peg barks loyally.

There's another chuckle as Doreen reaches down to stroke Peg's head. 'I dunno what you barked, Peg love, but I've a funny feeling you were telling Simon to put a sock in it.'

Simon shakes his head. 'Which is all well and good, but Eric here still needs a toast.'

'Too true, Simon,' Eric replies. 'And no more sips until we think of one.'

At such sobering news, everyone falls silent, each desperate to come up with something. Eventually it's Hugo that breaks the silence with a short, soft bark in Eric's ear.

'What is it, boy?' Eric asks.

'I've got an idea for a toast for you all,' Hugo replies.

'Go on then,' I bark, feeling a pang of affection for my son and his desire to help.

'Well, shouldn't you all just raise a glass to each other. After all, we've all been through so much this year,' Hugo whines.

'Or simply raise a glass to love,' I bark.

'Oh, Hugo, Percy!' Gail croons. 'That's wonderful.'

Eric looks tenderly at his best friend. 'It is rather wonderful, isn't it? And perfect for this time of the year. Well then, as our beloved pugs, Percy and Hugo, have so wisely barked, let's raise a glass to us and to love.'

'To us and to love,' everyone choruses loudly before taking a sip.

Just then the tune to 'Joy to the World', rings through the park and I turn around to see the little orchestra in the bandstand has started to play.

As the humans begin to sing, I look in wonder at all my family, feeling as though the hymn is directed at me. After so much worry, heartache and pain, all I now feel is complete and utter joy for the family I am blessed to be a part of.

In that moment, I catch Gail's eye and she offers me a smile of knowing as if she can tell just what's in my heart. Overcome with emotion, I lean over Jenny's arm to rub my snout against Peg's. In the past twelve months I have cheated death, become a father and survived, all because of the love that surrounds me. Now, standing in the midst of my family I feel grateful for it all, and want nothing more than to celebrate a very happy Christmas and embrace whatever lies ahead.

Acknowledgements

Huge thanks must firstly go to my agent Kate Burke and Diane Banks at Diane Banks Associates, who had the puppy power of belief in Percy from day one. A special thank you must also go to editors extraordinaire, Sally Williamson and Charlotte Mursell. Their endless support, vision and love for Percy and Hugo has made writing this sequel a huge pleasure.

I would also like to give thanks to all the wonderful pug owners and dog lovers out there who have taken time to talk to me, send me their stories, photos, pictures and generally be hugely enthusiastic about Percy. I have been blown away by Percy's popularity and am so lucky that animal lovers have taken him to their hearts. A heartfelt thanks must also go to all of the wonderful pug owners on Instagram who are so loyal and affectionate towards Percy it really has made being in Percy's world even more pleasurable than it already is. Your mentions, comments, shares, likes and general love is so appreciated.

This would not be a proper Acknowledgements page if I didn't take the time to thank the Alzheimer's Organisation, who I found to be an invaluable source of help while researching this book. Any mistakes contained within these pages are entirely my own. It also wouldn't be right if I didn't give my own pug posse a mention. So, to my wonderful husband, Chris; lovely parents, Barry and Maureen; the Lobina family and my fab friends, Becca Irwin, Kelly-Jane McLaughlin, Rebecca Marrion, Amisha Desai, Craig Evry, Karen Shaw, Barbara Copperthwaite and the Caversham running ladies, who are always full of ideas! I'm truly grateful for your tireless enthusiasm and support.

Lastly, but most importantly a huge thanks to you, dear reader, for picking up this book. There are a lot of books out there that deserve to be read and I'm delighted you chose me, Percy and Hugo to spend some time with; it really means a lot, so thank you and happy reading.